GOLD

A Mystery Treasure Hunt

Terry Acton

Dedicated to my wife Anita for her undying support and patience over the last two years.

CONTENTS

Chapter 1

Monday morning, sat at my desk, contemplating my future. My father had passed away three months earlier. I was now 32 years old and finding myself in the unexpected position of inheriting my father's publishing business, not sure if I even wanted it. I also had the responsibility of five staff to look after, but they seemed to be looking after me!

My father had given me the chance of a good education, for which I was extremely grateful. He never really interfered with what I did, he had left me to my own devices and told me I would find my own path through life.

The realisation that I had five people, including their families, to look after was quite daunting. The phone started to ring. I was awakened from my thoughts.

My secretary Jane called through, 'Good morning Mr Parker, a lady, Miss Sophie Appleby, staying at the Prince Edward Hotel, would like to call on you at your convenience; it is a delicate matter. Would you like me to make an appointment?'

'That would be fine, 2.30 this afternoon. Could you please make sure tea is available, Jane?'

At 2.30 p.m. prompt Miss Sophie Appleby arrived. She looked self-assured and was an elegant young lady, with fair hair and an attractive smile.

'What can I help you with, Miss Appleby?'

'I am a private investigator, Mr Parker, my client is quite old but still has all her faculties. It seems you bought an 18th-century Bracket clock from a London Auction House last September for £20,000. She now knows it was a great mistake to have sold it and would like to make a considerable offer to buy it back.'

Jane arrived with tea at this moment which gave me time to think of an answer. 'You say the lady is quite old, Miss Appleby. If it is not impertinent, how old is old?'

'I would say into her late eighties, early nineties, with fading health, Mr Parker.'

'This is not a request I normally receive.'

'Can I be frank, Mr Parker? She is one of my first customers since leaving college, I really think she is afraid of talking to anybody, perhaps that is why she chose me.'

'If you are so concerned about her, perhaps we could pool our resources?'

'Surely we would have conflicting interests, Mr Parker?'

'Not at all, I would not like to deprive her of a clock she loved so much. However, I would like you to clarify one or two points for me before going further: you seem to be very young for a private investigator.'

'Perhaps it would be better to explain to you, Mr Parker. My parents both died when I was quite young and I was taken in by a maiden Aunt in Nottingham; she helped with my education. When she died about two months ago, so did my funding and accommodation. While flipping through a newspaper, I saw a job in London for a book-keeper to include room and board at the Prince Edward Hotel.'

'Where on earth and when did you become a private investigator?'

I asked, intrigued by this unique young lady.

'My job leaves me with time to kill, so I thought I would try to promote myself in this exciting city of London.'

'And your experience up to now?' I said.

'My first job was to find a lost cat: I searched for several hours and I eventually found it in a neighbour's shed. They had gone on holiday, it had its nose on the glass window and was very hungry. My second job was to follow a man's wife; he thought she was acting very strange on Thursday afternoons, it turned out she was having chemo for breast cancer. She did not want him to know.'

'You are quite a remarkable young lady, Sophie, but you do realise that it could be a dangerous profession.'

'So can crossing the road in London, Mr Parker.'

'Perhaps you could make an appointment to see your client and we will see what is on offer? I do wonder what I am letting myself in for.'

At that Sophie was all smiles and departed.

On Thursday morning, Jane informed me of an appointment for quarter past three at the Prince Edward Hotel. Sophie would meet me outside, and we would proceed on foot to Sussex Place to meet her client. The afternoon duly arrived, and Sophie was waiting for me.

We set off with a good deal of trepidation, at least on my part. 'Sophie I will need to know your client's name for when we get there.'

'Her name is Virginia Brooks, I think she might be a Lady, Mr Parker. She lives on the second floor. This is Sussex Place.' Sophie pressed the intercom button and we were told to go up. Mrs Brooks was there waiting with the door open.

'Do come in both of you please. I do not get many visitors these days.'

She was not a particularly striking woman, nor had she ever been;

her features were plain at first glance, her face unremarkable.

'You have a wonderful view of Regent's Park Lake, Mrs Brooks. Have you lived here long?'

'We moved here some twenty years ago when my husband retired.'

After some more small talk and a cup of tea, I brought the main subject up. 'We do need to talk about the clock, that is the purpose of this visit.'

'I did not realise how much I would miss it, Mr Parker, I would make you an offer of £25,000 for its safe return.'

'Mrs Brooks you sold it in September last year, it seems a long time before trying to find it again!'

'Ah well, I miss its chime, you see. It is company for me, my husband recently passed away. I get so lonely on my own!' Sophie's eye caught mine.

'My father recently passed away also, it is now part of his estate so there are legalities, but I would be very happy to return your clock, Mrs Brooks.'

'How long will that take, Mr Parker?'

'I would think about six weeks or thereabouts.'

'But I can't wait that long, Mr Parker.'

'I can only do my best; I will ring you the moment we can make progress, Mrs Brooks.'

We said goodbye and let ourselves out. We were starting to walk back when Sophie said suddenly;

'There were three clocks in that room, none of them going, did you notice?'

'I will give you another surprise, Sophie! The Bracket clock I bought in the auction did not chime, it only had one keyhole for winding the clock up. That would make it a timepiece only. It would need additional key holes if it was a chiming clock.'

'You are sure about this, Mr Parker?'

'When I was younger my father was always interested in clocks, I used to like to hear them chime. He taught me about winding them up; regulating and servicing. I am absolutely clear in my mind.' I said good night when we arrived back at the Prince Edward Hotel.

'I don't think I will get much sleep, Mr Parker.'

'I have my doubts also, Sophie. Try to write anything relevant down, we will talk tomorrow.'

It was much later when I realised that I was sure Mrs Brooks was not telling us all the truth, she was very nervous. I decided on Friday to ring Sophie, I was put through straight away. 'Sophie do you have to work weekends?'

'I finish at 5 p.m. until Monday morning 9 a.m., Mr Parker.'

'Can I pick you up Saturday morning 9 a.m. sharp? You will need an overnight travel bag. I think we had better have a look at this Bracket clock. Well what do you say?'

'Yes, yes, yes, Mr Parker.'

Chapter 2

Saturday came and I drove over to the hotel, Sophie was waiting with her travel bag and we were away.

'I have never been in a Jaguar car before,' exclaimed Sophie.

'You will remember your cat in a shed long after this is all over. My parents' cottage is near Devils Bridge in Wales, we should arrive in the afternoon.' We pulled on to the drive at 3.30 p.m. having stopped for lunch. Maisie, my parents' housekeeper, was soon standing in the doorway.

'Master James what a pleasure to see you here! I have put Miss Appleby in the guest room at the front of the house, and you in your old room. I hope that will be okay, Master James.'

'Maisie I don't know how we would manage without you.'

'There is milk in the fridge, I will get back to my Jack, he never wants to be on his own for long. His health is not so good these days,' Maisie responded and then she departed.

Sophie seemed to be pleased with her room. I was quite happy to be back among so many memories.

Two cups of tea later I placed the Bracket clock on the table.

'Is it really worth £25,000?' Sophie inquired.

'Well Mrs Brooks seems to think so.' One hour later we were still none the wiser, having searched for secret drawers and exhausted our thoughts. We both needed another cup of tea.

'Mr Parker, why do you have two different keys that are different from one another?'

'They came with the clock wired together, one key is the old one, made with the clock, my father was one for originality.'

'But why have a modern key that doesn't fit tied to your old key? It must be important.'

On looking closer, I found four numbers in pencil on the inside of the back door, 1541. 'They are not service dates, that is also unusual, Sophie. Perhaps Arthur, our security man, might shed some light on the key on Monday. I suggest we are patient till then.'

On Sunday morning Sophie informed me she had slept well, but there was a large bird going around in a circle outside her bedroom window.

'That is a red kite, they live in this part of Wales. They have very beautiful colours and a forked tale. You will often see them hovering and gliding, you will soon get used to them.'

'You are very knowledgeable, Mr Parker. Do you think I could call you James? You are not that much older after all.'

'Sophie I am ten years older, but I can't see why not, just not in my office please. Do you agree?'

'Yes Mr Parker.'

'It is such a beautiful day. We will drive to Aberystwyth on the coast, have a short walk and then I will take you to lunch on the pier, their menu is always a delight. We can then set off back to London and arrive early evening.'

'We must remember the clock key, James.'

'Sophie you make me sound like a chauffeur.'

We set off and wended our way to Aberystwyth, with Sophie exclaiming, 'There is another red kite' every mile or so. The sea air, our walk, and the meal rounded our day off nicely.

Chapter 3

Monday morning was uneventful; by lunch time I had seen to my business chores. I told Jane I would be out for lunch and requested that she fend any calls till I got back.

I set off for The White Feathers public house. I was hoping to find Arthur, who ran the security firm that looked after my business. Sure enough he was supping a pint, and studying the racing paper.

'This is a surprise, Mr Parker.'

'Everything is okay at the office, but I would like your expert advice. I have a key from my late father's estate and it just fails to fit anything.'

'Have you brought it with you?'

'Yes, here it is.'

'It won't fit anything in your office, Mr Parker. Unless I am mistaken, it is a safety box key. There are about only five companies that make and do them in this area.'

'Which one should I try, Arthur?'

'I can do better than that, leave it with me. I will ring later this afternoon.' I then walked back to my office.

At 4.15 Arthur was on the phone. 'Good news, Mr Parker, I have found the key maker. They only made 2,000 of that type of key for a high-class jewellery store, which is on Bruton Street, Mayfair. They do confirm it is one of theirs. You will need the security number to have any chance of opening it.'

'Arthur you are a miracle worker.'

'It is nothing, anything for you, Mr Parker.'

He rang off. I shut up the office and headed for home, all in all a very successful day.

On Tuesday morning, Sophie rang.

'How did you get on with the key, Mr Parker?'

'Don't get too excited, we need to visit a jewellery store on Bruton Street. Could you slip out on Wednesday afternoon about 2.30 p.m.?'

'That's not a problem, James.'

'What did we agree about my name in the office, Sophie?'

'Sorry, Mr Parker.'

'I will meet you outside the hotel,' I said and put the phone down. Jane came into my office carrying an armful of papers.

'You need to look through these today, sir, some of them need signing.'

'I am straight on it, Jane.' The day soon raced by, I felt very excited about Wednesday and had an early night.

It was wet, cold, and not very invigorating first thing on Wednesday morning. The time to meet Sophie came more quickly than I expected. Sophie was waiting for me at the hotel. We set off on foot for Bruton Street.

'I find this terribly exciting, James. I have never done anything like this before.'

'You are not on your own,' I said.

We found the jewellery shop, rang the bell, and were admitted by a small man in a grey striped suit, looking the part of a successful businessman.

'In what way can we assist you, sir?

'My father has recently passed away and I have a key that belongs to a safety box. My security man from my company advised me to see you.'

'Can I see the key, Mr …? I did not catch your name, sir.'

'It is James Parker. I have the key and also I think the number.'

'If you will come with me, we will see if we can be of assistance, Mr Parker.'

With my heart racing and Sophie in tow, we proceeded down some stairs following the jeweller, with his large bunch of keys. He unlocked several doors and let us into a room. The walls were completely covered with silver boxes embedded in them.

'In order to inspect your deposit box, sir, we will need to put your unique four-digit number into our master computer. You will then have two minutes to open your box, Mr Parker. You must get it right first time. The computer screen is now set.'

I typed in 1541 with some degree of trepidation, and four green lights started to flash! I put the key in the slot and the door opened.

Our jewellery man placed the drawer on a table and said, 'It is all yours,' and we peered inside.

There was just an envelope. We thanked him and made our way back up the stairs out into the daylight. I realised with a small shock that Sophie was holding my hand, looking quite pale. My stomach was not the best either. I suggested a strong coffee while we open it. The first cafe we came to we went inside and sat down, looking at one another.

I slit the envelope carefully open. Inside was just a map and a church name: St Tudno's.

Sophie exclaimed, 'I know where that is! It is on the Great Orme at Llandudno; my aunt took me there last year.'

I was somewhat taken aback as the last thing I imagined I would be looking at would be a map. After twenty minutes I was still lost for ideas.

'Sophie I am not sure what we should do next.'

'There is part of the map missing, James.'

'Why do you think that? It looks all there to me.'

'But it is not all there, remember I keep books in my other job.'

'Would you come to the point, Sophie?'

'It is half of an A4 piece of paper.'

'Some people save on paper.'

'You are right about that, James, but the part we have is the front of the church facing the sea, it has been drawn looking down on it! We only have half the church.'

'I do agree with you, Sophie. You have to go back to work. We can meet on Thursday night at The White Feathers. I will treat us to a meal, we can then go over all we have learnt and see if there is a way forward.'

'Okay, seven thirty suits me, James,' and she quickly departed. The rest of the day passed uneventfully.

On Thursday I signed various letters for Jane. Our company books looked good, even when I took into account wages over the last month. All in all, quite a nice day.

I arrived early at The White Feathers; Arthur was propping the bar up in his usual position.

'Well, did we open it, Mr Parker?'

'We did indeed but it was not very exciting at this point in time. Let me top up that glass.'

Sophie came through the door, so I left Arthur with his pint of bitter. She was dressed in a blue blouse with a grey skirt and high heels. I realised Sophie was an attractive young lady and she was getting approving looks from two young men in the bar. I was pleased to be shown to our table in the dining area.

'Well, what did my private investigator come up with?'

'Actually, I had quite a shock when I returned to work. While we were opening that deposit box yesterday, somebody looked through my room.'

'Are you sure, absolutely sure?'

'I never have any person clean my room. I have a lot of paperwork, wages, bills, files, and the general expenses of the day-to-day running of the hotel. All my paperwork had been looked at and disturbed, only slightly but it was not quite as I left it. Some of them are legal papers I am dealing with, James. Who could have looked through my room, and why?'

The meal arrived and a bottle of wine at this time. I found myself concerned about Sophie and wondered if this was far more than we should have taken on.

'I would suggest you get in touch with the police if you are certain about this, Sophie.'

'When I was interviewed for the job of bookkeeper, it was stressed that hotel guests were never talked about at anytime. The hotel records and finance could only be discussed with the manager.'

'What do you intend to do then?'

'I do need my job, James. Perhaps I will leave it for a bit and see if anything else happens. Can I just add, our lives have been very interesting in the last two weeks. However, I do intend to carry on with our investigation.'

'So, where do we go from here? If you are determined to go on, a visit to Mrs Brooks, cards on the table, would probably be our next move.'

Chapter 4

On Friday evening we met outside the hotel, Sophie having rung Mrs Brooks earlier in the day.

We soon arrived at Sussex Place. On pressing the intercom button, we were told to go up to the second floor. Mrs Brooks opened the door.

'Please do come in, my dears, I did not expect you again so soon, I remember it would be quite a while you told me but do take a seat.'

'We have made some progress, Mrs Brooks. But Sophie's room has been searched! We both think you need to be open and frank with us, if we are to carry on. Your clock I can return but there must be far more than you have told us. It is your decision, Mrs Brooks.'

She sighed, 'I feel I must.'

Mrs Brooks began. 'It was about two and half years ago, my husband's brother turned up with an envelope. We were told to guard it with our lives. Now, George was known for getting into a good many scrapes, in fact he sailed quite close to the wind at times, and my husband felt he had to look out for him over the years. You see he was his younger brother.

George was down in Llandudno one night having a drink with one of the local fishermen, who told this amazing story. He had got up early one morning to dig for bait. It was only just light when he noticed a wreck sticking out of the sand.

It seems there had been a storm in the night, this does happen, all sorts of things get uncovered. He drove over to look at the hull. It was just the remains of another wreck. Then he looked closer and could make out what looked like a long trunk. He put it in his trailer, dug for his bait for the customers that day, then drove home and put the box in a safe place. Then, containing his curiosity, took out his customers for their fishing trip.

It was at this point in the story, the fisherman suddenly had a severe stroke, so severe that an ambulance was sent for. George thinks the fisherman knew he was not going to make it, as he thrust an envelope into George's hand. There was only one phrase the fisherman could say: Gold, gold, gold.'

'We were not expecting this, Mrs Brooks.'

'After telling this tale and entrusting the envelope to us, George left. My husband said that at least this time George did not want money, so the following morning he went off early, returned home and said it was all sorted. He then told me we must not lose the key, dear. This is very important, and he tied it to the bracket clock key.

My husband died in his sleep a few weeks after this.

I forgot all about the clock key. Then a few months ago I decided to start to downsize. I wanted a smaller place you see.

Then, about three weeks ago, George came to see me.

He was very excited about some new development, concerning the envelope.

He was driving to Llandudno that coming weekend. Then it came to me, I had sold the clock, with his key tied to the old clock key! I set out to make amends, I looked in the local paper and that nearly brings us to the present time.

I need a cup of tea and a tablet before I go on.'

We both looked at one another, not knowing what to say. She was soon back to carry on the tale.

'George left on the Sunday morning for Llandudno – but he never arrived. He was in a terrible accident, survived, but doesn't know anybody. The doctors say he was lucky to be alive.'

Mrs Brooks looked close to tears; I had no doubt she was telling the truth.

'Do you have any idea what George was up to, or where he was hoping to stay?' said Sophie.

'I can only tell you what I know, I have thought about it a great deal.'

'This fisherman, did he have a name?'

Mrs Brooks said, 'I did write it down, I think there were two H's in the name, I believe it was Henry Hendon.'

Sophie interjected, 'We could start by heading for Llandudno this coming weekend.'

'You do realise we might never get any further,' I said.

Mrs Brooks said, 'I know it is a lot to ask of you both, but I would be happy to pay all your expenses. You see, my husband would have wanted me to sort it out.'

I decided to tell her more. 'Here are the facts we have so far about the key. We have traced it to a jewellery shop in Bruton Street; your husband had taken a deposit box there and put an envelope in it. The key tied to the Bracket clock opened the deposit box. The envelope contained one half of a map. We think it is of the Great Orme and St Tudno's church, Llandudno.'

'That is rewarding, you have been busy,' she said.

'The problem is we have only half of a map, Mrs Brooks. Henry must have split it in half for safe keeping. How to start to locate the other half, that is if it still exists, will take a great deal of time. We might never find it! I do think we need to try and establish one way or another if it is in safe keeping somewhere.'

'George certainly must have found a new trail, if he was dashing off to Llandudno.'

'Would you like to dash off?' exclaimed Mrs Brooks. 'Why not go to Llandudno, I will pay all your expenses. You see, I haven't any children, so I have money to spare and you need not work all the time. It will stop me worrying about George so much if I know we are trying to carry on for him.'

'If James will go with me, I would like to give it a try,' said Sophie.

'I am sure he would like to take you away for a weekend. Now be off and enjoy yourselves, tell me when we have made progress.'

Mrs Brooks looked very tired. So we said our goodbyes, she showed us to the door and we got in the lift down to the ground floor, having not spoken a word.

I walked Sophie back to her hotel, then told her to bring an overnight bag and a good pair of walking shoes. 'I think we should leave at eleven o'clock sharp on Saturday morning.'

'You are going to continue to help me, James?'

'I do not know what alternative I have; you seem to have made your mind up to carry on.'

Sophie planted a kiss on my cheek. 'See you tomorrow.' Then she was gone.

It turned to rain as I walked back to my apartment with a spring in my step. I was enjoying this adventure, much to my surprise. I was already looking forwards to Saturday.

Chapter 5

The sun was shining when I drove round to the hotel, Sophie was all ready and waiting.

'Good morning James, take me to Llandudno,' she said with a big smile. We took the M40 out of London, then the M42 and the M54 to Wellington. Then to Shrewsbury where we had a very late lunch.

While we were eating, she said, 'Tell me about your father.'

I was rather taken aback by her abruptness, but I endeavoured to answer. 'He always had grey hair, at least that is my lasting impression. He managed to give me a good education.'

'What did he do job-wise, when you were young?'

'He worked in engineering, till he was about forty. He then started an antique business, travelling a great deal all over Europe, mainly buying clocks, he said it was a gateway into the lives of all kinds of people. The publishing business came later in life.'

'What about your mother?'

'She died when I was at boarding school, from a long illness. As my father was away a lot, he told me I would find my way in life when I got older, but I'm not really sure even now. I am not certain what to do next with my life! I do know I am responsible for my father's workers.

We must move on now; it will take at least another hour before we arrive and find somewhere to get our heads down tonight. I will tell you more another day.'

It was late afternoon when we reached Llandudno.

We found a nice guest house with bay windows and a parking space. They had a vacancies board in their window.

'It should not be too expensive, we must consider Mrs Brooks as she is paying for us,' Sophie said. We rang the brass bell that was highly polished and a lady came to the door. 'We are looking for two rooms for tonight, with breakfast.'

'Do come in, you can both have a room at the front of the house.' She took us to see them, they both had a bay window. 'Breakfast is from eight till ten, the keys are in the bedroom doors and the rooms are forty-five pounds each.'

'We would like to take them,' I said. We unloaded our luggage, made two cups of coffee, then we started to make our plans.

'I have made a rough plan of about twenty pubs. I think we could make a start to try and find the pub that Henry died in, Sophie. If you can come up with a better idea, I am all ears.'

'I haven't,' she said, 'But this is the thing, which pub do we start with, and what time do we start this pub crawl? We will need to buy a drink in each, the bar staff will try to help us more if we are spending money. I would suggest we drink tonic water with ice and lemon. Perhaps a six o'clock start, James?'

'That seems a good enough plan. Let us start at the far end of the promenade moving towards the pier. We can have our evening meal on the hoof so to speak. It is now five o'clock, we should set off, we must try to do ten tonight, and ten more by Sunday lunchtime.'

We set off at a good pace and just made our destination before six. Our first port of call was very quiet.

'Two tonic waters with ice and lemon,' I said. They duly arrived. I approached the barmaid and asked, 'Could you tell me if you ever remember a fisherman that might have drank here in the evenings? His name was Henry Hendon, it would have been about two years or more now.'

'I have worked here for four seasons, never heard that name, sir. You could try nearer the pier, fishermen are never far from their boats.' With that she returned to her duties.

Sophie said, 'I think we should stick to our plan, James, if we miss any, we could end up back tracking later.'

'I couldn't agree more. We have a long night ahead, let's drink up and move on.'

When we sighted our next pub, Sophie said, 'My turn, leave it to me. You can do the next.' She went up to the bar and soon returned with two drinks. 'The barman says he can find us a room, but he has never heard of our Henry.'

'If we had a gin with this tonic water it would taste better,' I said.

'James we still have at least eight or nine to go, that's only tonight and we have to start again tomorrow morning in all probability.' She gave me a smile and said, 'Drink up.'

At eight o'clock we decided to stop for our evening meal, we had taken twenty minutes for each pub. This was number seven.

'I think only food for me, I've had enough to drink for the time being,' said Sophie.

'Likewise for me, in fact a main course would be perfect for me.' We chose from the menu and enquired about Henry at the bar, same response as the last six.

At quarter to nine we started again. When my watch was just coming up to eleven, we had covered twelve pubs in total but had drawn a complete blank. We decided to call it a day.

The guest house was slightly nearer on our way back. We said good night. I was asleep almost before my head touched the pillow.

On Sunday morning we had a full English breakfast. The husband served while his wife cooked.

'You would be on a short break then,' he said.

'We are actually trying to locate a pub where a local fisherman used to drink some two years ago; his name was Henry Hendon.'

'Times have changed so much these last few years. The fishing boats are small in number, you could try the local lobster fishermen, they still take the day trippers out. I would try around the pier end; it could be as good a bet as any.'

We thanked them both and said that probably we would be back next weekend.

'You're very welcome, give us a ring, we will still be here.' They stood on the doorstep and waved goodbye. We parked on a carpark convenient to where we would start our next search. 'James it is too early to start at eleven, can we go on the pier?' Sophie said.

'We certainly can. This is one of my favourites; it is seven hundred metres long, it is the longest in Wales.'

'How come you know so much about piers?'

'My father took me to Aberystwyth when I was young, it was the last of the daylight and we watched a black swirling cloud of starlings. It was incredible, then they all went to roost under the pier on the supports.'

'But why would they do that?' said Sophie.

'The main reason is that they are safe from predators like sparrow hawks and peregrine falcons. There were hundreds of them, they would be picked off if they had landed in trees to roost for the night. So I became interested in piers, and birds at the same time.'

'Tell me more about the pier, please, James.'

'This pier is unusual in that it has two entrances; one on the promenade at the North Parade, the other at the original entrance on

20

another road. Between them is the Grand Hotel. The original pier was made of wood, built in the 1850s. It was severely damaged in a storm. It was decided to build a new longer one using iron castings, which we are sitting on today. It was opened to the public in the late 1870s. It is now five to twelve.'

Sophie gave me a kiss on my cheek, and said, 'Take me on a pub crawl, James.' We set off, keeping to our original plan.

It was towards three o'clock when we spotted the Weary Traveller.

'Certainly aptly named,' commented Sophie.

We fought our way to the bar in yet another pub, they all seemed very busy on a Sunday. It was as if everybody in Llandudno went out for lunch. On arriving at the bar we ordered two tonic waters. We had gone through our routine about Henry when we had our first positive answer, our fingers gripping the bar as if it was the edge of a cliff!

'You really remember Henry?' I questioned.

'I surely do, he passed away in here, some two years ago. He was telling a tale when he just keeled over! We sent for an ambulance but there was nothing anybody could do,' said the barmaid.

'Is there any way we could find more about his life?'

'He was a fisherman; you could set your watch by him, he always arrived at nine thirty. Many's the pint I have pulled for him. He told his tales to the tourists and they ended up buying his drinks. He always sailed with a full boat the next morning when he had a fishing trip organised. Henry was quite a character. I am sure he knew it and played on it. Everybody liked him, he was certainly good for business here.'

A customer needed to be served, so we sat down with our drinks to think what to do next.

'If George found a new lead, was it in here or somewhere else?' said Sophie.

'I would say we stop with what we have to go on, Sophie.'

'If you think that's the way to go, let us ask if Henry had family and what he did when he was not doing trips. He must have known a good many people around here.'

We stayed till most of the customers had gone. We caught our barmaid's eye, she came over.

'Hello again.'

'Did Henry have family or friends you know of? We would be so grateful to find out.'

'Henry had a brother, older than him, William was his name, he moved to a care home.'

'Did this happen before Henry died or after?' Sophie said.

'It was before, I think,' said the barmaid.

'There are still glasses to wash, we can all take a break then,' said her employer. She left us to mull over this new information. Just has we left, Sophie asked, 'You wouldn't know the road William lived on, by any chance?'

She thought about it, 'I am almost sure it was Chapel Street,' she said.

I glanced at my watch and realised the time; it was four thirty. We thanked her for her time and decided to move on. 'Let us start to make our way home now. We have a long drive.'

We arrived back in London quite late and I dropped Sophie off at the Prince Edward Hotel. 'We can chat sometime tomorrow,' I said.

''Bye James,' and she was gone.

In the morning Sophie rang and left a message.

'I have taken the liberty of booking a table at The White Feathers at seven o'clock on Wednesday. We also have an appointment with Mrs Brooks at eight o'clock.'

I rang and confirmed it was okay.

Monday and Tuesday soon disappeared. Wednesday arrived and I started to think of the new relevant points so far, for Mrs Brooks. We now know Henry had a brother. We still needed to trace him, but our only lead was Chapel Street in Llandudno.

Sophie was already there at The White Feathers before me, waiting.

'Hello James, I have booked a table by the window, it is the most private and quiet. I think we need to order straight away as we are on a tight schedule. We are due at Mrs Brooks at eight o'clock.'

'Just a main course and table water, fine by me, Sophie.'

We both ordered a lasagne and salad at the bar and we then sat down at our table in the window. Our meal was soon over. Our conclusions were; we had a lead, but not a great deal more. At eight o'clock we arrived at Sussex Place. Sophie pressed the intercom button and we were told to go up.

Mrs Brooks let us into her apartment and we sat down.

'It is nice to see you both, what new developments, if any, have we got?'

'Sophie, I will leave it to you to explain.'

'Henry had a brother, Mrs Brooks. We were told he moved to a care home, but, and it is a big but, we have no idea which care home he was admitted to, also if he is still alive. The barmaid in the pub where Henry had his stroke said she was sure William lived in Chapel Street. It is one road back from the sea front.'

'My word you have been busy. Well done. This calls for a cup of tea. I do hope you follow it up, my dears.'

On taking a further look around the apartment, there was a portrait of, I guessed, Mrs Brooks' husband. He reminded me of my own father and, as I looked around the room, I saw he had similar tastes in furniture. My guess was that he had been younger than her, she was in her early nineties in all probability.

While we sipped our tea I said, 'If you do not mind telling me, how did you meet your husband, Mrs Brooks?'

'Well, I never mind talking about him. He was in politics; I was his secretary. We worked together in many different countries, meeting people from all walks of life. We had a very exciting life together. Sadly, we never had children, we did not think it would be wise.'

What with discussing Mrs Brooks' life, and admiring the view of Regents Park, the evening soon disappeared.

Sophie looked at her watch, 'My goodness it is now nearly ten o'clock, James. We have both got to get up for work tomorrow, Mrs Brooks must be tired also.'

'I have really enjoyed you young people. I am already looking forward to your next visit.'

Upon that, we left and walked back to the Prince Edward Hotel.

'Can we continue this weekend coming and book our rooms in Llandudno, James?'

'You certainly can, I will pick you up at ten thirty on Saturday morning.' I said. "It should be a very different trip, no more tonic waters with ice and lemon; care homes, whatever next.'

'Ten thirty it is, 'bye James.'

Sophie soon departed back inside her hotel. I walked back to my apartment, very contented.

Chapter 6

Thursday and Friday were uneventful at my office. I seemed to do a lot of form signing for Jane, not much else.

On Saturday morning I arrived on the dot at ten thirty at the Prince Edward Hotel. Sophie was just coming out with her case.

We loaded up and we were away, the Jag purred along and we made good time. We pulled up for lunch in Shrewsbury.

'Tell me, Sophie, have there been any repercussions since your room was searched?'

'No, but a young man was found in a room with no explanation as to what he was doing there! His job was in the kitchens. Instant dismissal I am afraid.'

'That's one less worry,' I said.

We soon arrived at our boarding house. We rang the brass bell; the door was opened by our hosts for the weekend.

'We are pleased to see you again; we have put you in the same rooms. Sam will take your cases and I will put the kettle on. Please, make yourselves at home.'

Sophie said, 'They make me think I am on holiday, James.'

We unpacked, drank our tea, and decided on our plan of attack for Chapel Street. 'We will have to ring bells and knock on doors. That is the only way forward I can see.'

'At least we have only one street to contend with.' We set off. It seemed to be mostly boarding houses.

'Perhaps you could do one side, I will do the other,' I said.

With aching feet and the time coming up to seven thirty, most doors were left unanswered. 'Let us find somewhere to eat, then consider our options, Sophie.'

We walked to the end of Chapel Street. There was Tribells Fish and Chip restaurant on the corner of Lloyd Street.

'It will make a nice change from pubs, James.' Having found a table, we ordered cod, chips, and peas.

'It is going to be Sunday morning before we can start again,' I commented.

'Let's enjoy our meal when it comes, James. Then why not take a walk along the seafront, forget all the pubs we have been to, doors we have knocked, bells we have pushed and make the most of our break tonight, before we start again tomorrow.'

'That sounds a great idea. Mrs Brooks said not to work all the time. I think it is your turn to tell me about some of your life. Tell me about your parents.'

'There is not much to say, my father worked in some form of insurance, my mother worked for a small building firm part time, doing secretarial work. I would be about six when my aunt took me on as her responsibility. My parents were both killed in a car crash. I was too young for many memories. I have photos though of the three of us. I had a very sheltered upbringing with my aunt Irene. She was the only person in my world. I miss her so much.'

Our meal arrived. The revelation that Sophie did not have anybody to look out for her was a surprise, it disturbed me more than I let on. The fish was beautifully cooked, we sang their praises and told them we would come again.

Walking along the promenade with Sophie holding my arm made

a perfect ending to the day.

Sunday morning, blue sky, I could smell bacon wafting up the stairs. I was soon dressed and went down to breakfast. Sophie was sitting reading the local paper.

'Good morning James, did you sleep well?'

'Very well thank you.'

'I have come up with a new idea to trace William. We will stand still in Chapel Street and then wait for someone to take their dog for a walk. We will be reasonably sure they live there.'

'I have not got a better one, let's give it a try,' I said.

Breakfast was soon over and we set off with renewed vigour for the day ahead. Having stood for nearly one hour we spotted our first dog walker, it was also our first blank. We decided I would knock or ring on doors, Sophie would look for dog walkers.

Two o'clock came around, we had missed lunch, then we got our first break! The lady said, 'William you say, he lodged with my friend at number twenty-seven. He had been a fisherman, if that's who you are looking for.'

'Do you know where he is now, we would be so grateful,' I said.

'He moved to a care home in Penrhyn Road, it was the something 'Margaret' I think.'

We set off with new hope.

At three thirty we were standing outside a care home, the sign said Saint Margaret.

'This looks a good match, Sophie, let's ring the bell.' A lady appeared.

'Can I be of help?'

'We are inquiring about a William Hendon, we think he moved here about three years ago,' I said.

'You will need to talk to our manager, I will see if I can find her.'

She disappeared down the hallway. Sophie was standing with her fingers crossed. What seemed a long time was only four minutes when I checked my watch. A very elegant lady arrived at the door.

'Hello, my name is Mrs June Harding, I am the manager here, how can I help you?'

'We are trying to trace a Mr William Hendon, would he be in your records please?'

'Before going any further, are you relatives and why are you interested in him?'

'We are not related Mrs Harding, we are trying to piece together William and his brother Henry's life, who were both fishermen.'

'Come with me please.' We were shown into a room with filing cabinets covering most of the space. 'Please take a seat. We have a total of forty rooms that are occupied at any one time. William Hendon you say.'

Ten minutes later she said, 'I have found him! He was here, he passed away some three years ago. His health was very poor when he came to us. He was with us twelve weeks in total, before he passed on.'

'Could you tell us if he had many visitors, did he leave anything to anybody, was he close to anyone?'

She looked at the folder on William, 'He was in room eleven on the ground floor. It only mentions a Mrs Thomas from twenty-seven Chapel Street, she came on Friday afternoons.'

'What about possessions?' Sophie said.

'Very few I am afraid. This is the end of their lives when they come here. We normally keep their things for a time and if they are not claimed, we dispose of them. I will need to go to our stock room to check. I will get one of the staff to bring tea for you both.'

One pot of tea and a plate of biscuits arrived.

Having missed lunch, we devoured the biscuits and were enjoying our second cup of tea when Mrs Harding came back, with a plastic shopping bag.

She said, 'This is all he left, we keep them for about two years. You are in luck we haven't had a clear out recently. It is long overdue to dispose of them, if they are not claimed by somebody. We never keep clothes. If there is anything worth saving it goes to a charity shop. The proceeds go towards the Christmas party, the rest gets binned.'

We looked in the bag; one driving licence, a bus pass, national insurance card, and two books on shipwrecks of the Great Orme.

'It is not much at the end of a lifetime, the books will go to a charity shop. If you would like to make a small donation for them, I will give you a receipt, you would be very welcome to take them,' said Mrs Harding.

We thanked her profoundly. I gave her twenty pounds to put in the Christmas fund, she gave us a receipt and we were on our way.

'That must be one of the shortest investigations up to now on this case,' said Sophie.

'You make us sound like professionals, Sophie.'

'We will be if we ever get to the bottom of this adventure.'

It was now coming up to four thirty by my watch. 'Let's find the car. We can eat in The White Feathers if I put my foot down.'

It was just before nine when we arrived back in London. Arthur was propping the bar up, he gave me a wink, 'Quite a regular, Mr Parker, these days.'

Having eaten our late Sunday lunch, we looked at our bag containing the possessions of the late William Hendon from the care home.

'Not much, James, two books,' said Sophie as she passed me one. 'Let's make a start.'

It seemed there were a large number of shipwrecks off the Great Orme. An incalculable number of vessels had perished over the centuries, their very existence totally forgotten. Nevertheless, many shipwrecks are still remembered, and their stories told to countless generations of Llandudno people.

These books must have been very important to William, but what was he searching for? Having read to near closing time, I decided to call it a day and suggested we each take a book back to read. Sophie said, 'I will go too, and we can talk on Wednesday.'

I dropped Sophie off at the Prince Edward Hotel and drove to my apartment. Having parked the car safely, I proceeded to bed with my book and a cup of coffee.

Once started, I was soon lost in another world of shipwrecks.

The first large boats were sail driven, taking goods and people around the coast of England, then later to other parts of the known world. If and when the wind dropped they would have to sit it out, sometimes with little water or food, it could be for many days. In the event of a storm, if they were near the coast, they would drop anchor to stop the boat from being driven in by the storms. If the chains parted from the seabed, the boat and people on her would be lost on the jagged rocks around our coastline.

Fire was another big problem, the ship's hold could be filled with raw cotton which would get hot on its way to the mills in Lancashire, exotic timbers like mahogany which was once growing where they were now planting cotton, or maybe tea which was all the rage in England. Sometimes wreckers with lights on the cliffs would try to lure them on to the rocks.

A life at sea was a very dangerous occupation, but men had always been drawn to the sea and the riches the world had to offer. They saw it as a natural highway, much as we see motorways of today.

Soon I decided I had read enough, and sleep overtook me.

Monday morning, I was early for work. Jane, my secretary, was even earlier, she was hard at work. Her desktop was covered in papers. She was a very articulate person that would stand out in any environment. My guess is that she was in early forties. I was very lucky to have her working for me.

'You are early, James, perhaps we can go over our last month's figures, also the accounts today.'

'No time like the present. I should be asking you,' I said.

'We all need our jobs and enjoy working here together, James. I will get the necessary paperwork.'

She soon returned to guide me through the last month's workload. Much to my delight we had paid all our employees, paid several bills, and made a small profit.

'It is not much different from when your father was looking after us, James. He took a more active role, but that will come with time. We all like to think we are part of this publishing business and try our best to make it work for you, and our families.'

'Jane I am so grateful to you all. I will do my best to keep it going. My father would have wanted it so.'

On that note Jane left me to my thoughts. I had realised she was a very efficient employee from day one, really she was running the business for me. Perhaps in the future I should give her a rise. I spent the rest of the morning going through filing cabinets, hoping to grasp some part of this business I had inherited from my father. Lunch time came around and my thoughts drifted back to the weekend and Llandudno.

Sophie with her detective agency had turned my life upside down. There was I, left a publishing business which seemed to be running itself. I now had more responsibility than at any time in my life and was enjoying it all immensely. I decided to ring The White Feathers to book a table for Wednesday evening. I then rang Mrs Brooks to say we would call at a quarter to eight, with our latest updates.

Sophie rang on Tuesday morning to confirm my booking at The White Feathers. 'How did you know?' I said. 'I have not left you a message yet.'

'We detectives have our ways, 'bye James.'

Wednesday was uneventful at work. I arrived at The White Feathers at seven o'clock. Sophie was sitting at our usual table by the window. She looked very happy, she was wearing a white blouse, with a beige skirt and matching shoes. I was the lucky chap about to have a meal with her.

'You look very happy with yourself, if I may say so.'

'I have had two young men trying to buy me a drink, and then in walks Sir Galahad. I also have something very important to tell you, when we have had our meal.' We both ordered the dish of the day and two glasses of wine. It all came quite quickly. It was soon consumed, and the plates were cleared away.

My watch said seven thirty-five.

'How did you get on with the book?' she said.

'I have read only about half of it. The pages look well thumbed, he had probably looked over it many times, or the people before him.'

'Well I can do better than that! I had reached the middle pages when I thought there was a page loose, it wasn't.'

'You are going to tell me we have found the missing half of our A4 map.'

'You have hit the nail on the head, James.'

To say my pulse quickened would be putting it mildly, I wanted to dance Sophie round the pub.

'I only found out today in my lunch break, it was such a shock! I can't think straight. We have something very positive to tell Mrs Brooks tonight, James.'

'She will be very pleased; it is the next step in our quest for her brother-in-law, George. We need to set off with our progress report.' It seemed we walked faster; we were there with time to spare.

Sophie pressed the intercom button and we were told to go up. Mrs Brooks waved us in, 'Please make yourselves comfortable. I will make us a cup of tea.'

'James you are looking at Regent's Park through the window. This is the first time we can put the two halves of the map together. Aren't you thinking about it?'

'I am putting on a calm front, this latest development will be quite a shock to Mrs Brooks.'

She returned with the teacups and saucers, 'Now, what progress have we made?'

When Sophie told her about the map, I could see her hands visibly trembling as she held the tea pot.

'Sophie will you go over the facts up to this point in time? We can think about them, study the map and come up with our own conclusions.'

The three of us sat round the table, needless to say with three cold cups of tea. Mrs Brooks was the first to speak.

'My thoughts are, that when Henry first found the wreck early that morning, he put the long box in the trailer, took it home and put it in a safe place. He then took his boat out on his fishing trip. Afterwards he then told William. They found out what the box contained, realising it was very important! In fact, so important they would have to bury it again. Logic says in the ground. Hence the map.'

'My thoughts go along the same lines,' said Sophie.

'They must have decided not to go public for a reason. It was their chance to be in the newspapers, the story alone would have fetched a sum of money.'

'They could have been celebrities,' said Mrs Brooks. 'James what are your thoughts?'

'It could have been for any number of reasons. They did not know the value of what they had found, or who to approach about it, or that what they had found was part of a much bigger story.

My conclusion is that the answer to all these questions lies in those books William was reading. They probably knew a lot more and exactly what they were looking for!'

We talked in circles for quite some time. Sophie pointed to her watch, 'James we must not worry Mrs Brooks anymore tonight, it is nearly ten o'clock.'

'Before you go, why not let me go over the books to see if I can find something more. When I was younger, I could speed read two pages a minute, I used to check all my husband's paperwork before he committed anything to do with the Government to any part of the world.'

'I will drop them off at eight thirty tomorrow morning,' said Sophie. 'We need to be off now, James.'

I wished Sophie goodnight when we got back to the Prince Edward Hotel, then headed for my apartment.

Chapter 7

Thursday morning, back down to earth. I spent time trying to master our filing system again. It covered the last ten years of my father's life. I now wished I had taken more interest in what he did for a living. He had left me to my own devices, which must have been a huge sacrifice on his part, although he was always there for me. Jane bought me a cup of tea with a biscuit, 'Miss Sophie Appleby left an envelope for you, sir.'

'Thank you, Jane.'

When I opened the envelope I saw that Sophie had taped the two halves of the map together. You could see it was of the Great Orme. Clearly marked was St Tudno's church.

There were quite a number of crossed marks, which seemed to make a rough triangle when I held the map away from me. On conjecture, the opinions from the three of us would be pure guesswork. The logical step must be a ground survey to establish the crossed marks on the map. Then we could draw our conclusions on the next course of action.

With my lunch break over, I went back to the filing system. With Jane's help it was starting to make sense. By four thirty I decided to call it a day.

Sophie rang early on Friday morning, 'James, would it be okay to take Mrs Brooks to Llandudno this coming weekend? If she is up to it, she could see what we are up against, we do seem to be spending a lot of her money.'

'That is an excellent idea, you must make sure they have a downstairs room with toilet. I will pick you both up at ten o'clock Saturday morning.'

Mrs Brooks answered the call, 'If you can put up with me, Sophie, I would love to come. What time must we leave?'

'Five past ten, we would enjoy your company very much.'

On Saturday morning Mrs Brooks was waiting outside her apartment building, we soon loaded her bag and we were away.

It was just coming up to two thirty when we arrived at our bed and breakfast in Llandudno. Mrs Brooks had a lovely en suite room downstairs. We drove to the sea front, had a small late lunch and then discussed tactics.

Mrs Brooks said, 'I have brought both books with me. I have gone through them twice without coming up with anything. I thought it would be best to go through them again, but with a magnifying glass. I would be very happy if you left me here, I can hear the seagulls and the sea. I am very content to sit here in the sun with my memories.'

We left her there and proceeded to 27 Chapel Street. On ringing the bell, a lady answered the door.

'We are looking for a Mrs Thomas.'

'That would be me. What can I do for you?'

'We know you visited William Hendon in the care home before he died, did you also know Henry?'

'I was very close to both of them. You had better come in.' We were shown into a nice room, brightly lit by the afternoon sunshine.

There were two alcoves each side of the chimney breast. A picture of Henry in the left one and William on the right-hand side.

She was much as I expected, probably around William's age. 'Now what do you need to know about them?'

Sophie said, 'We are investigating William's brother's death, it seems when Henry died that night in the pub, he thrust a piece of paper into our client's hand and the last words he spoke were "gold gold".'

'Henry, William, and I played together when we were children. Most of the younger ones, on becoming of age, moved to the cities because it was easier to make a living there. We looked out for one another over the years.'

'But what about Henry and his last words?' said Sophie.

'The streets of Llandudno are awash with tales of wrecks and precious cargos, if they were all true we would have gold paving slabs along the promenade. Over the years the tales seem to keep coming. We have a storm, another wreck pops up out of the sand, only to disappear again within a short space of time.'

'You must have been very close to them, Mrs Thomas.'

'I was very fond of them. But it is a fact that if you visit any of the pubs towards the sea front at just before closing time, you will find a story being told. The person telling it will be drinking a pint, paid for by the tourists. It is a way of life in Llandudno.'

I gave her a business card, thanked her, and said goodbye.

Mrs Brooks was still sitting on the bench, where we had left her earlier on the sea front.

'I have had a lovely afternoon; it has been a while since I have been to the seaside in Wales. Did you find Mrs Thomas?'

'We did, only she dismissed our tale as being just another yarn. The locals tell so many stories she said. If only half of them were true, the paving slabs would be made of gold along the promenade. Those were her words.'

'If you are ready for something to eat, we thought you might like fish and chips for tea, Mrs Brooks.'

'That sounds a wonderful idea, I am in your hands.'

We were soon sitting down enjoying our meal at Trebells Fish Restaurant.

Sophie said, 'Did you find anything to help us in the books, Mrs Brooks?'

'I think I have found another lead. There had been a circle drawn in pencil round one of the wrecks. It had been rubbed out. You could see it quite clearly with my magnifying glass.'

'It may have just defaced the book.'

'That was my thought, James. Then to my surprise the same wreck in the second book had a pencil ring rubbed out! I believe it can't be a coincidence.'

'What was the name of the wreck? said Sophie.

'It was a three-hundred-and-sixty-ton Liverpool Brig named Albatross.'

'Did it say when, and any other information, Mrs Brooks?'

'You are going to find this hard to believe. One of the books confirmed the Brig named Albatross set out from Liverpool in the year 1812. It was carrying a cargo worth £60,000!'

I looked at Sophie, she looked at me and we both looked at Mrs Brooks.

'You did say £60,000, Mrs Brooks?'

'I most certainly did, James.'

'That must have been an incredible amount of money in those days.'

'It still is today; I will have to work at the Prince Edward Hotel for several years to earn that sort of money,' said Sophie.

'This seems a lot to take in on top of our meal. We can research this new information in the coming week. Where to start I am not sure,' I said.

'Sophie will you sort the bill, I will fetch the car and meet you both by the door. Give me ten minutes please.'

They were just coming out of the door when I arrived with the car.

As I drove the car back to our boarding house, I found myself at a loss, trying to contemplate all that had happened in the last few weeks. My weekends had taken a whole new dimension. Sophie and Mrs Brooks were both taken with this adventure. I was beginning to wonder what we had got involved in. There could not be any turning back now, we all three were well and truly hooked.

'Would you like to join us for a night cap, Mrs Brooks, before going to bed?'

'That sounds a nice end to the day, Sophie.'

We were sitting down drinking our coffee, thinking our own thoughts, when Mrs Brooks said;

'I came to Llandudno many years ago with my husband. We stayed at the Grand Hotel. It is between the two entrances to the pier. It was very hush-hush. There were heads of state from different parts of the globe. You might have heard of the Cuban crisis; it was late 1950s early '60s. The Russians tried to move nuclear weapons to Cuba. The Americans said not in our back yard. Turn those boats back or we will blow them out of the water.'

'To think you were involved in all that, you have had an amazing life,' Sophie said.

'I was so young; I can still remember being young and in love with my then-to-be-husband. My job involved taking the minutes at these meetings. I was sworn into secrecy. It all came back to me this afternoon, sitting on that bench by the pier.'

We wished her goodnight and retired to our rooms.

Sunday morning, the smell of bacon was drifting up the stairs.

It was very inviting to get up to. I had become used to my quiet life in the apartment back in London. It was eight thirty by my watch, I quickly dressed and went downstairs.

'Good morning James, we are both awaiting your instructions for the day, sir,' said Sophie.

'I would suggest a good hearty breakfast, it may be late in the day before we eat again.'

'Have we got a plan, James?' said Mrs Brooks.

'I think we should take the road from the coast that takes us up to St Tudno's church. We then establish where the crossed marks are from the map. The decision of what to do next when we have located them should suggest itself to us.'

We thanked our hosts, packed our bags ready to leave and Sam insisted he carry them to the car. We were soon loaded and away.

The mountain road was quite steep with the sea on our right, we started the long climb up Marine Drive, towards the summit. We were charged two pounds fifty by the toll house, being informed the first three and half miles was a very winding scenic drive, it was also for one-way traffic. The final half a mile would become two way for cars. It was in total four miles to where we would come down on the south side of the Great Orme.

The side road that would take us to Saint Tudno's was clearly marked well before the summit. We had been told the church lies in a slight hollow on the northern side of the Great Orme.

'It was worth two pounds fifty for all that information,' said Mrs Brooks, 'what a lovely start to our day.'

You could feel the drop in temperature as we climbed the long twisting road, it was still early in the day.

'Why were there so many wrecks around the Orme?' said Sophie.

'Perhaps they didn't always have lighthouses.'

'There is a sign saying Llandudno Lighthouse, let's take a look.' We arrived to find the glass lantern missing. The building was now converted to a boarding house.

The plate on the wall said the lantern could still be seen at the visitor centre near the Great Orme summit.

Mrs Brooks said, 'I think we should drive to the summit, before the church, James. We need to establish as many facts as are reasonably possible. When was the lighthouse built, and why did the Albatross flounder on the rocks. I think at this moment in time we are scarce on facts. It is mainly conjecture but Henry and William must have reached this point. They had found something very, very, important. They were stuck trying to take it further.'

The Jaguar took the winding road in its stride. Eventually we arrived at the summit, having passed the Tramway's halfway station, also the sign for the Great Orme Bronze Age copper mines.

'We are certainly finding a lot of facts just on the drive up, Mrs Brooks.'

'The two pound fifty toll ticket gives us free parking, James,' said Sophie.

Once inside the visitor centre, there was the glass lantern from the top of the lighthouse. The sign said it had been erected in 1862. It stood some three hundred and twenty-five feet above sea level.

After the light was switched off in 1985, the lantern had been taken to Liverpool, for display in the Harbour Board's office. As the lighthouse was a listed building, it was pointed out that the lantern had been removed illegally. In 1993 the lantern was returned to Llandudno.

'That is an established fact. We now know in 1812 when the Albatross was wrecked there wasn't a lighthouse. Even the smallest of boats have radar systems in this day and age. Lighthouses are not needed now,' said Mrs Brooks.

'Our boat could have been wrecked in a storm or it might have been sabotage, it was carrying a very expensive cargo,' said Sophie.

'I suggest we have a cup of tea in the Randolph Turpin bar.' It was a pleasant surprise. It had got its name from a famous boxer. He had been the British and Commonwealth middleweight champion during the 1950s. There were pictures and the story of his life on the walls. All facts, but not relevant to the task in hand.

Having finished our tea, we returned to the car and set off down to the church. We parked in front of the wall and opened the gate to the churchyard.

A sloping path led between the gravestones up to the church door. We turned the latch it opened with a large creaking sound. Sophie said, 'Wow!' Just inside the door to the left, was the font.

'The notice says this font has been here since the twelfth century.'

'This is a very special place of worship, Sophie,' said Mrs Brooks.

A lady appeared, 'Can I help you? I am a parish helper.'

'Anything you can tell us about the church history, we would be very grateful,' said Mrs Brooks.

'Very briefly, the present church was built in stone in the twelfth century, the porch was added in about 1500. There was probably little change to the building until a severe storm destroyed part of the roof, in 1839. The church authorities decided to build a new church on the south east slopes of the Great Orme, rather than repair St Tudno's.'

We were so fortunate to have been here with this fountain of knowledge from this lady. She said, 'Would you like me to go on?'

'Yes please.'

'The church continued to deteriorate until 1885. Then a rich businessman from Birmingham paid for the restoration of the church, with a new roof. His daughter had regained her health while staying in Llandudno. It would have been a thank offering. It was then discovered that the font was missing. Surprisingly it was found on a nearby farm, it was being used as a water trough!

'Please enjoy our churchyard. We also do outside services. You will see the pulpit and seats on the right wall of the church outside. The next one is at eleven a.m. this coming Sunday. We have services, weather permitting, throughout the summer. If you have a specific grave to look at, I would do my best to help.'

At this she soon departed, new visitors had arrived.

We retraced our footsteps back into the sunshine and the graveyard. The pulpit was on the side away from the sea, there were seats laid out to form a crescent, row after row. The three of us took seats facing the pulpit.

'You can probably hear every word the priest says to the congregation, the sea being the other side of the church,' said Sophie.

Having looked at our map for some time, we were unanimous that one of the crosses on our map, without a shadow of doubt, was the pulpit. The rough triangle seemed to be behind the church on our map.

We each set off to look at the graveyard. Some twenty minutes later we regrouped in front of the pulpit.

'I have noticed that the ground is rising behind us,' said Sophie. 'The road seems to wrap itself round the churchyard wall, I do think we need to go higher, James where do you stand about this?'

'I agree, we should move the car to a higher place. We now have a further problem. There is a later churchyard joining this one.'

'Perhaps this one is full up now. Llandudno is a popular place for holidays, or even retiring to. When our boat the Albatross was wrecked, the population would have been in the hundreds. We are now looking at probably several thousand,' said Sophie.

All agreed, we moved back to the car to go higher behind the church. We parked alongside the wall behind the church, leaving Mrs

Brooks in the back of the car. There were steps opposite, leading to higher ground, then a gentle slope of grass.

From where we were standing high above the church, we could see all of the church grounds, also the new adjacent churchyard with a building in the centre of it.

There were two gates into the churchyard through the wall we had parked alongside, they each had a gable roof. We still climbed higher.

'James,' Sophie called me over to where she was standing, 'If we take a line from the pulpit, over the right-hand gate to where we are now, then look over the left-hand gate, you will discover a straight line would arrive at the door on the building in the new churchyard!'

'I am with you all the way on this, Sophie. This is definitely the position of the third cross on our map.' Where we were standing was in a small hollow of about fifty feet wide, there were rocks behind us, then the grass slope continued up above us.

To say we were delighted with our discovery would be putting it mildly. We set off back down the slope to tell Mrs Brooks.

'Sophie I can see another car parked alongside the wall, nearer to the left gate.'

'It is just people on their holidays, James!'

When we had got back safely in the car, Mrs Brooks said,

'You were without any doubt being watched as you climbed higher up from here.'

'It was somebody that thought we had a better view, probably nothing more,' said Sophie.

We told her about our deductions about the crosses on the map. 'It may be common ground, but you need to tread very carefully, if you are going to go digging it up.'

'If we took a metal detector, it would mean we only turned the turf back, then replaced it. James, you seem to be our decision maker, what do you think?'

'I cannot see any way forward if we don't. Let's drive down into Llandudno, have a cup of tea, then head back to London.'

'James that car is following us, I am quite sure he or she never knew they in turn were being watched,' said Mrs Brooks.

'Write the car number down, let's see what he decides to do when we reach the bottom.' With our follower behind we drove back into Llandudno. I drove to the small roundabout by the pier.

I set off along the main promenade. 'The car is still behind us, James.' I turned right, heading for Betws-y-coed, it was still there in my mirror after the third roundabout, I was sure Mrs Brooks was right.

'I am going to follow the hospital signs, if he follows us into the hospital grounds there's no doubt about it.' The entrance to its carpark was on our right. I indicated and turned, he followed us in, I took a ticket and parked the car. The car followed us and parked some several cars along.

'James what should we do? We can't just sit here.'

'Mrs Brooks, there is nothing we have done that makes it okay for he, or she, to follow us. We need a change of plan!'

'I want you both to stay in the car. I will walk past the car into the hospital, if he follows me into the hospital I will try to lose him. My guess is that he or she will stay put having seen there were two of us. You must both stay in the car and keep the windows shut, I will return in twenty-five minutes, do not worry it's all under control.'

'I am not sure what you are doing, James, we will do as you say, just be careful.'

Having locked all the doors, I walked into the hospital. Much as I thought our car follower stayed with his car. I now knew it was a middle-aged man, having glanced on my way in. Twenty-five minutes later I walked back to the car, looking as casual as possible.

The car was still parked up, he was looking at a newspaper. I slid into the driving seat, started up the engine, and drove towards the barrier. He pulled up behind me.

Looking at my watch, I had one minute left of free parking time, so I put the ticket in the slot, the barrier lifted, I inched forward until we were clear of the barrier and switched the engine off. I stepped out of the car and raised the bonnet.

'James is the car okay?' said Sophie.

'Just two more minutes then we can be on our way, nothing to worry about.' I pretended to look at the engine. I shut the bonnet down, got back into the car, turned the key, and drove on to the road.

'We seem to have lost him, he is still in the hospital carpark,' said Mrs Brooks.

'Until he buys a ticket he won't be going anywhere, free time is for thirty minutes only. He will have to go back in the hospital to buy a ticket.'

'James you are brilliant, drive us home please!'

It was just coming up to nine p.m. when we arrived back in London. I dropped Mrs Brooks off, with her parting comment, 'Enough excitement for one day, see you both on Wednesday.' When I pulled up outside the Prince Edward to drop off Sophie she was quite hesitant to leave the car.

'Are you all right, Sophie?'

'I was very nervous with that car following us. It must have been a shock to Mrs Brooks, she is much older than us.'

'Look, by Wednesday, you will have had time to think more clearly.' I gave her a hug of reassurance. 'Now off to bed, think about all the positive things we have discovered.'

At that she said, 'Thank you James, see you on Wednesday,' and she was gone.

All in all, quite an eventful day! What our next step could be would need a great deal of thought.

Chapter 8

Monday morning, Jane was in work before me, her desk just covered in papers.

'Did you enjoy your weekend, Jane?'

'I most certainly did, my husband took me to the Lake District, we travelled up on Friday night. We climbed mount Skiddaw on Saturday and went to the theatre in Keswick in the evening.'

'Tell me what I can do to help with all this paperwork, you seem to have a terrific amount this morning!'

'It is not a problem; you will need to sign some of it for me later. If you would look at our dispatch area, we never seem to have enough space for all the books when we are sending them off. There are two main problems, one is the weight, a small run of books of even 300 in hardback form, average out around five hundred pounds minimum weight. That is not counting packing and a wooden pallet to stack them on.'

'I will look into it this morning, Jane.'

'The second problem is the company has grown and created a bottleneck in the dispatch part of our works. If you can solve it, we all would be very grateful.'

On inspecting the dispatch area later, I saw that the lorries backed into our yard to load the books. There was adequate room for the stack truck to load the books on to the lorries. The main problem was inside the dispatch room. The conveyor was against one wall. This did mean that the boxes and books were all loaded from one side. I could well imagine people falling over one another. If we moved the conveyor to the middle of the room, flat-packed cardboard boxes could be assembled on one side, while books would be on the other side. In my mind there would be less frustration, hopefully it would make it easier to work when we had deadlines to meet.

Monday soon came to an end. I had a feeling of being happy, I had decided on a plan to take my publishing business on to another level.

Tuesday, Jane seemed to be very pleased with my ideas. I told her I would talk to Arthur on Wednesday evening. He would have specific instructions to move the conveyor weekends only. There would not be any disruption to our normal working day.

Tuesday afternoon, I confirmed with Arthur that he would be in The White Feathers on Wednesday early evening. I booked our table in the window for seven o'clock. I then rang Sophie to enquire if she had stopped worrying about last weekend.

'Thank you for your concern, James. We have all been run off our feet at the hotel with guests from Japan, France, and other nations. They are over here talking about wind power. I am looking forward to Wednesday, 'bye for now.'

On arriving at work on Wednesday morning, Jane came to me first thing.

'James, we have a chance for you to see first-hand this morning the problems in our dispatch area. We have a run of 2,000 books to be packed and loaded for two o'clock.'

On arriving in our dispatch room, we had one person putting the cardboard packing cases together and one person packing books into them. I then realised I had not any idea of how the books got in or out of our dispatch room. Two of my staff of five in total were beavering away, there was a good deal of stacking boxes one on top of another. Then one would load the conveyor, while the other drove the stack truck to load the lorry with the boxes.

At this point Jane came to see how I was getting on.

'I do realise you have been thrown in at the deep end, James, any thoughts of improving in anyway, please say.'

'I had not thought how much you are all dependant on each other to multitask and I am extremely grateful. Perhaps the way forward would be for me to roll my sleeves up and help out in here on some of the production runs. Small changes without too much disruption are probably the best way.'

She soon went back to her desk in the office.

Having seen first-hand 2,000 books safely packed and loaded on to the lorry, I watched it back out onto the main road. I now felt I had some understanding of the problems facing our firm for when I talked to Arthur in the evening.

On getting back to my office, I decided to draw up some plans for Arthur. I would need his valuable advice and where to obtain the materials to make our alterations. I was also hoping for some idea of the cost.

Wednesday evening I arrived at The White Feathers for six thirty having left work early, Arthur was there before me.

'How can I help, Mr Parker?'

'I have decided to improve our dispatch area. I have made a drawing of the alterations for you to look at. It will involve moving the conveyor from the wall to the centre of the work area. It will mean one person can make up the cardboard boxes on the one side, the second person will pack the books on the other side. I would like a five feet square table on four-inch wheels with brakes, one on each side of the conveyor. The tabletop must be level with the conveyor.'

'We could make the tables first, Mr Parker. Then I would need another helper when we do the change over.'

'Could you also make an overhead means of lifting the boxes? It must run from side to side over the conveyer. Hopefully there will be the minimum amount of lifting after it is installed.'

'I can work out the cost and come back to you in a few days, Mr Parker. If you approve, we could change over in the Bank Holiday weekend at the end of the month.'

At this moment Sophie came through the door into the bar, it was now seven o'clock. Having filled Arthur's glass, I left him and I joined Sophie at our table in the window.

'Good evening James, you were early tonight.'

'Hello Sophie, I am trying to make some improvements at work. Arthur will carry them out for me.'

'Have you had time to think about last weekend in Llandudno?'

'I have had some thoughts. Let us enjoy our meal then talk when we are at Mrs Brooks later.'

'We have had such an assortment of people this week staying at the hotel. All the high up people that have come to England for this wind power convention have brought with them bodyguards, speech translators, and secretaries. We have been so busy. I have a mountain of paperwork to get through. Some of it is not even in English!'

'It seems we have both have had a lot of decisions to make this week, Sophie. I must say I am beginning to enjoy our meetings and meals here; I can't imagine what we will do with our lives on weekends if we ever get to the bottom of our investigation with Henry. Mrs Brooks is our next port of call.'

With Sophie by my side we set off to walk to Mrs Brooks' apartment. 'You can press the intercom button, James.' We were soon told to go up and she was waiting with the door open.

'Please do come in make yourselves at home. I have put the kettle on for a cup of tea.'

We were soon all sitting down round the table.

'I think we would like your thoughts, Mrs Brooks, first. We have both had a busy time at work this week.'

'I have rung up the Vehicle Licensing Agency. For a small fee they will send the address of our car follower. It should be here in a few days time.'

'That is an excellent idea, Mrs Brooks. I have some thoughts on retrieving what Henry probably buried on the Great Orme. We will need a spade and probably a metal detector. Do any of us have a spade? I live in an apartment, never had call to use one.'

'That makes two of us, James,' said Mrs Brooks.

'We don't have call for one at the hotel. At least I have never seen anybody using one,' said Sophie.

'It is probably for the best that nobody knows that we are digging on the Great Orme,' said Mrs Brooks.

'We will be only lifting the turf then replacing it, Mrs Brooks. James, what do you think?'

'I cannot see any other way of moving forward in our quest, it may well all come to a close. To my mind Henry hid whatever he found on the beach that morning when he was digging for bait. It was important, very important, hence the map.'

'Hopefully the DVLA will be sending the address of our follower in Llandudno in the next few days, James.'

'Until we know why, and who he is, we need to tread carefully. He should be top of our list of things to find out,' said Sophie.

'James, can you sort out a suitable spade from somewhere? I will contact you both once we have that address,' said Mrs Brooks.

'Arthur seems to be a fountain of knowledge; he will send me off somewhere I am sure. We could try to pick a rainy day, when we go for it.'

Mrs Brooks said, 'Last weekend must be my most exciting for years. You do realise the chap in that car is on to us now. Both of you must not take any risks. Three deaths if we count my husband, we do not want any more and poor George is in a home.'

'Let's miss this weekend coming, we can regroup next Wednesday evening.'

'That sounds a good idea, Sophie,' said Mrs Brooks.

At that she showed us to the door and we said goodnight. 'She is quite a brave old lady, James, you know I am quite fond of her, plenty of metal is a good way to describe her.'

We walked back, each in our own thoughts, to the Prince Edward Hotel.

'I might be able to help you with the French papers, Sophie.'

'You are very kind but I will survive, you try and find a good spade.'

She gave me a kiss on my cheek, 'I will miss the weekend trip. See you next Wednesday,' she laughed and was soon gone into the hotel. As I walked back to my apartment, I wondered how three people, total strangers, who had met for the first time only a few weeks ago, could be so close now.

On Thursday morning I decided to ring Arthur, he answered straight away. 'What can I help you with, Mr Parker?'

'Do you know where I can buy a spade?'

'I can tell you where, and when. The best time to go would be on a Saturday morning. You need to ask for Mr Jack Berryman, he is only there on Saturday mornings. The shop's name is Berryman's Hardware, it is on Shylock Street. He likes talking, James, so allow plenty of time, you will be in for quite a treat.'

'Thanks again, Arthur'

'Any time for you, Mr Parker.'

Thursday and Friday soon came to an end. On Saturday morning I looked at the map and decided to walk to Shylock Street. Having found the shop, I proceeded to enter. A smart young man was standing behind the counter.

'I have been told to ask for a Mr Berryman please,'

'That would be my grandfather sir, I will see if I can find him for you.'

When he arrived, I realised he was long past retirement age. 'You would wish to speak with me, sir?'

'I have been given your name by my security man, he looks after my works, his name is Arthur.'

'I have known him from a lad, how may I help?'

'I would like to buy a spade.'

'We stock the finest spades in the UK. Whatever the label says no one really makes spades in England anymore.'

'My great grandfather worked a forge in Wigan for many years. The last forge shut down twenty years ago and moved to India. I would recommend craftsmen-made Dutch tools, they are still hand forged. What sort of spade would you be looking for, sir?'

'Just a small spade, not too heavy'

'But what will you specifically use it for, may I ask.'

'I would say a rocky terrain, covered in earth and moss. I think probably no more than twelve inches deep.'

'We have a small collapsible spade, they were used by the plant finders on the mountains, for alpines and other species. We also hire out metal detectors at very reasonable rates, and I would suggest a small steel bar to test the depth of the soil, sir.'

'That sounds as if I have come to the right place.'

'Make no mistake, you most certainly have.'

At that he disappeared into the depths of his spade shop. He was soon back carrying a special heart shaped shovel with a collapsible handle, one metal detector for me to hire, and one steel bar, shaped like a letter T.

'The steel bar will stop you jarring your wrists when digging if there are rocks present, sir.'

I paid and thanked him profoundly. All told, it was a very interesting morning.

On Sunday morning, having dressed and shaved, I decided to go out for a cooked breakfast. I was missing the smell of bacon drifting up the stairs. It was Llandudno, Sophie, and Mrs Brooks that I was missing too. Being with them was like being part of a small family, totally different from my work.

Monday was not such a worry at work. I was now getting to know my staff of five. Our filing cabinets with their systems were becoming easier to understand. To handle so many books that were sent in for proofreading, and to get them into a workable product, I was beginning to think they were all miracle workers. My father had chosen well, I was going to do my best to look out for them all.

On Tuesday morning I asked Jane what she thought of my going around all the staff, with the idea that any suggestions they made to improve our workflow, would be considered. If we chose to implement them and they were a success, a bonus or some treat would be a reward that they would enjoy.

'That is a very good idea, James; we all feel part of this firm. If we can improve it, you can rest assured we will all do our best.'

On Wednesday evening I arrived early at The White Feathers, Arthur was propping up the bar reading the sporting life newspaper.

'I had better fill that glass again, Arthur.'

'Mr Parker, it is a pleasure to help. I have looked to Mr Berryman many times over the years for advice. I hope he did sort things out for you.'

'He was not just trying to sell me something, he made me think of old-world courtesy in his manner, it was a very interesting morning. I am quite sure he would soon have a room packed if he was doing talks on early digging tools for miners, canal builders, and others. We soon forget these things of the past.'

Sophie arrived and she came over to us. 'Hello James.'

'This is a good time to meet Arthur, who you have heard me talk about when we need help, we seem to lean on him more than we ought.'

'That's nonsense, Mr Parker, your father was a good friend to me over the years. It is a pleasure to meet you, miss.'

Having got a glass of wine for Sophie, we made our way to our table by the window.

We ordered the dish of the day and I told her about my adventure to the spade shop.

'While you were doing that, I was doing endless paperwork, it has been my biggest challenge at the hotel. The diplomats all departed on Monday morning. Everybody worked right through the weekend. The manager told me we had made a nice profit. He was pleased with my bookkeeping. Having worked the weekend, I was owed two days off.'

Having enjoyed our meal, we said goodbye to Arthur. Then we set off for Mrs Brooks' apartment.

'Although I worked really hard over the weekend, I still missed Llandudno.'

'Perhaps the only word is snap, Sophie.'

Having arrived, she pressed the intercom button and we were told to go up. The door was open. 'Make yourselves at home, I have just put the kettle on.'

There was something nice about sitting drinking tea with Mrs Brooks.

'I have traced our car follower to Church Walk in Llandudno, the DVLA sent the letter on Monday,' she said.

'We should make him our top priority; I do not want anything happening to you.'

'It seems quite appropriate you spotted him, and have now found where he lives, Mrs Brooks,' said Sophie.

'James, tell us about getting a spade.'

'I have bought a collapsible spade. It will fit in a bag discreetly; they were used by alpine plant hunters in the past on mountains. I have also hired a metal detector and small tee-shaped bar for testing the soil depth.'

'When do you propose to make use of this new information?' Mrs Brooks said. 'James, you're the driver.'

'My thoughts are; we concentrate on our follower, you say he lives in Church Walk, Mrs Brooks.'

'I have been given an address: 3A Helms House. It sounds like a flat or apartment. I also think it would be a good idea to go in the daylight when we confront him.'

Sophie said, 'It sounds a good plan, shall we take a vote?' All three hands were raised.

'Next on our agenda, when do we dig?' Sophie said, 'Perhaps we should wait for a mist and rain weather forecast. I have two days holiday owing me, if we go then, there will be fewer people than on a weekend.'

'Since we do not want to bring attention to ourselves, I would agree to that, Sophie. Mrs Brooks, have you any thoughts?'

'It would be a good idea to take me with you, I could be your lookout. We could arrange some sort of signal if anyone parks by the wall. If it is all clear when I see you making your way down, I will open the boot and rummage for something.'

'The best time for our dig would be without a doubt mid-week. I could still drive us down this weekend coming. We could confront our follower and see what he has to say for himself.'

'Mrs Brooks do you think you can find out anymore about this Liverpool Brig from 1812? Is there a maritime museum that might help us more concerning the cargo? £60,000 must have been worth noting.'

'I will start first thing tomorrow to make subtle enquiries, James.'

'I will pick you both up at ten thirty on Saturday morning.'

'It is getting late, James, let us walk back now.'

Mrs Brooks showed us to the door, we wished her goodnight, stepped into the lift and went down and out into the night air.

While walking back to the hotel, Sophie said;

'James are you sure you can handle this person who is following us in Llandudno?'

'We will play it by ear, stop worrying, off to bed, you have books to do tomorrow.'

'Goodnight James.' I walked back to my flat.

Chapter 9

On Friday morning, Arthur had sent me a breakdown of the cost of alterations to our dispatch area. Jane seemed to think we could afford it. All in all, quite a week.

On Saturday morning I drove round to the hotel. Sophie was waiting with her case; she was full of smiles and we went to pick up Mrs Brooks. We loaded her case and were soon on our way. 'There were a lot of people about in the park this morning, maybe one of the animals escaped,' Mrs Brooks said.

'Let's hope it is not dangerous,' said Sophie.

We pulled up in Shrewsbury for a late lunch, at two thirty. Over lunch Mrs Brooks told us she had sent a letter to the Maritime Museum in Liverpool, requesting any information they had on the brig called the Albatross.

'You must have been a great asset to your husband's work,' Sophie said.

'I hope I was, my dear.'

We finally arrived in Llandudno at our lodgings. Sam, the proprietor, helped us to unload. His wife soon appeared carrying a tray with a pot of tea. 'We missed you all last weekend, come into the lounge, it will do you good to unwind after your journey.'

'Would you happen to know where Church Walk is, and is it possible to go there on foot?' Sophie said.

'There is a small traffic island by the pier, with your backs to the sea walk up that road, you will pass the Great Orme tramway on your right and that is all Church Walk. Beautiful period houses, sadly most converted to flats now. The traffic island is about fifteen minutes from here.'

Mrs Brooks said, 'Why don't you two get off, I would only slow you down too much, I will enjoy another cup of tea, you can take me out tonight.'

We set off. 'James, I am quite concerned about what we are going to do and say when we confront our follower.'

'If you leave it to me, I will sort it out, Sophie.'

We soon came to the traffic island and set off up Church Walk. 'I can see the Great Orme tramway on our right,' said Sophie, holding my hand.

I must admit I was apprehensive about the coming confrontation but decided not to show it to Sophie. Helms House was on the right, a short distance from the Tramway Station.

It was behind a high old mellow brick wall. We entered through an impressive archway; it had a huge turnaround driveway. The garden must have been in its heyday a wonderful delight on the eyes. There were two giant monkey puzzle trees, one on each side of the turnaround, rhododendrons and old exotic shrubs all looking sadly neglected.

'The Victorians sure knew how to live, the upkeep of a place like this does not bear thinking about.'

There were two steps up to the massive front door, it was ajar, and we stepped in to a huge hall. There were post boxes on the one wall. 3A was on the second floor. Having arrived outside 3A, the brass plaque said Mr William Jones Esq.

Sophie pressed the bell. After our third attempt, she said, 'He's not there, James, now what do we do?' Our problem was solved by a lady carrying a mop and bucket. 'Can I be of help?'

'We need to speak with Mr Jones.'

'He is not in today, I know he will be here Sunday morning, he plays the organ at our church service.'

'What time is the service?' I said.

'Ten, till eleven. The church is on the other side of the road a bit further along. The locals all call him 'Snoops'! Anybody will point him out to you, he drives a blue estate car.'

We thanked her and went down the stairs and out onto Church Walk.

'Well, I feel in a much better frame of mind now.'

'I have noticed you have stopped holding my hand.'

'Just be serious, I was expecting our follower to be wearing a suit with arrows on it. If he plays the organ on Sunday mornings in a church, he can't be too bad.'

'You won't mind if I reserve my opinion until we have spoken to this guy and find out why he was following us.'

'Sorry James, you are right, we must only stick with facts and never draw conclusions.' We were soon back at our boarding house.

Mrs Brooks was in the lounge enjoying a sherry with Sam's wife. 'We have stayed so many weeks now and I am still not sure of your name.'

'It is Branwin, it means beautiful in Welsh, my husband says they made a mistake,' to which we all laughed.

At seven o'clock we were changed and ready to go out. 'Do you think we could go Tribells Fish Restaurant again tonight, I enjoyed it so much the last time,' Mrs Brooks said.

One of the staff recognised us as we entered the restaurant and we were shown to a table. 'Welcome back, Mr Parker, we have fresh caught haddock on the menu straight from the boats, delivered this morning.'

Having chosen our drinks and meal, Mrs Brooks asked, 'I am just dying with curiosity, there was nowhere I could ask back at our guest house, how did you both get on with our follower?'

Sophie said, 'You are going to find it hard to believe, we found Helms House in Church Walk, a very impressive house from the 1850s. It had been converted to flats, number 3A was on the second floor. We knocked on his door several times, all to no avail. But we have been assured by one of the cleaning ladies that we may find him at the church a few yards along on the other side or the road. He plays the organ there on Sunday mornings.'

'That's not at all what I imagined; it looks like we are all going to church on Sunday morning. Did the cleaner lady offer anything else about him?'

'She did say the locals call him Snoop,' said James.

'Perhaps he's a bit weird, likes to poke his nose in other peoples' affairs, James.'

'We are about to find out tomorrow morning, if both of you go to the church service: stay there to the end, do not let him out of your sight. I will park out of view, on the road. If he is going off somewhere after the service, it would be logical to take his car to the church. If he is going back to his flat, the car will be left there, we will confront him when he has walked back to Helms House.'

Mrs Brooks said, 'I am so glad we have you to plan the scary bits, James.'

'Let tomorrow take its course. Would you both like another drink?' I said. Having ordered more drinks, Sophie said,

'What else can you tell us about Llandudno, Mrs Brooks?'

'You know I was here in the Cuban crisis in the late 1950s, early

'60s. I was studying at college when the second world war broke out. People never think about the money that is needed to support wars. At the beginning, in 1939, due to the threat of bombing over London, the government moved its tax offices to Llandudno. Most of the hotels were taken over by the inland revenue, they played an incredible part in the second world war, by finding and structuring the cost. It must have been a huge task.'

'You seem to know so much, Mrs Brooks,' Sophie said.

'I am so much older than you both, I studied this sort of thing at college, that is why I ended up in politics with my husband. Church Walk would have been a much different place in the beginning of the century. It would have been home to lots of sprawling mansions with beautiful landscaped gardens: ageing magnates, foreign diplomats, industrialists. The upkeep after the second world war was just too much: I imagine some have been demolished or turned into flats, like Helms House.'

'I have noticed further down one or two boarded up,' said James.

'You would need very deep pockets to even consider taking on the restoration of one.'

'The restaurant staff are starting to clear up, we need to depart now,' said Sophie.

We drove back to the boarding house, with very little conversation, each to our own thoughts.

Sam said he would lock up. 'You are our only guests this weekend. Branwin has put tea, coffee, and biscuits in the lounge.' At that he said, 'Goodnight all' and retired to bed.

Mrs Brooks poured the tea. 'I have had further thoughts about tomorrow morning. When we confront our follower, it would be best if it is where other people are near, by his flat he would not want too much commotion. On a Sunday there will be lots of people coming and going. If we catch him on the street, he might just drive off. The surprise attack will be to our advantage!'

'You make it sound like we are going to war, Mrs Brooks,' said Sophie.

'She is absolutely right, Sophie, he is part of this puzzle we are trying to solve, we must not pass any avenues if we are ever to get to the bottom of it.'

Sunday breakfast was a good start to our day. We were all very anxious about the day ahead. At nine thirty we were parked up between the church and Helms House. By quarter to ten it seemed everybody in Llandudno was going to our church.

'It is now five to ten, sit towards the back of the church and do not let him out of your sight. I am relying on you both to recognise his face. He could walk past me, be sure to stay close.'

After what seemed the longest hour of my life the church bell struck eleven. People started to leave the service soon after. I was just beginning to think something had gone wrong when Sophie and Mrs Brooks appeared from the entrance to the churchyard.

They crossed to other side of the road from where I was sitting in the car, heading for Helms House.

I locked the car and proceeded to follow them, they stopped by the gate, I caught up.

'He seemed to know every person in the church, we thought he was never going to make a move,' said Sophie.

We set off across the courtyard up the steps, passed though the massive oak door into the hall. 'Will you manage the stairs, Mrs Brooks?'

'I am not missing out on the next part, James, I will make it!'

We arrived outside number 3A. Sophie said, 'This is it.' She pressed the bell.

We heard footsteps from within, then the door swung open. 'We would like to speak to Mr William Jones.'

'That's me. What can I do for you?' he asked.

He had receding grey hair and looked in his late fifties. 'There is quite a delicate matter we need to discuss with you.' Having looked us up and down, he invited us to come in.

We were shown into a large high-ceilinged room, it was more like an office than a lounge.

'What is it you wish to discuss?' he said.

'Why were you following us two weeks ago on Sunday afternoon?'

'It is my own business who I take an interest in.'

'You have not denied then that you did follow us all round Llandudno, we eventually lost you at the hospital.'

'So what?'

'You cannot do that; I could report you to the police for harassment.'

'That is my job most of the time!'

'Would you please explain yourself, Mr William Jones, I am at quite a loss.'

'What did you say your name was?'

'I did not say my name, but it is Mr James Parker.'

'Now we are on the same footing, Mr Parker, I will tell you. I am a reporter; I work for the Llandudno Echo.'

To say we were speechless would be putting it mildly. Sophie regained her composure first.

'That is why people call you Snoop, I get it now.'

'If you do not mind, I would prefer you not to use that name. I belong to a very honourable profession. I am the eyes and ears of my newspaper. I report deaths, births, sport, in fact anything to do with Llandudno.'

'That still does not explain why we were being followed,' Mrs Brooks said.

'Some two months ago I was collecting the darts result at the far end of the bay, it was a Saturday night. You, Mr Parker, were there with this young lady. You were enquiring about a Mr Henry Hendon, am I right?'

'You are, please go on.'

'You just happened to be in the Weary Traveller a few weeks later, it was on a Sunday afternoon. You were still asking questions. It happens I knew old Henry very well, and his brother William. They were both born and bred in Llandudno, and so was I. Then yet again I am doing an article for the copper mine, just a few weeks later. There you are with your young lady on the Great Orme. I do find it an amazing coincidence, that you are down here in Wales most weekends. If there is a story, I am the man to print it. Hence why I followed you.'

'We do not have to tell you any of our business, Mr Jones.'

'You can be sure I will be watching you; I might even be able to help you.'

'We will keep that in mind, we might need you, you never know, you have been honest with us.'

'You may be assured of my service at all times, Mr Parker.'

At that he showed us out. Having helped Mrs Brooks down the stairs we were soon back in the car.

'I thought you handled that well, James,' Mrs Brooks said.

'At least there was no malicious intent on his part, we will still need to watch our step. He knows we are up to something.'

'He probably knows the people and Llandudno like the back of his hand, we should stay on the best side of him,' Sophie said.

'Let us go down to the sea front, I will buy us an ice cream each, watch the gulls, and then I will drive us home.'

With the sound of the waves and sea gulls it was a lovely end to our day. We set off back to London.

Chapter 10

Monday morning, Jane informed me we now had two metal tables in the dispatch area. I set off to inspect them, they both had castors on the four legs, moved with very little effort, and could be adjusted for height. Arthur had come up trumps with them.

On getting back to my office, I rang to thank him.

'Glad you're pleased, Mr Parker, each table has two castors with brakes, it should make them more stable when loaded. We need the overhead track, plus the electric hoist next. I have ordered a five hundred weight minimum lift hoist, running on a four-wheel bogey on hard rubber wheels. The firm supplying them say two weeks delivery. If it all pans out, we should be able to change at the end of the month, in the bank holiday weekend.'

'I will see you on Wednesday evening, Arthur, at The White Feathers, 'bye.'

On Tuesday I helped load fifteen hundred books; it was an exhausting experience. Books in quantity are very heavy, I felt the changeover had been long overdue.

I arrived early at The White Feathers on Wednesday evening. I then paid Arthur for the tables and filled his glass. Sophie came in and we sat down at our table in the window.

'I've not had many ideas of what to do next, James.'

'Likewise, Sophie. We can start to listen to the weather report, that is about it. We will just have to be patient, we can start digging when the weather turns, not before.' We had soon eaten our meal and set off for Mrs Brooks' apartment. On arrival Sophie pressed the intercom button, we were told to go up.

'Do come in, I will put the kettle on,' she soon returned with three cups of tea.

'We have not made any progress, Mrs Brooks, we can only listen to the weather forecast.'

'Never mind, I have received a letter from the Liverpool Maritime museum, it confirms the brig called the Albatross did go down off the Great Orme in 1812.'

'That means it is not just in a book,' said Sophie. 'Furthermore, any information they have we can look into.'

'They do not send any ancient paperwork through the post. If we would like to ring them and book for two hours of their time in advance, they need two days notice to do this. Any information concerning the Albatross could be made available for us to inspect when we go there. I could manage most days in the coming week, for a trip to Liverpool.'

'Wednesday is probably my best day, what about you James?' Sophie said.

'That seems fine by me. If we are all agreed, perhaps you will go ahead and try to book it, Mrs Brooks.'

'It would be a good idea to compose a list of questions for when we get there:

The number of survivors.

How many crew did she sail with? What was her cargo?

Where was she heading?' said Mrs Brooks.

'We could ask about any report in the newspapers, if they had papers back in 1812, there would be a record of the wreck. It did say a cargo of £60,000 in both books.'

'Hopefully we will find out what she was carrying,' said Sophie.

'It seems we will not be going to Llandudno this coming weekend. I will go to see George on Sunday,' said Mrs Brooks.

'How far do you have to travel to see him, and would you like a lift?'

'He is only about twenty minutes from here, James, that is a very kind offer. You could both come! That is if Sophie would like to.'

'I almost think I know him, I would be delighted,' said Sophie.

'Visiting time is three till five. We would need to start from here at two-thirty. I will wait downstairs for you both.'

'James, the time is now ten o'clock, we should be saying goodnight to Mrs Brooks.' She let us out and we went down in the lift.

'Liverpool next week, whatever next,'

'Promise me you won't give up on me, James, will you?'

'There is no fear of that, Sophie!'

We set off back to the Prince Edward Hotel, with Sophie holding my arm which seemed to happen more often than not these days. Having said goodnight with a peck on my cheek she disappeared into her world of books and guests. I set off to my apartment. Meeting George in the flesh on Sunday was a new part of our quest to solve this riddle that had taken over our lives.

Thursday and Friday seemed to pass very quickly. On Saturday morning I decided to drive out of London, to somewhere with open spaces, and plenty of grass, having taken the metal detector. I dropped two or three coins by my feet and proceeded to try to find them. Having gained confidence, I decided to go for the real thing. With my back to the grass verge behind me I tossed three coins over my shoulder.

Within a short space of time a rather crusty old gentleman appeared, 'Are you some sort of nutter, what do you think you are doing?'

'I am trying to find some coins I have hidden in the grass.'

'You have just thrown them there?'

'That is correct; I am learning to use a metal detector.'

He soon departed muttering and scratching his head. Much to my surprise in less than fifteen minutes all three coins were found. Going for the real thing on the Great Orme could not come quickly enough. I drove back into London.

On Sunday morning I rang Sophie. 'I am just ringing to see if you would like me to take you out to lunch?'

'I would like that very much, James, I feel at quite a loose end not waking up in Llandudno! When can I expect my carriage to arrive?'

'I will pick you up at quarter to one, that will give plenty of time before we pick up Mrs Brooks at two thirty.' I rang off.

Having cleaned and washed the car, at twelve thirty I set off to pick up Sophie. I arrived with two minutes to spare; she was just coming through the door of the hotel. 'I have cleaned and washed your carriage, miss.'

'James you have forgotten your cap, all chauffeurs wear a cap. Where are we off to?'

'The Royal Oak, it is not very far from here.' We were soon sitting at a table enjoying our lunch.

'James have you thought about our digging trip to Llandudno?'

'Yes, but it might seem over the top; I would like you to wear walking gear, with a cap, I will do the same. We have a Volvo estate car we use for small deliveries at my works, we will take it and hopefully we will not come to the attention of Mr William Jones, or Snoops, whatever you want to call him.'

'If Henry decided to bury the long box he found on the beach, it will fit in the Volvo much better. What are we going to do with it if we are lucky enough to find it?'

'Take it back to my work. There will not be any staff there in the evenings, you do realise we might find nothing.'

'James, Henry made that map and did his best with his brother to hide it. If not the box, we can be sure he buried something very important.'

'We need to move on now, we have Mrs Brooks to pick up.' She was already standing outside the apartment block looking very smart when we arrived.

We set off for the hospital. She said, 'Do not be alarmed when you meet George, he is not in any pain, just not able to converse with anyone.'

Having parked the car, we set off following Mrs Brooks into the hospital. George was in a pleasant room with a nice view of the garden.

Much to our surprise, he was in his dressing gown sitting by the window. 'George, this is nice to see you up,' said Mrs Brooks. There was no answer. A nurse came into the room.

'We have dressed George for you today, it might help him to regain his memory, his other injuries have healed now, being on his feet might help. I am not trying to raise your hopes, you are never sure if things will improve.'

Sophie said, 'Hello George,' but he did not answer. 'He seems such a nice man.'

'He was a lovely man,' said Mrs Brooks.

Having stayed with George for an hour we decided to leave.

'You know I am sure George was trying to lift his arm by the window then!' Sophie said.

'It is just wishful thinking, my dear, take me home, James.'

We dropped Mrs Brooks off, I drove Sophie back to the Prince Edward Hotel.

'If we get a reply from Liverpool, we might be going there in the coming week.'

'If only George would wake up, I feel sure he knows more than us, perhaps we are missing something?'

'I really thought he tried to move his hand; I did not imagine it.'

'We should start to think about Liverpool docks now, we are certain the Albatross sailed from there. It was an important journey she set out on to carry a £60,000 cargo. The Albatross sailed but where was she heading? We need to establish that. It must be the next part in this puzzle, Sophie.'

'Thanks for a lovely lunch, James.'

She departed back into the hotel. I drove home to my apartment. On Tuesday morning Sophie left a message for me to ring her. 'Hi James, Mrs Brooks received a letter from Liverpool, we can have two hours on Thursday with a Mr Dennis Ramsbottom. He will assist us with all known records they have at their disposal. We can take photos and he will answer our questions to the best of his ability. Our time given is one thirty till three thirty. Mrs Brooks must confirm our booking today by twelve noon.'

I dialled Sophie straight away. 'Is that a yes, James?'

'Tell Mrs Brooks I will pick you both up at nine Thursday morning. We can get lunch before we meet Mr Dennis Ramsbottom. I will bring my camera. Two hours in nautical time is not much!'

'You sound more like a sailor than a private detective,' she rang off.

On Wednesday Arthur rang. 'Good news, Mr Parker, the lifting gear has arrived. I need to come in on Friday to talk about picking the boxes of books up with the crane.'

'Four in the afternoon would suit me.'

'Likewise, Mr Parker,' and he rang off.

Thursday morning, I was up early. I had not slept well. It seemed a mammoth undertaking we had taken on!

Sophie was already outside and waiting at the hotel when I pulled up.

'Morning James, I have bought a folder to make notes on, we can compile the facts from Mr Dennis Ramsbottom. Did you remember the camera?'

'I did, thank you.' We were soon at Mrs Brooks' apartment.

'Take us to Liverpool, James,' she said as she climbed in the car. 'I have been thinking a great deal about this trip, we need to establish all the people involved in our ship from 1812, however small. All these facts will help us to move forward.'

Chapter 11

It was just coming up to twelve when we arrived in the Liverpool dock area.

'There is an arrow pointing to the Maritime museum, Albert Dock.'

Sophie was out of the car before I had switched the engine off.

'Just look at that building, it's got two huge clocks on the roof, one on each end, there are some type of giant birds on top of them.'

I helped Mrs Brooks out of the car. 'It must be twenty years or more, Sophie, from my last visit here, they are called the Liver Birds. I will tell you about them over lunch.'

We soon found a nice restaurant with a wonderful view of the Liver Building and the waterfront. We sat down and all ordered lasagne and salad, and three drinks.

'Please tell us about the Liver birds,' Sophie said.

Mrs Brooks, who seemed to be a fountain of knowledge on these occasions, began. 'If my memory serves me well, the Liver Building was built before the first world war. We are looking out on the river Mersey. Ships have been sailing from Liverpool for several centuries. In its day it was the tallest building in England. They used reinforced concrete, which was a first, it is over three hundred feet high and I think thirteen floors in total.'

'What can you tell us about the birds, they look huge and must be important?' Sophie said.

'It was decided to build two large towers, one on each end. My husband told me they were to house two huge turret clock movements. The dials are even larger than Big Ben in London. One to face out to sea for passing mariners to tell the time, the other to look out over Liverpool. There were over six thousand workers in the offices, all working here for the Royal Liver Group.'

'You still need to tell us about those bird sculptures, I have become as intrigued as Sophie.'

'If my memory is correct, they are mythical liver birds. A cross between an eagle and a cormorant. There are so many tales about them. You will notice from where we are sitting, one faces out to sea, the other faces towards the city. The one facing inland is a male looking for the pubs to open, whilst the one facing the sea is a female, looking out to sea to see if there are any handsome sailors coming up the river. It is often said if one of the birds were to fly away the city of Liverpool would cease to exist. There are many tales of Liver birds going back through history.'

'You could have made an incredible storyteller, Mrs Brooks,' Sophie said.

'I feel quite worn out. Next on our list is Mr Dennis Ramsbottom, you can ask most of the questions.'

On looking at my watch, the time was one fifteen. 'We need to present ourselves at the museum for one thirty.' I paid the bill and we set off along the waterfront.

'It says on the notice by that red ship it was a lighthouse ship, I find that very strange,' said Sophie.

'I have never heard of them, but they must exist.' We soon arrived outside the maritime museum entrance.

'This is our sole objective today, we must get maximum

information from here, take a deep breath,' said Mrs Brooks. The electric doors opened, and we went inside. I paid for two adults and one concession.

'Would you like a guide, sir?' said the young lady behind the counter.

'We have an appointment with Mr Dennis Ramsbottom for one thirty.'

'He will see you in the meeting room. I was told about your visit this morning, if you would follow me, I will take you there.' We set off down a long corridor. 'You are lucky, Dennis only works part time, he is the best person in England to talk to about shipwrecks.'

She stopped by a door and knocked, a voice from within said, 'Enter.' We were shown into a long room with a table running lengthwise which had several chairs round it, three walls had gilt-framed pictures of ships. The fourth wall seemed to be made of glass entirely, it looked out over the river Mersey.

'Thank you, Lillian,' and she departed.

He shook hands and said, 'Please take a seat, now how can we help?'

He sat down on the opposite side of the table with his back to the window.

He had an impressive and striking face, topped with silvery hair. His eyes were almost a liquid blue looking out at us, he wore a blue blazer with a bright yellow tie. We all took to him immediately.

'James perhaps you would start our enquiry,' said Sophie.

'We would like any information you have on a ship called the Albatross, it sailed from Liverpool in 1812. Two books we have acquired say it was wrecked off the Great Orme in Wales.'

'May I ask why you require this information, James?'

'It came to our attention that two fishermen brothers from

Llandudno were totally convinced there was a great deal of gold on that ship. Unfortunately, they are both dead now. Mrs Brooks' brother was very excited about some new development. He was going down to Llandudno when he had a terrible accident. Having survived, he is now brain damaged.'

Mrs Brooks took over, 'Dennis, if I may call you by your first name?'

'That is perfectly okay, please continue.'

'I feel I owe it to him, you see.'

'Where would you like me to start, Mrs Brooks?'

'The ship, we know the name, was the Albatross but not a great deal more.'

'We do have a number of enquires very much like this from time to time, most never end up satisfactorily. This ship called the Albatross, I have spent a considerable number of hours going over her history, you will be intrigued, I have no doubt. I will arrange for Lillian to bring you tea. I will gather all the relevant details.' At that he disappeared into the corridor we had come in by.

Sophie said, 'I really think he likes his job. He walked with a limp when he moved, perhaps he was an ex-navy captain.'

We stood looking out of the glass wall admiring the ships. Lillian arrived with a pot of tea for three and milk.

'I can't stop, I do find Dennis so interesting, but there is only me on the door today, 'bye.'

We had looked at the gilded framed pictures in great detail and were just starting to get restless when Dennis came through the door, carrying armfuls of what looked like old papers. He quickly unrolled one of them on the table.

'This is where we should start. It is the Albatross in all her glory. She was what we call a Brig Sloop, three hundred and sixty tons in total, built in the year of 1808. She had two masts, the depth of her hold was twelve feet, her keel was seventy-three feet long, with a gun deck of ninety feet. She was what we call a Cherokee class brig and sloop. This design was much criticised, also called coffin brigs, due to the deck being frequently awash with water.'

'You say it had a gun deck,' said Mrs Brooks.

'Perhaps I should tell you some of the history of 1812 to help you form a picture of that date in time.'

'I know we had just defeated Napoleon,' said Sophie.

'Well done, young lady, but the British Empire was fighting battles everywhere. America declared war in the same year. We had been weakened by the Napoleonic war. England sent a huge army of veteran soldiers to invade New York, raid Washington, and capture the key control of the Mississippi river at New Orleans. The French decided to help the Americans.'

'The population of England was about twelve and half million then,' said James. 'While the population of the thirteen colonies of America was only estimated at two and half million which included five hundred thousand slaves.'

'I can see I have some very knowledgeable pupils here today. Now the brig ship with its square sails was used by merchants all round the coast but a hazardous journey to America that could take two months or more, that was entirely something else. Days without wind to fill the sails, pirates intent on stealing their goods. In order to protect them, the brig sloop was born, with its extra sails it was faster. It could carry as many as sixteen thirty-two pounder carronades, plus two six-pounder guns. Try to imagine a ship broadside with six-inch cannon balls. Carronades would be mounted on a slide instead of a carriage, they needed fewer men to man them.'

'You are saying the equivalent of today's modern destroyer,' said

Mrs Brooks.

'That is entirely right. If you will bear with me a little longer, we will come to the main part of this discussion. The war of 1812 was a military conflict that lasted from June 1812 to February 1815. We had far more soldiers, many thousands fighting for the British Empire. We defeated their regiments all along the coast. The outposts inland that we tried to set up were soon found impossible to maintain. The cost of supporting the men in clothing, food, and ammunition was impossible at that distance from England. We could stop their supplies from the sea with our superior cannon power from our ships. When their troops moved inland, they could grow crops to feed themselves.

The outposts we had tried to set up were soon taken back. Eventually Major General Jackson became President of America. After that the United States of America and Britain never went to war again.'

'So the Albatross was just part of the story, for sending goods and men to fight for the British Empire.'

'Yes, that is the picture I have tried to present to you.'

Dennis started to lay out more old ledger books and pieces of old parchment paper on the long table in the middle of the room. It was completely covered.

'You are now looking at all the available data we have compiled here at our museum in Liverpool on the known facts of the Albatross. This inventory has been put together over many years by my predecessors and historians. You are welcome to take photos.'

Mrs Brooks said, 'The books we have looked at say it was rumoured that the ship was carrying a £60,000 cargo. Do you think there is any possibility it could be true, Dennis?'

'It is more than possible, but we can only deal in facts, Mrs

Brooks. You will need to go through the goods that were loaded, the list of merchants, and number of crew, who was on it and why. You have a very daunting task ahead of you.'

'Thank you for your help, we are very grateful to you for your valuable time,' Sophie said.

'I am very interested in your quest, you must remember newspapers help to cement things together through the years, such as what the weather was like on the day the ship went down. There are small birds called the turnstone, they keep looking under stones. It is what you will be doing to move forward. You never know it could be the find of the century and will help you in your endeavour to add more to our known history.'

'James, you need to take photos now, our time is nearly up,' said Sophie.

What with Sophie's notes, the extensive photos I took, Mrs Brooks making a filing system that we all three could understand, Dennis clearing the table we hadn't realised how time had flown. It was now four o'clock. Dennis said he was impressed with our approach to the coming task. We wished him and Lillian all the best and started the journey back from Liverpool. My passengers were soon fast asleep in the back of the car. I arrived in London just before nine.

'I have had enough excitement for one day,' Mrs Brooks said when we dropped her off at her apartment. 'We can catch up on Wednesday.'

'Back to the hotel, or The White Feathers for a meal, Sophie?'

'If they are still serving, I would like to eat with you, James.'

We sat eating our meal in silence, both thinking of the day in Liverpool.

Sophie said, 'It is quite hard work being a detective, James, do you wish we had never started?'

'There are times when I think the three of us must be crazy, but it has brought us all together, with a common purpose. I do not think I want to pack up yet.'

'The weather forecast is not good for the long-range weather report, for the coming two weeks. Our dig on the Great Orme will have to be put on hold, James.'

'There is no way we can even contemplate our dig, but we could take the metal detector down this coming weekend, establish where to dig, and mark the spot. What with carrying the spade and the depth bar, we may have to carry a long box down that hill on wet grass.'

'Supposing Henry did not bury the box …?'

'Let us not cross that bridge yet, Sophie, I will drop you off at the hotel, we both have to work tomorrow.'

Chapter 12

On Friday morning, Sophie rang sounding very excited, 'James, my maiden aunt who I lived with in Nottingham – I can't believe it – when she died, she left a will mentioning me! The solicitor said he could meet me there on this Saturday at twelve o'clock at the house. I can go on the train, I just wondered if you would like to come, I could treat you to lunch.'

'What time train are you thinking of booking? I need to see Arthur in person to speak to him about the lifting gear in our dispatch area, but I will come if I can.'

'There is a train at nine forty-five, shall I book it?'

'Yes, I will be there, looking forward to a train journey, meet you at the station.'

I arrived at St Pancras station with two minutes to spare.

'Just starting to get anxious, James.' We boarded, and the train was on its way.

The train pulled into Nottingham station on time and we set off on foot for Sophie's maiden aunt's address. It was just coming up to twelve o'clock when we arrived. It was set back from the curb without a driveway, behind a mellow brick wall with a wrought-iron gate. It had a small front garden with a yellow privet hedge.

Sophie pressed the bell. The door was answered by a man in in a fawn suit.

'Miss Sophie Appleby, I am very pleased to meet you.'

'How do you know my name?'

'There is a picture of you with your aunt on the mantel shelf, please come in.' He took us into the front sitting room, 'If you would take a seat, I will proceed. My name is Mr Simpson.'

'Mr Simpson, this my very good friend James.'

'Pleased to meet you, sir. Now Miss Appleby, your aunt appointed me as the executor of her will concerning the property we are in today. You have been made the sole beneficiary of the house and contents.'

'I did not know she had made a will, she never told me, Mr Simpson.'

'It was made in my office some three years ago. I have brought several papers for you to sign for me here today. There is also a small amount of money I will need to sort. If you could come to my office in about three weeks' time, we should be able to complete all the paperwork and I will pass it on in its entirety. The world is full of surprises, Miss Appleby.'

Having put all his paperwork in order, we shook hands and he left.

Sophie said, 'I have been left a house, James, I have been left a house!'

'The best thing for you is a cup of strong black coffee, I will look in the kitchen and see if there is any.' When she had regained her composure, she took me on a tour of the house. It had a beautiful coloured Minton tiled floor in the hall, two rooms and a kitchen downstairs. There were three bedrooms and a bathroom upstairs. The back of the house had a small neatly laid out garden.

'This was my bedroom at the back of the house, my aunt slept in the front, we shared the bathroom. I was at college with no income when she was alive. I knew a solicitor was sorting things out but I had no idea of the outcome, hence I moved to London.'

'You have at least three weeks to think this out. I have a similar problem with my father's house in Devil's Bridge, if you remember, when we started our investigation of Henry. My advice would be to tread water for a while.'

At that we set off back to the station, with Sophie saying every hundred yards, 'I own a house, James.'

'How about you treat us to sandwiches, we can eat them on the train, instead of lunch out and wasting time.'

'Okay, I will buy them from the station.'

We were soon on the two thirty train travelling back to London. 'If you can get your mind back on the investigation, would you like to come to my works on Sunday morning?'

'That's a yes, James, what are you planning to do?'

'I would like to download all the photos I took in Liverpool. We can then print them in A4 size and make up three sets, one for each of us. We can study them individually on our own, over the coming days.'

'If it was not a wreck due to a storm, then it had to be sabotage, but what are we looking for?'

'Who was on her; there must have been an inventory of passengers, crew, goods she was carrying, et cetera.'

'It is going to be an immense task, but so is £60,000 in 1812. It was also an immense amount of money in those days.'

'Well, now we have got you back on track, let us say ten thirty tomorrow morning.'

At four fifteen the train pulled into St Pancras station, I walked her back to the hotel, and said goodbye.

Her parting comment, 'I own a house, James.'

I walked back to my apartment and decided to ring up Maisie, my parents' housekeeper, in Devil's Bridge. She answered quite quickly.

'Hello Maisie.'

'Is that you, Master James?'

'I am ringing to see if everything is okay, with the house and you and Jack.'

'Everything is fine, you need not worry, Master James, the house is fine. We are slower than we used to be but more than able to manage here. Would you be coming down to us?'

'Not for a while, let me know if there are any problems,' I said 'Goodbye' and rang off. After a light meal I retired to bed with a book. On Sunday morning, having washed and shaved, I set off on foot to work.

I had not been in my works on a Sunday very often. The total silence was uncanny, I was soon cheered up when Sophie arrived. 'Morning James, I feel quite privileged to see behind the scenes of your publishing business, how can I help?'

'I have started to download the pictures from my camera into our computer.'

'This is all very advanced, James, I did not know we could do that.'

'We do use some high-tech equipment, I can then send them to a printing machine. If you can take them and sort three copies of each, we can sort them into groups and we will have something to look at individually and think about.'

'We can start to add the cost of everything in the goods loaded, James, it will be interesting to see if they add up to £60,000.'

'With Mrs Brooks looking, she has a fine pair of eyes, she found those rubbed out circles which enabled us to get this far. Perhaps if she has not gone to see George, we can drop a set off later today.' It was just coming up to twelve when we started to clear everything up.

'Would you like me to take you to lunch at The White Feathers, Sophie?'

'I was hoping you might ask me.'

I switched off the lights, locked the doors, and we set out for The White Feathers.

On arriving I ordered two drinks. 'And have you a table for two for lunch please?'

'We can find you a table, Mr Parker, the table in the window has been reserved, if you could follow me, sir.'

'It seems everybody goes out for Sunday lunch in London, James.'

We ordered and sat looking round, there was a totally different cliental on Sunday lunchtime, not one of the Wednesday crowd did I find. In no time two roast dinners arrived like magic.

'Can I suggest we walk to Mrs Brooks after lunch, it will be nice after we have managed this huge meal.'

'This time next week we will be eating sandwiches on the Great Orme. It will be a perfect distraction if people come by while we use the metal detector.'

'We should take a tablecloth and make it a proper picnic and use it to cover up the tools you think we might need.'

'That is a good idea. I will pack that depth tee bar; it might give us an idea of how deep Henry buried this box when we do dig it up in the rain in the coming weeks.'

'If we do not find the box, what next?'

'Positive is the only way to think. I will settle the bill, let's see if Mrs Brooks is in,' with Sophie in tow I set off.

We were soon let in and seated.

'I did not expect you both till Wednesday; it is a nice surprise!'

'The photos I took at Liverpool, we have printed three sets, all A4 size, at my work this morning. I have a set for you to start to look at, we will each do the same. We can compare our thoughts and notes on Wednesday evening.'

'You are efficient, James, have you got time for a cup of tea both of you?'

We said, 'Yes,' she disappeared into the kitchen to put the kettle on.

'There are so many people in Regents Park this afternoon,' said Sophie.

'One weekend when we have solved this case I will take you there. Mrs Brooks will miss the view when she downsizes to somewhere smaller.'

Three cups of tea on a silver tray arrived, they were put down on the low table between us.

'My husband always liked tea in a china cup served on this tray weekends. He looked forwards to it.'

'After Thursday in Liverpool, we went to Nottingham on the train on Saturday because Sophie has been left a house there by a maiden aunt.'

'You have had an exciting week.'

'One day in the future, I shall invite you and James to stay for the weekend.'

'I think we will both accept, my dear. Now has anybody thought about what we are looking for, we seem to have a lot to look at.'

'James, where do we start?'

'Number of survivors, if any, how many crew did she sail with, who and what sort of people they were. The cargo will be a quite extensive list, but we have to do it. Make sure we know where she was heading and why. And lastly Dennis said newspapers are a good source of information.'

'I am not sure you could get a paper in 1812, James, if you leave that to me I will put it top of my list to find out about,' said Mrs Brooks.

'Can I start on the list of cargo? If it had all those guns to protect it, there must have been some special items on board,' said Sophie.

We said goodbye, took the lift down into the lobby, and started to walk back to the Prince Edward Hotel.

'Do you mind me holding your arm, James?' Sophie said. 'We seem to spend a great deal of time together.'

'Let me say I enjoy it and do feel protective for you. I have not thought about it anymore than that. We are back at the hotel! I will see you on Wednesday at The White Feathers.' She kissed my cheek and departed into the hotel.

The alarm woke me with a start, it was Monday morning. I had not slept well. The last week had been both mentally and physically tiring. The visit to Liverpool Maritime Museum with the huge task we had set ourselves, Sophie being left a house in Nottingham, Mrs Brooks paying for endless trips to Llandudno had worn me out. I also had a business to run. I showered, made strong coffee, then set off for my office.

Jane was already hard at it. 'Morning James, Arthur left a note for you to ring him sometime today.'

'There's no time like the present. I will get straight to it.' Arthur picked up the phone on the first ring.

'Good news, the lifting gear is ready, Mr Parker. If I pick it up on Thursday, we could install it on Saturday. That will leave Sunday for any hitches but I am not expecting any!'

'I will be down in Llandudno this coming weekend, but I can give you a set of keys at The White Feathers on Wednesday evening. If there are any problems, we can sort them on Monday morning.'

At that I said goodbye and he rang off. Having decided to get to grips with another part of the works, I asked Jane for suggestions. 'You could see how Roger goes about book cover designs. He has been here the longest, he started with your father many years ago, he is an inspiration to us all.'

My first impression when I walked in the room where Roger worked was that he was a very precise and tidy person. The walls were covered in books with their faces looking out to the centre of the room. In appearance I would say he was in his early fifties, he had a round face with slightly wavy hair. He wore tortoiseshell glasses.

'This a pleasure, Mr Parker, what can I do for you?'

'I would like to get to know you all in person, so please call me James. Perhaps we could start with book covers. How do you choose them when advising?'

'I will try to tell and show you very briefly of how we go about it, James, but remember it takes several years of training to become a good graphic designer.'

'If I can understand a small part of what you do, Roger, I would be very grateful. At least on the phone I would not feel so inadequate.'

'Let us make a start! We have to try and provide a cover that tells a story. Ideally a story that evokes the words behind the cover. Most people that write books need a graphic designer. A book cover will determine whether the reader even gives it a second glance on a bookshelf in a shop or library. We try to give an eye-catching cover, the contrast between the font and the picture needs to be just right. There are so many tricks we use to make the person who picks up that book unable to put it down.'

'I should want to buy them all, Roger, if you were running a book shop! Thank you, I will try and remember your words of wisdom.'

'Any time I can help, I have enjoyed the chat, James.'

It was just coming up to lunchtime when I arrived back in my office.

'You have to sign some letters for me later today, James. How did you get on with Roger?'

'Well I have certainly been inspired by him. I am so glad he is working for us and not anybody else, we are indeed lucky to have him.'

'Enjoy your lunch, I will see you later.'

In between eating my sandwiches, I started to look at the list we had prepared on Sunday morning concerning the Albatross. Mrs Brooks finding out about newspapers, Sophie tackling the cargo list, I would make a start on the crew and passengers that were on board on that fateful day in 1812, the captain or commander and second commander as they were often called. The first commander and crew would sail the Brig and the second commander was responsible for the guns she carried and ammunition, at least fifty men plus, in total.

Jane disturbed me from this train of thought.

'Can we sign these papers, James, I need to get them in the post please.'

She had soon set off for the post. My mind soon drifted back to our wreck. How could that ship with all those disciplined men not have been saved, only the best would have been chosen for a voyage to America, unless it was sabotage. But then the crew would have been no match for trained solders, so we could rule that out. The clock was soon showing four thirty in my office, I decided to leave early and have a quiet evening.

Having made a meal accompanied by a glass of wine, I then took a book to bed. I was just unable to concentrate. Perhaps the Albatross was overloaded, she could have been low in the water. The hold would have been full, the weight of all those guns and ammunition was a possibility to think about. I eventually drifted off to sleep.

Tuesday and Wednesday were uneventful at my office. I was looking forwards to meeting Sophie at The White Feathers. Having arrived early, I gave Arthur a set of keys for the overhead conveyor change-over he had planned for the coming weekend.

'You seem to be coping well with your father's business, Mr Parker. I would like to buy you a drink, what would you like?'

'A pint of bitter would be very nice, thank you.'

Sophie had just come through the door, so I left Arthur to his pint and newspaper. We were soon seated at our table in the window. The waiter brought her a glass of red wine and took our order.

'This cargo list I have taken on, it is quite daunting, James, it is in old English script, crates, boxes, livestock, guns, ammunition grain, and that's only the start of it. I need to break it down into sections. I am not sure what we are looking for.'

'You are not on your own, there were over fifty crew in total, some for sailing the ship, and then all the military men to look after the armament. Perhaps Mrs Brooks will have some ideas.'

'I would like to treat you tonight, James.'

'What with Arthur buying me a pint, and now you treating me as well, I feel quiet spoiled.'

'I am a lady of property now.'

'I can't argue with that.'

Having paid the bill, we set off for Mrs Brooks apartment, we soon arrived, and I pressed the intercom button.

'Hello, come straight up.'

We were seated at the table in no time at all, she had made tea and joined us.

'Now who is going to be first?' she said.

'We are hoping you might, Mrs Brooks.'

'I have found out that there were newspapers in 1812. In fact, they were about in the 1700s, much to my surprise.'

'These are known facts, then,' Sophie said.

'They certainly are, but the papers were not in the modern sense, my dear. If you wanted a paper you would subscribe to their company, it would be a limited number of people that could afford one to be delivered to the door. I think the London Gazette is probably the oldest, another old paper was the Cumberland Pacquet, and I am sure there were many more.'

'That is now an established fact, well done.'

'James, I can do better than that. Both newspapers mention the United States of America, the USA had declared war on England in 1812. To my mind the Albatross was carrying goods for feeding our soldiers, and weapons.'

'You are right on both counts. James reckons there were over fifty men on board. There are crates of muskets on the cargo list. That ship was going to America.'

'Now Dennis said it was probably on the way to America. It stopped off at the bay of Llandudno, we know that. Was it to avoid a storm or a last time to go to shore?'

'If you will go on searching the papers, Mrs Brooks, anything you find that was unusual that fateful day, however small, around Llandudno will help to fill in the picture.'

'Sophie you must carry on with that cargo list.'

'If I only had more ideas, James.'

'When you have divided it in sections, treat it like a maths equation, we can cancel out livestock and probably most of the food items. Gun powder and weapons we need to think about. Leave large crates on the list, they could conceal a safe. If there were £60,000 on board, it would have to go somewhere.'

'You have given me a thought. What about all the merchants that supplied goods to the ship? Can we link their names with the goods supplied? Perhaps their names might be in the ledger books that

Dennis showed us. The British Government would only have been dealing with very up market traders, it would not have been small businesses,' said Mrs Brooks.

'I think we could all go down in Davey Jones' locker trying to solve this riddle.'

'Remember what Dennis said, James, about the turnstone bird, we have to keep turning things over. Henry and William were stuck, there are three of us to sort it out,' said Sophie.

'You can be sure we will be drinking something stronger than tea when we do,' said Mrs Brooks in a nonchalant way.

'Are you coming this weekend with us to Llandudno, Mrs Brooks?'

'This weekend I am going to see George, to see if he is improving. Best of luck with the metal detector. Ring me on Sunday night when you get back, please, I do not want to wait till Monday.'

At that we wished her goodnight. We went down in the lift and outside into the cold night air. Sophie was soon holding my arm, and I walked her back to the hotel.

Chapter 13

Saturday morning I walked to work and backed the Volvo estate out of the yard at the rear of the building. I then collected the metal detector from my office, and a flat cap. Arthur was already hard at it.

'Morning Mr Parker, it will be up and running when you get back Sunday night. There is a small problem. The makers supply a lifting hook, but you will need to come up with the best way to get the boxes attached to it.'

'I will give it my full attention on Monday morning, Arthur, best of luck with it.'

Sophie did not recognise the Volvo when I pulled up at the hotel, it took a sharp beep on the horn to get her attention. 'Morning James, I forgot we were going in the Volvo.'

'Did you remember your hat and walking gear?'

'I certainly did. All present and reporting for duty, sir.'

'Let's hope if Mr Snoop is around, he won't be looking for the Volvo.'

Having put Sophie's case in the back we were on the way. It was just coming up to two o'clock when we pulled up in Shrewsbury for a late lunch

'I have quite missed not going to Llandudno last weekend. Are you sure about how to use the metal detector, James?'

'We are about to find out. You will have to be patient till Sunday, our best shot at it is after three in the afternoon.'

We arrived quite late in the afternoon at our boarding house, we had taken our time over lunch. Sam soon appeared to carry the cases in.

'We missed you both last weekend.'

'Likewise, Sam.'

'Branwin has just put the kettle on, make yourselves at home.'

Having unpacked we went down to the resident's lounge. 'We seem to be the only people staying this weekend. I wonder if Sam and Branwin would like to go out for a meal.'

'That is lovely thought, James, I will take the cups into the kitchen and ask.'

In no time at all they said, 'We would like that very much, but can we go halves with the bill?'

'Let us see what it is first. Where would you like to go?'

'We both like Italian food. Mario's serves the best pasta in Llandudno.'

'Then Mario's it is.'

Branwin said, 'I will book it for eight o'clock, we do not get many people for rooms after seven thirty, then we can lock up for the night.'

Sam said, 'We normally walk to the restaurant, would that suit you both?'

We set off, Sophie holding my arm, Sam and Branwin leading the way. We arrived to a very warm welcome as soon as we walked in, by Mario himself. We were shown to our table with a flourish of hands and our coats soon wafted away. Luigi from Naples was our waiter for the evening. Sam introduced us to him. 'Tell me, Luigi, what you would recommend in your knowledge of Italian food for us all?'

'If you are new to our food, I would suggest for your Primo, which is a starter, try our wild garlic butter on music paper. It is a very special thin bread. For your Secondo, main course, pappardelle with rabbit chestnut ragu. It is the chef's speciality flat pasta strips tossed with a rich meaty ragu, and creamy chestnut and fragrant orange zest.'

'Thank you, Luigi, for your help, we would like two of those please.'

'You had better make that four, and a bottle of Merlot wine,' said Sam.

'And a bottle of table water,' said Sophie. The wine and table water soon arrived.

'James, I thought I should mention,' said Branwin, 'our local newsagent told me the reporter from our Llandudno paper had been making enquiries about where you were staying. What he did not know was that the lady running it is my sister.'

'Nothing to worry about, we know him as Snoops. He plays the organ in Church Walk on a Sunday morning.'

'There is nothing that goes on in Llandudno, James, that William Jones can't tell you about. He comes from a long family line of reporters stretching back several generations. Your business is without any doubt your own, but tread carefully.'

'One day we will tell you, Branwin, and Sam.'

Our first course was served by Luigi, 'Enjoy your Primo,' he said with a twinkle in his eyes.

'He certainly makes you feel important to him,' Sophie said.

'That is because he is a professional head waiter, their job is to make you come back for more. We have seen film stars and many celebrities here over the years,' said Sam.

The plates were soon cleared and the main course, Pappardelle, arrived and our glasses filled with wine. 'Enjoy your Secondo.'

Sam told us about life when he was younger and the night seemed to just disappear.

When Luigi cleared the table, having enjoyed the first two courses, we were unanimous that he should pick the Italian desert for us. He surprised us with a cannoli type desert that was out of this world. The dishes were cleared. Luigi was soon back with an after-dinner drink of grappa. 'It's on the house,' he declared, 'Enjoy.' Later, when Sam asked for our coats, Luigi even came outside and waved a taxi down, 'Safer for you, come again,' and he was soon back to the last guests.

Having been dropped off by our taxi driver we were soon saying goodnight.

'Make breakfast a bit later please,' said Sophie, 'I am not used to nights like this.'

On Sunday morning I was up before Sophie, 'My head is not very clear, James.'

'You will soon be okay when we walk along the front later, it will blow all the cobwebs away.'

Having enjoyed our later breakfast, we said goodbye to our hosts, and started to drive down to the sea front.

'I do not think we should walk along the front yet, we would be better making sure Snoops is playing the organ in Church Walk. If you pull up a short distance from the church, I will pop my head round the door. We can set off knowing he is not playing the organ at Saint Tudno's on the Great Orme, there is an outdoor service this morning, it started at eleven o'clock.'

While Sophie checked on Snoops, I looked for his car, it was parked back at his flat.

We set off on the long climb up Marine Drive. It was just coming up to twelve when we arrived at the church.

'The outdoor service is still in progress, James. We need to give everybody time to leave, before we park by the rear wall.'

We carried on driving till we reached the summit. 'Let us take some time out in the Randolph Turpin bar, Sophie.' Having made two coffees last the best part of an hour, we decided to make a move. We set off down to Saint Tudno's church, parked the Volvo by the rear wall. The last of the congregation were still leaving. We took our time putting macs and hats on. The metal detector was in my rucksack.

Sophie walked to the front of the church; she was soon back. 'The coast is clear, let's make a move.'

'That does seem a very appropriate thing to say given the circumstances.'

'James, be serious.'

I locked the car and we crossed the road and took the steps opposite from where we had parked. The steps soon ended, we took the path to higher ground, then a gentle slope of grass till we were looking down towards the two gates in the churchyard wall. 'It is just above us now, the small hollow with rocks behind it.'

The flat shelf about fifty feet wide was invisible if you looked from below, the grass slope carried on up above us.

'Somebody further back in the churchyard might see our heads but we have to take that chance, James, I have bought a ball of string and two small sticks. If we start at the back and move the sticks forward two feet at a time, we can be sure not to miss anything.'

'The hollow is only no more than ten feet wide, my guess it will be towards the back, let us make a start.'

It was on our third pass in the middle, Sophie had moved the sticks three times, when the metal detector started to make a shrill noise, it was over an area of about a foot square. We both sat down looking at one another.

'It could not be a tab off a drinks can, a walker certainly did not drop something a foot square, Sophie.'

'I will try your depth bar, let me do it.'

She immediately hit a wooden object only three inches down through the turf. On further investigation it was about a foot wide and three- or four-feet long.

'I wonder if it is just a wooden truss, from when the church roof was blown off, one thing for sure it is too narrow for a coffin.'

'James, my guess is it's just a plank, you do have a vivid imagination. Underneath we will find what Henry and William buried. It must have been terribly important to go to all this trouble.' Let us go over the rest of the shelf and make sure we have not missed anything, however small.'

'I wish I had brought the spade now.'

'You will just have to contain yourself, James, not only do we have to dig it up we have to get it down to the car. We have no idea what it is or how heavy it might be.'

'You are right. Let's clear up and get out of here.'

Having put two sticks to mark the spot, we made our way down onto the road, metal detector safely packed, we started to drive down into Llandudno.

'I never thought I would be looking forward to a poor weather forecast, James.'

'Let us hope we enjoy it when it comes, clues are thin on the ground at the moment.'

'You do realise that is a joke, James.'

When we arrived in Llandudno it was just coming up to four. We set off back to London.

Chapter 14

On Monday morning, after a good night's sleep, on reflection the weekend trip was without doubt a step in the right direction. As usual, Jane was already working hard when I arrived at work.

'Did you enjoy the weekend, James?'

'I certainly did.'

'I viewed the loading area when I arrived, that was why I came in so early. Very impressed so far, Arthur is a very tidy worker.'

'He is, would you like to come with me? I would value your input, Jane.'

With the conveyor in the centre of the loading bay, the two tables each side of it on movable casters, the track above the conveyor at ninety degrees to it all looked an impressive piece of kit.

'Are you intending to load from both sides?'

'We are, flat-pack boxes put together on one side on the table the same height as the conveyor. The person this side will fill them with books. The crane will lift them on to the conveyor, from there straight into the vans, and away to the customer.'

'How do you pick them up with that hook on the crane?'

'I will be getting Arthur to make a strong steel coat hanger. It will fit on the hook on the crane, we will lay nylon lifting straps on the tabletops, the boxes on top. When they are packed, the nylon straps will go over the bottom bar of the steel coat hanger.'

' So there will be no more lifting boxes full of books by hand?'

'That will be a thing of the past, any age will be able to pack and load books.'

'I think all our employees will all want to try this.'

We were soon back in my office. Jane made us both a cup of tea, while I rang Arthur.

'All okay, Mr Parker?'

'It most certainly is, I will drop you off a sketch of the lifting hook arrangement on Wednesday, at The White Feathers.'

'If you're pleased, then I am too, 'bye Mr Parker,' and rang off.

The rest of Monday was uneventful. I decided to finish early from work and watched the television after eating, then I took an early night.

Mid morning on Tuesday, Jane said,

'We seem to have a well wrapped parcel for you, it came with the post this morning.'

'I was not expecting one, Jane.' On opening it there was a letter on the top of the box.

It began,

My dear Mr Parker, it must be some five or six weeks since you and the young lady called Sophie, came to see me about Henry and William's life here in Llandudno. I was not very helpful at the time. The death of both of them had left me with a big gap in my life, and I do apologise to you both.

I recently decided to clear an old shed in my garden. It was where William and Henry kept old tins of paint, jars of slotted screws, also many boxes full of old papers and things to do with Llandudno through the years. In the bottom of a box was another box so to speak. I don't ever throw anything away without looking at it. There were several old maps, I am quite sure some of them were Llandudno before we had a pier! and some of the early town, probably 1850s or even earlier. They had probably picked them up at one of the auction houses over the years.

Now you might think why I am telling you all this, Mr Parker. In amongst the old maps was a piece from an old newspaper. It had to be old, some of the script was in old English. It is very difficult to read. One of my neighbours said the letter S and F and other letters were hard to understand.

Now to get to the main point, the newspaper cutting was all about a Brig ship called the Albatross. She had set sail from Liverpool and dropped anchor at Llandudno, this was her last night before setting sail for America. The paper says this ship carried goods like most of the merchant ships, it also had a ninety-feet gun deck to protect our fleets, on the way to America.

The soldiers that looked after the guns had gone into the town looking for whores in the taverns, getting drunk in the process. Even the cook had gone with them. Now the story in the newspaper, who had printed it in good faith, was told by a local; it seems the bay was lit up like daylight. The ship had gone up in flames and loud explosions, there were several local people who could verify this.

The local person who told the story to the newspaper said he had gone down to the beach just as the light was coming up. He found a fellow strapped to a rigging pole, who had survived. He told the local chap there was only seven men left on board to look after the ship. They had all had a lot to drink, then one of the crew lit a fire to cook some fresh meat. A spark had ignited a keg of gunpowder which exploded. It set off a chain reaction all down the ship. Now he said he had some sort of stomach bug, he was at the far end of the gun deck, he was a sail trimmer and looked after the rigging on board.

When the gun powder and ammunition started to explode, he grabbed a rigging pole and put a rope onto it and jumped overboard. His next memory was waking up when the local man came along, early next morning.

The following morning the Welsh Fusiliers sent twenty men to guard the beach, some of the locals were arrested.

Beach-combing was carried out whenever there was a wrecked ship. The spoils of the sea. The British Government never saw it that way. The soldiers had all absconded, they were redcoats and a rough lot.

The paper had tried to find the only survivor, who had told the story to the local chap. But the sail trimmer just disappeared, the local was accused of making up the story and the newspaper of being liberal with the truth. Two weeks later the Welsh Fusiliers packed up and left Llandudno.

Perhaps, Mr Parker, this will help you with your quest into Henry and William's lives. The maps will give you an idea of the past in Llandudno. Please feel to do as you think fit. When you have finished with them, perhaps a museum would like them, it is entirely at your discretion. I do hope you and Sophie are well and you would be most welcome any time you are in Llandudno.

Yours, Mrs Thomas.

I found it so hard to concentrate on work the rest of the day. Wednesday was not any easier, this huge step in our investigation had left me quite exhausted.

On Wednesday evening I met up with Sophie at The White Feathers at seven o'clock. I gave Arthur the sketch of the lifting hook.

'It will be early next week before I can do it, Mr Parker. I will make a spare, you will be better off with two.'

I left him a pint behind the bar and joined Sophie.

'I can't stop thinking about that steel depth bar I had in my hand hitting a box or plank when that metal detector started up, James.'

'Let us enjoy our meal and wait till we get to Mrs Brooks. Have you heard anymore about the house in Nottingham?'

'Not a thing, I am quite glad really. My job is so demanding, and this investigation is more than I can cope with. I do need you, James, will we still see each other when this is all over?'

'Of course you will, and Mrs Brooks, now forget it all, think about all the pleasant surprises we have had together.'

Having eaten a very nice meal with a glass of wine, we set off for Mrs Brooks apartment. I managed to contain my fresh knowledge until we were seated at her table with a cup of tea. 'Now who is going to go first this week?'

Sophie said, 'I will start; amongst the cargo on board were a large number of bales of red cloth. Without any doubt they were to make uniforms for the red coats of the soldiers.'

'But why have red coats?'

'I rang Dennis in Liverpool, James. The main reason was to recognise your fellow men. The weapons were not good enough for long range, it was mainly hand to hand combat. He also said discipline was harsh in the army. The redcoats had little self-discipline; heavy drinking was a common problem among all ranks alike. Mostly they had enlisted in the army for life for the money, some were ex-convicts with no civilian life, the regiments were their homes.'

'My thoughts,' said Mrs Brooks, 'They could have something to do with the ship going down, they were a rough lot!'

'You can say that again, I had better tell you about the parcel I received through the post from Mrs Thomas in Chapel Street Llandudno, William's friend and landlady. It seems she decided to clear an old wooden shed in her garden. It mainly contained William and Henry's things from the past. Mostly it was tins of paint, metal screws, boxes of useful things for boats. She found a box in a box so to speak, her own words, it contained old books, maps, very old, from the first half of the 1800s. The biggest shock is part of an old newspaper in old English. It is all about the night the Albatross was wrecked.'

'Did it say how it came about, James?' said Mrs Brooks with hands clenched on the top of the table.

'I think you had better both read it before we say any more. I have put it through the copier at work. You have one each to look at.'

Chapter 15

Sophie looked as white as a sheet; Mrs Brooks did not look much better when they had each read their copies that I had given them.

'I need another cup of tea with a spoonful of whisky after reading that.' She disappeared into the kitchen to put the kettle on.

'What on earth will Dennis make of this?'

'That is the least of our worries. How we proceed with this new information is very important. We must be so careful about it.'

'I have put whisky in all three cups, we need it,' said Mrs Brooks.

'I have been thinking about the £60,000 we think was on board our brig ship. If it was coins of the realm, when the ship blew up, they would have come down like rain. There would be so many coins in the sand people would have been digging them up ever since.'

'There are always metal detectors combing the sands. I do not think it was coins on the ship, Mrs Brooks,' said Sophie.

'It had to be gold.'

'But where would you hide it, James?'

'I think that somebody was on that ship who knew about it! He was not supposed to know. It had to be linked to whoever loaded it.'

'The person who loaded it might not have been aware. But the Merchant for certain would, James, he would know for sure.'

'Out of fifty people on board, there will be only a few merchants trusted by the government, with a cargo like that. That will help to narrow the search down.'

'Sophie you have an extraordinary mind for one so young.'

'Gold would be very heavy, it could not have been put in a crate, you would never pick it up,' said Mrs Brooks.

'Sophie, I would concentrate on boxes; you can cancel all the large crates that will make your list shorter. If we can link specific boxes with merchants, we will narrow it down even more.'

'I wonder if Dennis could find out from Snoops when the first Newspapers were printed in Llandudno. He could be inquiring on behalf of Liverpool Museum. If it was done subtly he would not know we were involved.'

'James, we should not take that line of enquiry unless it is essential.'

'You are right, this could be the story of the century if we can ever find that gold. There again, it is his hometown, he knows every nook and cranny in Llandudno, past and present.'

We talked round and round in circles, the long-case clock struck eleven o'clock.

'It is time we let Mrs Brooks go to bed, James.'

We went down in the lift and out into the night air. Sophie tucked her arm through mine and we set off back to the Prince Edward Hotel.

'Perhaps if we don't get to Llandudno this coming weekendm James, we could go to see George again with Mrs Brooks?'

'Until the weather turns to rain and mist there is no way we can go digging on the Great Orme. It would be very foolish to even contemplate it.'

We soon arrived back at the hotel.

'There is a man on the other side of the road, he is looking in that shop window, I think he might be watching us!'

'You need to be sure before you say things like that.'

'If you turn with your back to him and kiss me, I could make sure, we do need to be certain.'

I turned with my back to the shop opposite and kissed Sophie for about two minutes. 'What do you reckon, was he or wasn't he watching us?'

'James, I had my eyes shut, I am not sure,' she said with a smile. 'You try working it out.'

At that she disappeared into the hotel.

The penny dropped. I had to smile as I walked back to my apartment, I would need to make some important decisions in the near future, and it wouldn't be about Henry and William.

On Thursday we had a book run of six hundred copies. Even without the lifting hook, we used the tables to make up the boxes and fill them with books in a much easier fashion. We had saved quite considerably on the time taken. Jane was all smiles. All in all, a very nice day.

Friday mid-morning Sophie rang.

'The weather forecast is sunny again for Saturday and Sunday, can I ring Mrs Brooks to see if we can visit George with her on Sunday?'

'I could take you both out for lunch, pick you up at twelve thirty, why not.'

'You are a darling, James,' and she rang off.

Whatever next? I had enjoyed our weekends together but was not sure about anything more.

'James, are you alright, you look so far removed this morning!'

'Never felt better, Jane.'

'We need to go through the wages bill this month sometime today.'

Having checked through our expenditure, and money taken over the month, I was very pleased to see a small profit. I did not want to dig too deeply into our capital when I paid Arthur. At five o'clock I wished Jane a nice weekend, then left her to lock up, walked back to my apartment, very happy. What a week!

Saturday morning; I awakened feeling refreshed, so I decided to make a start on the list of merchants from Liverpool, as that was where the Albatross was loaded. There were so many it was difficult to know the best way to tackle it. If I cancelled the arms and ammunition crates, the Merchant would know he could not hide anything in them and they could be opened anytime if the ship was attacked. The grain merchants would also know their crates might be opened anytime. During two months at sea the crew must eat a lot of food.

Several tons of pig lead, packed by a dealer in paints and oils from Whitehaven, I put a question mark against his name. Next one hundred sacks of prick fine flour, another possible hiding place. Barrels of tar, it wouldn't be that merchant. Then I came across, amongst the many papers Dennis had gave us permission to take pictures of, an article on cooking at sea. It was dated 1833. Somebody had gone to the trouble of putting it in an envelope.

From Liverpool each passenger would receive five pounds of oatmeal weekly, two pounds of biscuits, one pound of flour, two pounds of rice, a half pound of sugar, one half pound of molasses, and two ounces of tea. They are obliged to cook it the best way they can in a cook shop twelve feet by six! Sometimes they would not get cooked food for days and nights when a gale of wind is blowing, the sea could be mountains high breaking over the ship in all directions.

There was also a second article in the envelope with the date after the war, which lasted from June 1812 to February 1815. It was about how shipping expanded its reach, it became safer to travel, it became the lifeblood of the American nation in the first half of the nineteenth century. Ships and sailors connected manufactures and customers, immigrants with new homes, very much like a modern telephone system of today. By one o'clock I stopped for lunch.

I then carried on with what seemed endless lists of merchants and their goods.

On Sunday morning the sun was shining through the windows of my apartment. The lounge was covered with paperwork, small piles on chairs, there was nowhere even to sit down. I wondered if Mrs Brooks and Sophie were in the same state that I was. With nobody coming in the near future I left it all and went out for lunch.

Sophie was waiting outside the hotel; it was just coming up to twelve thirty.

'Good morning and how was your week, James?'

'Well apart from my apartment looking like a bomb has hit it and nowhere to sit down with piles of paper on every piece of furniture, it was okay.' Mrs Brooks was also waiting outside when we arrived at Sussex Place. 'The two ladies in my life on time, what have I done to deserve it, Mrs Brooks.'

'Well, you are taking us out for lunch, James.'

We were soon on our way to visit George in his care home.

'We need to look out now for a place for lunch, we are halfway there,' I said after we had driven for thirty miles.

'What about the Rising Sun on the left?' said Sophie.

'I think that is the symbol of optimism,' Mrs Brooks said.

'We certainly need plenty of that.' I drove on to the carpark and parked up. It was an old coaching inn, the dining area had oak-panelled walls with a log fire burning in an old huge chimney place. Tablecloths on the tables looked very nice. We each ordered from their lunch menu, and three glasses of wine. 'Two white and one red while we wait, please.'

We all looked round the room and admired the pictures of days gone by. Mrs Brooks was the first to broach the last week's progress.

'I have not made any more headway with the newspapers. We have established there were newspapers all around Britain when our wreck went down, what about you, Sophie?'

'My week has not been very good. I worked hard every day and then got told off for all the papers I had laid out quite neatly, there was a lot of them! The manager said we do not want conflicting interests in this hotel. I told him it would not affect my work in anyway. I had not got anywhere else to do them. He was not very pleased and gave a huge frown before marching off.'

'You poor girl, why not bring them round to my apartment, we can lay them out and work on them in the evenings. If we need to make phone calls I can do them in the day time.'

'When you see how many boxes and crates were loaded on that ship it might make you change your mind, they had not invented containers, Mrs Brooks, it was all put on by hand.'

'Now look here, four eyes are better than two! and you won't get told off.'

'If you really don't mind, I will say yes, please.'

'That is all sorted. What about you, James, and your list of merchants?'

'I have nobody to tell me off, but I can understand your manager being worried. There are piles of papers on every bit of furniture in my flat. I am trying to divide them into three piles. Grain merchants have large boxes, they could be opened up any time and if gold was in them you would never pick them up. There are several large crates I need to link with merchants. These will be in my first list. Then my second list will be smaller boxes, and their merchants, such as buttons, hats, gloves, garments. Now my last list will be barrels of tar, gunpowder, rifles, fresh-water barrels, places you would never hide anything in.'

'If it was gold to support the war, they would be the same merchants that supplied arms, gun powder, et cetera,' said Sophie.

'That is a very good point you are making, Sophie,' said Mrs Brooks.

Our lunch arrived. 'The amount of food on our plates, I wonder how they make a profit,' said Mrs Brooks.

We all tucked into a delicious Sunday roast.

I settled the bill, and we were soon on our way for the last leg of the journey. We were all in agreement that the Rising Sun Inn would be seeing us again.

'My turn to pay next time,' said Mrs Brooks.

It was coming up to three o'clock when we turned into the care home in West Horndon. We had made good time in the London traffic.

'George won't go back to the hospital; this is his home now.'

'I like the garden, there are seats with lovely views everywhere,' said Sophie.

We were taken up to the second floor.

'George has a view looking out over a nature reserve, then the Langdon Hills in the distance, Mrs Brooks. You need to have no worries, we will do our best to look after him,' the lady said. 'Any problems just press the bell to the right of the door and I will be straight up.'

She left us to look round George's new home. 'How are you today, George?' No answer.

'He still could improve, Mrs Brooks.' Sophie held his arm and George let her take him to look out of the window.

'Just look at your beautiful view, you have birds to look at, there is a black bird, George.'

I could see Mrs Brooks wiping a tear off her cheek.

We spent the next hour sorting out cupboards. We moved the table by the window so George could look out, we made a cup of tea, and Mrs Brooks looked so much better. Moving the furniture round made it feel like a home.

George let Sophie move him to the table, 'There you are, that is a nice view.'

'Time to go, I hope you two will come again with me.'

'You can be sure of that,' I said. We let ourselves out and down the stairs. The lady who took us to George's room was sitting behind her desk.

'Is everything okay and does it meet with your approval?'

'I am very pleased,' said Mrs Brooks.

'If you're happy we will do our very best for George.'

We said our goodbyes and found the car, I was just starting to let the handbrake off when Sophie said, 'You will say I am being silly but I think George tried to lift his arm again by the window.'

'It is probably your imagination running away with you,' said Mrs Brooks.

'Unless he was trying to tell us something. Next time I will tell you straight away if he does do it again.'

'That would be three times, you are being optimistic, I agree with Mrs Brooks,' I said.

I put the car into gear, and we started our drive back into central London.

'Sophie, if you would like to bring your set of papers from Dennis tonight you would be very welcome, my dear. If your manager looks in on Monday, it will all look nice and tidy for him. Perhaps get you back in his good books.'

'James, what are your thoughts?'

'I agree with Mrs Brooks, no time like the present!'

'Why not both of you, I can do salmon and cucumber sandwiches about seven o'clock?'

I dropped them both off and proceeded back to my apartment. I started to look at my endless lists and papers. It was a firm conclusion in my mind that it was somebody high up the ladder, logic said it must be one of those merchants. If the government entrusted a cargo of gold to feed the war against America, it would be all very secretive about it. We needed to eliminate the merchants one by one. I must have drifted off to sleep. When I awoke, it was six o'clock.

The phone was ringing, it was Sophie.

'It took you a long time to answer, James.'

'I was fast asleep, it is not like me, we did say seven o'clock.'

'Could we walk, please? It is a lovely evening.'

'I will start out and see you at quarter to seven.'

'I will be waiting,' and she rang off.

I set off at twenty to seven, I arrived at the Prince Edward Hotel as Sophie was just coming out of the entrance.

'Good timing, James,' she said as she took my arm. We set off for Mrs Brooks' apartment.

'It is not often we go out on Sunday night together; we are normally saying goodbye, James.'

'You are right. We have mostly just come back from Llandudno by this time. Tell me, any news on the house in Nottingham?'

'Not as yet, it is early days, it will be quite a responsibility when it all goes through. I would like your help when the time comes.'

'I might be older, but I have never bought or sold a house, but I will help when you need me. At the moment this investigation is taking up every hour away from work! I feel like we are part of story in a book.'

'We just need a happy ending to it.'

'That's one way of looking at it.' She kissed my cheek and pressed the intercom button when we got there. Mrs Brooks said, 'Come up,' and we were soon shown in. She had laid the table and there were salmon and cucumber sandwiches on a plate, plus a chocolate cake.

'The kettle is on. I will join you in a minute,' she disappeared into the kitchen.

She had put tables and flat-topped furniture all along one wall, so that Sophie could lay out the various paperwork and maps we had acquired.

'You have been busy this afternoon, Mrs Brooks,' said Sophie. 'If we can create some form of system, we can all delve into it. There will no reason to move it once we start. I have plenty of room.'

We soon had eaten our sandwiches and she cleared the crockery away into the kitchen. Sophie laid out the paperwork into various piles, there seemed to be a lot of them. 'James, what are your thoughts?'

'Well the first is; we should link goods with merchants. This will in theory halve the piles.'

'I have nothing better to offer,' said Mrs Brooks.

'That includes me, let's go for it,' said Sophie.

One hour later and a lot of to-ing and fro-ing, the piles were starting to shape up. Some had more papers than others. We were all pleased with our efforts.

'I would like to start to look at the maps on Monday,' said Mrs Brooks, 'If there was gold on the Albatross, where did it go to? There would be very few roads or houses in 1812 compared with today. They could not have hidden it far from the shore. One person or two at the most would be needed to get it off the brig, then a horse perhaps. If you open the leaf on the table by the window we can put the maps on there, starting with the oldest first.'

When it came time to pack up, Mrs Brooks said, 'Do you feel better now, Sophie?'

'I do and I appreciate you letting me work here. I can't come on Monday night, but Tuesday would be fine by me.'

'Then Tuesday it is, seven o'clock.'

We said goodnight and went down in the lift. We walked back to the hotel. When we were near to the entrance, I said, 'Can you see any strange men following us?'

'I can't but you can still kiss me goodnight, James.'

On Monday morning Arthur rang.

'I can drop off the lifting hooks later today. Will you be about?'

'In the office all day, Jane will show you up when you get here,' and I rang off. The morning soon disappeared. In the dispatch area I set up three boxes of books with straps under them on the tabletops. When the lunch break was over Arthur arrived with the hanger frames, which I had designed.

'I have made them from one eighth steel strip, James, plenty strong enough but not too heavy.'

I took Arthur down to the dispatch area. We put a lifting frame on the crane hook and gently lowered it over a box of books. Arthur pressed the button and hey-presto we lifted our first box of books up in the air and over to the conveyor.

'Arthur, you are a very handy man to have around.'

'The staff are going to like you when they find there is no more lifting, James! Can I make a suggestion; if you paint the top of the table with an oblong shape for placing the boxes on and also positions for the straps, it will mean anybody can load up and place them on the conveyor, you want the straps to fall away from the box. When the box goes down the rollers into the vans. the strap will remain in between the rollers. You can then place them back on the painted template on the table, ready for the next box.'

'I think I had better put a shot of whiskey in your pint on Wednesday night, Arthur.'

'Any time for you, Mr Parker, I have another customer to see so I will be off now.'

In the late afternoon when I was getting ready to lock up, Jane came to see me.

'I thought I would ask, James, are you pleased with the lifting hooks?'

'Very pleased. Arthur is a good workman, we tried them out with some boxes I made up. I still need to mark the table tops out for the best position of the boxes and straps for lifting from the table to the conveyor. First job Tuesday morning I will see to it.'

'We have a run of five thousand books over Thursday and Friday. Perhaps it would be a good idea to have all our staff for one hour in the dispatch area so you can supervise them?'

'From the safety point of view that is a splendid idea, Jane, I will leave you to organise it.'

'It will be done. Goodnight James, see you in the morning.'

I locked up and set out for my apartment.

Chapter 16

After making my evening meal I decided to take a leaf out of Mrs Brooks' life. I moved all the flat-top furniture along one wall after a lot of pushing and shuffling about. I then laid out my piles of paperwork and maps. Much to my surprise I still had somewhere to sit down and a table to eat off.

On Tuesday morning I set off early for the local hardware store, I bought a roll of masking tape and an aerosol of cream paint. On arriving at work, I made a template with the masking tape on the tables in the dispatch area. I was very pleased; you could see quite clearly where to place the straps and the box in position. The cream paint stood out clearly on the tabletops. By Thursday the paint would be dry, it would be all systems go.

Jane came to see me after lunch. 'It all looks very technical with your painted templates, James.'

'Hopefully it will halve the loading time. When you consider the number of cartons of books when you load five thousand of them, I am surprised we have any staff staying with us. The sheer weight of lifting that many books by hand is quite daunting.'

'On Thursday morning at eight thirty you will have half of our staff to help, then a new crew in the afternoon. Fingers crossed and good luck.'

She left me to my thoughts. When I walked back to my apartment at the end of the afternoon, it was with some degree of in trepidation, but I was very happy.

Evening meal over, on my one remaining chair and table that were not covered in papers, I started to place them in some form of order. There were around fifty people on board. I decided to leave them be for now and concentrate on merchants' names. It soon became apparent there were a lot of them. I put them in alphabetical order, for want of a better idea. Some had supplied various items from the same warehouse, all based around Liverpool.

My original thoughts had been to link merchants with goods. Sophie had reminded me not to rule out arms merchants with their barrels of gunpowder, rifles, and ammunition; they would all be working alongside the government. If there was gold on board to pay for the war in America, they were as good a bet as anybody. Ten o'clock, with my head spinning, I decided to call it a day, and retired to bed with a book.

On Wednesday morning, I was glad I was going to work, my home did not look any tidier than when I arrived back on Tuesday. I shut the door and set off for work. Jane was there before me, hard at it.

'Fingers crossed for Thursday, James. You need to sign some paperwork later today, then have an early night, tomorrow will be one hard day. There are several titles in those five thousand books, they are going to different places.'

I took Jane's advice and finished work early. It was quite depressing when I opened the door and went into my apartment. I realised how difficult it must be for Dennis, the curator of Liverpool Maritime Museum, and his staff, to make sense of the past. I must have laid papers out then changed the piles several times. Perhaps Mrs Brooks, with Sophie's help, had made more progress than me. I decided to forget it all and set out for The White Feathers public house. As I walked through the door, I could see Arthur was propping the bar up, reading his paper. I went over and joined him.

'Evening Mr Parker, are the lifting hooks working?'

'Tomorrow is the big day, we have a run of five thousand books.'

'You will have worn them out, never mind trying them!'

I ordered a pint for Arthur and one for myself. Sophie arrived and came over to join us.

'Now what are you two planning?' she said with a smile.

'I was just telling James what a lucky young man he is, with you, Miss Sophie.'

'Flattery will get you a long way, but I have no doubts you have had your moments, Arthur.'

At that cheerful note we made our way over to the table in the bay window.

'Are you in your hotel manager's good books again?'

'He dropped in on Tuesday, full of smiles and said, "That is much better, Miss Appleby" so I feel happier.'

'Well now that is out of the way, how did Tuesday night go with Mrs Brooks?'

'She is a real trooper, James, full of ideas for her age, absolutely marvellous. We started by laying everything out in alphabetical order.'

'I did the same, Sophie!'

'Yes, but did you make a list of the number of items each merchant put on that brig?'

'I did not, I am not sure of where this leading.'

'We both think there are fewer merchants than boxes and crates. There are several hundred in total. If we can break down the list of merchants to a smaller number, possibly five or six …'

'We would be looking at a smaller number of boxes and crates in which the gold could have been hidden.'

'James, you have got it in one.'

Our meal arrived and a glass of wine for Sophie.

'How many books have you published this week with the new set up, and was it easier?'

'Thursday is the day; we have five thousand to get loaded and sent away to our customers.'

'I think they are all lucky people'

'If you do not look after them, we would soon be out of business. You know that by your manager keeping everybody on their toes at the hotel.'

'So, I have seen where you work, when do I see your apartment?'

'Not until there is somewhere to sit down.'

'You are going to invite me one day then?'

'Patience, young lady! It's quarter to eight, we need to be on our way.'

Sophie pressed the intercom button, Mrs Brooks told us to come up. The door was open, she was making cups of tea in the kitchen. 'Welcome to you both, how have you got on, James?'

'Not very well as yet. I have tried to form some sort of order to my pile of papers, it is so hard to know which is the best way forward. My main thoughts are; when we get to dig up whatever Henry buried on the Great Orme, we can try to connect what it is with the merchants.'

'If we can get a name, perhaps Dennis at Liverpool can help us,' said Sophie.

'You do the digging, I will find that merchant, we just need one small clue to help me,' said Mrs Brooks.

'The long-range weather forecast is rain over Wales this coming weekend, it was on after the six o'clock news tonight. Let's hope they have got it right.'

'James I can get Monday off, the hotel owes me some extra time from when we had all those people from abroad for the convention, I worked all weekend for them.'

'Why not book it provisionally, if it is blowing a gale we might dig on Sunday afternoon.'

'Thunder and lightning, let's hope it's a real gale!'

'You won't be saying that when you are up there, Sophie,' said Mrs Brooks.

When we had all stopped laughing, I said, 'Perhaps it would be better if you left it to us, Mrs Brooks, sitting about in cold cars in nasty weather, we are both a lot younger. We will ring the moment we have any news.'

'I just hope you have not been arrested for digging up the Great Orme when you ring.'

'If we have, you can come down on the train with a file in your handbag to get us out,' said Sophie.

'You just be careful both of you, but you have made me smile. I will get a lift to see George this coming weekend. If you do dig anything up, please let me know.'

'Perhaps it would be best to ring Sam and Branwin first thing tomorrow, James. My manager will also need to be told just in case we are still down in Llandudno on the Monday morning.'

'I will be out of action with five thousand books to dispatch over Thursday and Friday, ring me on Friday night. Now remember waterproofs, good shoes, most of all warm clothing, Sophie.'

The rest of the evening we seemed to keep moving piles of paper from one piece of furniture to another.

'There is one thing I am sure of,' said Mrs Brooks, 'There were very few roads in Llandudno at that time, the total population was only three hundred and one in 1801.'

'That's not many people, Mrs Brooks.'

'If you remember, James said the total population was only twelve and half million for the whole country. When we were with Dennis, he confirmed it.'

'If there were few roads at that time, the gold must have been hidden very close to that beach, perhaps even buried there and moved at a later date.'

'I can remember when we were researching the lighthouse, just four hundred yards west on the beach is the Homby Cave. It was named after the two hundred and eighty-ton Liverpool brig Homby which hit the cliff below in a storm on New Year's Day 1824.'

'Perhaps the cave was not common knowledge,' said Sophie.

'You could well be right.'

'James, think about what you just said; if that did happen then there must have been at least two people involved!'

'One with local knowledge of the cave,' said Sophie.

'We also know the gold could not have been moved far, there wasn't sufficient time,' said Mrs Brooks.

'This is all conjecture at this point in our investigation. I do think you are on the right track, nevertheless we have to go to work tomorrow, Sophie.'

We wished Mrs Brooks goodnight, and set off walking back to Sophie's hotel.

'I can remember when I used to go home and watch the television, then go to the pub for a drink at ten o'clock, just like normal people!'

'It was not as much fun, James,' she put her arms round me and gave me a kiss on my lips. 'I bet you did not get kissed goodnight like that,' and disappeared into the Prince Edward Hotel.

As I started to walk back to my apartment, I had to admit Sophie was right. It was for sure not two people just involved in an investigation anymore. I came down to earth from my thoughts when

I opened the door of my apartment. Papers, maps, and ledger books were on every piece of furniture. Perhaps the next case she chose to investigate would be one with less paperwork.

On Thursday morning my alarm clock went off at six thirty. I quickly got washed, dressed, and set off for work. Jane was still there before me.

'Morning James, I have arranged for three staff to be here for eight o'clock. Is there anything you would like help with, we still have one hour for last minute things?'

'Jane if you can field the phone calls and manage the change over with staff at lunch time, twelve thirty, I would be very grateful.'

'Of course. Well, I wish you the best of luck, you have three different customers, make sure they get the right books, I will leave you to it.'

The first van backed into the yard at quarter to eight, shortly followed by my three staff. I soon had them sorted with the cardboard boxes, how to position them and the straps on the templates. With one person making up the boxes on one side of the track and two people putting the books in the boxes on the other side, the first van with its order was on its way at ten thirty.

One of the staff backed the driver in with the next van, and we were on the next shipment. By twelve thirty we had cleared another thousand books. I thanked the first three staff profoundly. Jane issued the next delivery note to the driver and he was on his way.

'That is the most books that have ever left these premises in one morning! I have been with your father from the start, and if he were still alive he would be very proud of you.'

Lunch break over, at one thirty my next helpers arrived for the afternoon shift. They were the older section of the people that worked for me. Roger, our book cover design and illustrator, and

Ted, our master printer who I still had to get to know. I decided to make up the boxes and leave them together to pack them. They soon adapted to the new system, the third van was on its way by five thirty, with one thousand eight hundred books. I did suggest they could take turns by changing with me.

'We are happy working together, James.'

Much to my surprise I only just kept up with them.

'James you have cleared three thousand seven hundred books in one day, that leaves another thirteen hundred tomorrow, I am amazed. I will say goodnight, let us see what tomorrow brings.'

I set off for my apartment, with a spring in my step, happy with my day. Even the paperwork everywhere, when I arrived back, could not take the shine out of my day. I had a late meal, took the Ledger books to bed to read and was soon in another world of merchants and ships in Liverpool.

On Friday morning I was awake before the alarm. Up, dressed, and soon in the delivery bay at work for quarter to eight.

'Morning James, I have decided to let Roger and Ted help this morning, I will see you later.'

Jane was soon on her way back to the office. Keeping up with my employees was no mean feat. The delivery note was signed and the lorry backed out of the yard with its load, on its way by twelve o'clock. Having thanked them both for their efforts, we all went for lunch. I decided to go round them all in the afternoon and thank them all separately, they all seemed pleased and gave the new ideas unanimous approval.

I set off at four thirty for my apartment and it was beginning to rain. Sophie rang at six.

'How did the book run go, James?'

'I could not have had a better two days; it was a huge success thank you.'

'I have just rung Sam in Llandudno, he is saying the weather is absolutely awful so we are either mad or in love, but if we want to come this weekend they will be happy to see us.'

'One day we will tell all. I will pick you up at ten thirty, try not to forget anything,' and I rang off.

Chapter 17

On Saturday morning I was awake early, waiting for the weather forecast, the last few weeks had been constantly frustrating. This weekend we were going to dig for whatever Henry had found on the beach early one morning while digging for bait. With a great deal of trepidation, I turned the key in the work Volvo, the engine fired into life.

Sophie was waiting on the step by the door of the Prince Edward Hotel.

'Good morning James, did you sleep well?'

'Not much, I feel like a student again before exams. All the uncertainty of it is not easy to cope with.'

'We do have so much riding on this weekend, we need some positive lead to move on. On a lighter note we could end up in jail. I would not mind if I was with you, James.'

'Digging up the Great Orme you would probably get two years or more.'

'If we solve this mystery, Llandudno would be the most talked about resort on the Welsh coast. Can we run through the list of things we both need?'

'I have one collapsible spade, twenty feet of strong rope, a waterproof coat and leggings, complete with a flat cap and one pair of studded boots for the wet grass.'

'I have a water-tight coat with leggings and a hood. I have also bought a torch, not sure why. Take me to Llandudno, James.'

'Did you ask about staying over on Monday, Sophie?'

'My manager said it would be alright, but I must let him know on Sunday evening. If I haven't rung, he will expect me to be on duty first thing Monday morning.'

'Now that is out of the way, I have been thinking about the drive up Marine Drive to get to the church. We normally pay a fee which includes parking at the top. Due to the weather it might be closed!'

'We could take the road we usually come down from on the other side, James.'

'You are probably right, the road next to the open sea is exposed to the worst of the weather but we will still be able to get there. My second thought is about where we are staying; Sam and Branwin must be curious about what we are up to, I am sure we would be if we were running a guest house.'

'They would not be taking us off to Italian restaurants if they thought we were up to no good. They are pleased to have regular bookings, and, James, they do genuinely like us. They know we like them or we would not keep going back there, plus we are paying guests. Can we pull up for lunch earlier today? It is my turn to treat us.'

It was just coming up to twelve thirty when we pulled onto the carpark at the Blue Bell Public House, 'Two for the price of one, all lunch time meals.'

'There are several cars even if we seem to be in the middle of nowhere, James, let's give it a try.'

Having parked up we proceeded from the carpark into the Blue Bell. I ordered two halves of cider, 'Could we just have your soup of the day please?'

'Pea soup and freshly baked bread by our chef this morning, sir.'

'That would be perfect.' We were soon seated and admiring the pictures and glass cases with birds and animals.

'We seem to have stopped at the right place, James. I quite like it here.'

Some ten minutes later two soups with homemade bread arrived. 'Mrs Brooks is off to see George again this weekend. She really is quite remarkable, she has so much energy for her age.'

'Her mind is sharper than mine. She was certainly a great asset to her husband in politics, of that I am in no doubt. This soup is good, and the bread, James. I would like to come here again in the future.'

We were soon on our way, having paid and sung their praises about the soup. We set off, the Volvo eating the miles up. By two thirty we were passing though Shrewsbury. The road was awash with water, pouring from the gateways of the fields, we were now doing twenty miles an hour.

'You did say let's hope it is gale-force!'

'I did not really mean it, James, just drive carefully.'

We were now in slow-moving traffic and it was getting late when we finally arrived at Sam and Branwin's.

Sam was soon at the door, 'I did not think you would make it, the wife said you would have rung if you had changed your mind. Let's get you settled in.'

Having unpacked we joined them downstairs.

'This weather is so awful we wondered if you would like to join us tonight for a meal about seven thirty? It is very unlikely we will have any other guests.'

'That is a lovely idea, we will take you up on that,' said Sophie.

'There are papers and drinks in the front room, we will see you later. Branwin is quite a good cook.'

'The local news said not to travel unless it was necessary, due to high winds coming in from the sea, Sophie.'

'You could say it is perfect weather, James!'

'You will not be saying that in the morning.'

'Would you like to come through, we have put out water and a bottle of wine,' said a voice from the kitchen.

We were soon seated, and Branwin said, 'I enjoy cooking and Sam likes to serve.'

Sam sat at the head of the table and Branwin placed a huge plate covered with thinly cut meat for him to serve.

'We are having Welsh venison tonight; I hope you enjoy it.'

Sam had soon laid the meat out on our plates, 'Please help yourselves to the leek and potato rosti.'

'I have also done some red cabbage,' said Branwin.

Our wine glasses were soon filled, 'Please help yourselves to water.'

After the meal, I asked Sam what he did when he was younger. 'Before I had even left school, I helped my dad with his business, he was a general builder. We would set off on Saturday mornings with a hand cart loaded with slates, ladders, even the odd chimney pot, it was quite hard work. There are not many places in Llandudno we have not worked in. I would foot the ladder and pass the tools up to him. We built garden walls, a bit of carpentry, painting, it was very interesting and varied work.'

'How did you end up running a boarding house, Sam?' said Sophie.

'That would be partly my fault,' said Branwin, 'but it is Sam's tale.'

'Most of the young men were leaving for the better paid jobs in the cities but I became restless and wanted to see the world. I applied to join the navy, passed the medical and soon left Llandudno to sail round most of the world during the coming years. I came home on leave and met Branwin at the local dance.'

'I had to fight all the other girls off, they all loved him in his uniform,' Branwin said with a laugh. 'When he next sailed we wrote to one-another.'

'We had both been brought up in Llandudno, anyway, to cut a long story short, the next time I was on leave I popped the question and Branwin said yes. It was goodbye to the navy, we married and moved into the bed and breakfast business, we eventually ended up here.'

'That was a lovely tale,' said Sophie, looking at James.

'I saw that look! James you need to look out!' said Sam.

'Now don't you tease them, they have plenty of time,' said Branwin.

We could hear her laughing in the kitchen, when she cleared the table.

Sam said, 'Let us go into the lounge for coffee, we can look at the news and weather report. Gale force winds and rain tomorrow predicted all up and down the coast here.'

'If you go down by the sea front in the morning, you must stay on the side opposite the sea, the locals do this, it is far safer. The flower beds and bus shelters have all been blown over, holding on to one another is the safest way.'

We thanked them both for a lovely evening and retired to bed. I told Sophie to try and get a good night's sleep. Tomorrow was going to be one hell of a day. I eventually fell asleep.

A curtain of rain was beating down when we departed the boarding house the next morning.

'There was thunder rumbling and flashes of lightning in the night, James, did you hear it?'

'I have to admit I did not, I must have slept better than I thought.'

We drove down to the sea front, it was virtually empty of people.

'Most people are staying indoors.'

'After Sam's advice, we should stop in the car.'

We drove along to Marine Drive, it was not closed much to our surprise! The ticket office had its shutter down.

'They are not expecting many customers today.'

The cliff road was awash with water pouring from the rocks above us as we drove slowly up to St Tudno's Church, some twenty minutes later we parked by the church wall behind the graveyard. We were soon dressed in our gear for the climb.

'I am quite nervous, James.'

'Do not worry, keep close when we get out of the car.'

Our eyes were watering with the wind in the short time it took to gather our tools together, then we crossed the road and started to climb. I soon became aware of the clouds which were very close to the ground. I decided to not say anything to Sophie. We were soaked even with our macs on when we reached where our hollow lay. Thankfully our sticks we had placed for the coming dig were still there. Two goats were huddled against the rocks at the back of our hollow, keeping out of the worst of the weather.

'It looks like we have company, James.'

With our spade and depth bar we started to cut back the turf, the two goats quite oblivious, huddled down out of the wind.

Some twenty minutes later the turf was neatly rolled back from what looked like a short railway sleeper.

'Perhaps it is a beam from when the church roof was blown off all those years ago, James.'

'It could well be, we still need to look under it, let's try to lift it out.'

Much to our surprise one end was so much heavier than the other.

'It's a box, James.' Sophie was quite excited. 'Who would have thought it! we did it, we really did it.'

'If you can contain yourself, we have still to get it down to the car, we cannot carry it down the wet grass, it is too slippery. I must admit it has made my heart race a little. Calm down and think.'

'We did bring a rope, I will put the turf back while you go down for the rope. We can pull it down between us. The goats will keep me company till you get back, I will be quite alright.' With some degree of concern, I set off back down the slope back to the car. The rope was coiled on top of the spare wheel. It was only when I shut the boot lid down and turned to cross the road I realised I was struggling to see the other side. Visibility was far less than when we arrived.

With the rope over my shoulder I crossed the road and set off back up the slope. I was sure the ledge was slightly to the right from where we had started to climb. My heart was thumping, I must be nearly there. I shouted 'Sophie, Sophie,' at the top of my voice.

'I am over here!'

The sound of Sophie's voice was below me! I started to go down. I was higher than I had expected. Suddenly a torch light was making an ark below me. If I had gone any further down I would have fallen down on top of the goats onto the ledge. I made my way down onto the ledge. The goats were bleating, Sophie shouting, it was quite a bedlam. 'Could you calm down and make less noise.'

'I thought you would never find me.'

I gave her a wet hug. 'You are safe now, I am back, let's get this rope tied round the box and make our way down.' We roped the spade and depth bar to the box. Sophie said goodbye to the goats, we then started to make our way down. It was easier said than done to drag a heavy box on the wet slope down to the road. Having fallen over too many times to count we finally arrived at the road, but we were not able to see the car.

'We need to cross over to the wall of the graveyard. The car is between the two porches set in it, James.'

We eventually found the car, although the cloud was still making it hard to see more than a few yards in front of us.

'I don't think we need to worry about anybody seeing us.'

Having packed the box and tools in the back of the Volvo estate, we took off our wet macs and climbed in the front. I then noticed Sophie was physically shaking. I was shaken up myself.

'Let us go back to the boarding house. I will ring your hotel manager and tell him we need another day here. I cannot face the journey today, Sophie.'

At that she burst into tears and we sat for a while. Then I started the car and set off slowly back down into Llandudno.

We drove round to the front of the church facing the sea, with the road descending before us. Soon, below the low-lying cloud the rain was less, but the road was still awash with water pouring from the gullies in the rocks.

Some twenty minutes later we pulled up in front of the boarding house. Having locked the car after making sure the box was out of view of prying eyes, Sophie rang the bell. Sam soon appeared at the door.

'We did not expect you back today, I thought you would be in London by now!'

'Could we stay another night, please?'

Branwin arrived at the door. 'Come in out of weather, don't keep them on the step, Sam. What can we do for you?'

'They would like to stay another night, dear.'

'We have a Mr Jones and his mother here, they booked in this afternoon. He is in the front bedroom where Sophie sleeps, his mother is in the room downstairs. He plays the clarinet in the band from up North, they are down here for a competition. We are going to see him play tonight, there is only the one room not occupied.'

'Could we take that, please?'

'Of course you can, James, get warmed up both of you. I will put some soup on in the kitchen. Help yourselves, we will be gone before you get down, we will see you in the morning. Have some tea or wine, whatever you want, you are very welcome.'

With our bags safely back upstairs, I ran the bath, told Sophie to get in it and went down to make a cup of tea. She was drying her hair when I came back with the teacups on a tray.

'You do look after me, James.'

'Anymore cases like this one climbing about the Great Orme in this sort of weather I will not be helping. I will get in the bath, see if you can bring the soup up on a tray please.'

She said, 'You are a dear,' planted a kiss on my nose and set off down the stairs.

'I will expect to see you dressed when I get back,' she called.

I was soon feeling better after a bath and putting clean dry clothes on.

There was a knock on the door. 'James can you let me in with this tray, please? Branwin left a note saying help ourselves to a piece of cake from the fridge for afters.'

We soon settled down at the table in the window enjoying our cauliflower soup. 'We need to ring my manager and also Mrs Brooks, we must not ring too late; she will be starting to worry. What a day, James, we actually did it! From a deposit box with half a map we now have Henry's box he dug out of the sand and buried again.'

'You do realise it may be just an empty box!'

'Not with one end heavier than the other.'

'It could be a workman's toolbox from the time they repaired the church roof.'

'We have to think positive about this, it has taken several months to get this far. Have you finished your soup?'

'Yes, but I could eat some more.'

'Let us make those phone calls, then you can warm up the soup again.'

We went downstairs to use the house phone. Sophie dialled the hotel manager. When he answered he said, 'I was beginning to think you were coming in tomorrow morning.'

'We have been detained, Mr Buckley.'

'You make sure you are here on Tuesday morning at nine o'clock sharp, young lady.' He said 'Goodbye' and put the phone down.

'That is now over and done with, I will heat the soup while you ring Mrs Brooks.'

I dialled her number and she picked up straight away, 'Hallo, it's James, that was quick.'

'I have been on tenterhooks all day, James. I went to see George this afternoon, there is no change in him. I have not settled down since, through anxiety worrying about you both.'

'Can I just say mission accomplished, Mrs Brooks. Make yourself a cup of tea, and can you come to my work at seven o'clock tomorrow evening and we will open the box?'

'I hope you have not got into trouble and you're both okay.'

'We are quite alright but could not face the journey home today. We were so wet when we finished. We will see you at seven.'

'I am so excited, I will be there, 'bye James.'

'I expect that phone call was a shock for her.'

'She will have a tablet with a cup of tea. I think we should celebrate with a glass of alcohol.'

'That is more the spirit. You can carry the tray upstairs; I will see what I can find in the drinks cabinet.'

Having had two more bowls of cauliflower soup and a piece of cake each, Sophie poured two glasses of wine for us.

'James you were a hero! Finding your way back to me on that ledge.'

'When the cloud cleared you would have soon found your way down.'

'That is easy to say but I was frightened; what if you had got lost or hurt, then what would I have done?'

'The point is I didn't, and you have found a dangerous job as a private detective, you could give it up.'

'There's no way I am doing that, James, what, and miss all the times we have had in Llandudno. Do you think when it's all over we might still come and stay with Sam and Branwin?'

'I cannot see any reason why not. You had better pour another glass of wine.'

'When we have opened the box, this case will probably be over. I think we should think of a name for our detective agency.'

'You seem sure I will want to come in it with you. Do not imagine this case is anywhere over yet. It has a long way to go, we will both have grey hair by the end of it.'

'You will look nice with grey hair, quite becoming I should think. I will ask Mrs Brooks when we get back.'

'You will do no such thing.'

'I am only teasing you, James. Shall I pour the rest of the wine. Will we need to pay for the bottle?'

'It does say in my daily paper men can drink three units a day, ladies only two units.'

'I do believe you are teasing me. Now, let's make a list of what we think we are going to find in the box when we get it open.' Having talked in circles and finished the wine bottle, I decided it was time for bed. 'Which side would you like to sleep on Sophie?'

'I have never slept with anybody before! You choose.'

'Left side for me, we can sleep back to back, it would be safest. I will use the bathroom first if you don't mind.'

With the wine we had consumed, I was nearly asleep when Sophie climbed into bed, she kissed my back and said goodnight.

When I woke up Sophie was on my side of the bed with her back to me, fast asleep. It was then I had an uncontrollable urge to make love to her, having lifted her hair I started to kiss her neck. She was soon awake making loving noises.

'I could not sleep so I got in your side, I did have my back to you, can I turn over please?'

She turned over and kissed me back. 'Oh James this is my first time, please don't stop.' We were so frustrated it did not last long. We were still clinging to one another when I heard the gong summoning us to breakfast. I quickly set off for the bathroom. Sophie was still curled up in bed.

Having finished in the bathroom I ran a bath for Sophie. She was still under the sheets with a great smile on her face.

'James if you only knew how long I have waited for you to make love to me!'

'Would you like me to drop you in the bath?'

'You wouldn't.'

'I might! But we have to go down for breakfast, and not look like two love-struck young people.'

In all of ten minutes Sophie was in and out of the bath, ready to go downstairs.

'Will I do, James?'

'You look ready for anything, though I would say you look a bit flushed.'

'It was all that horrible weather yesterday,' she said with a smile. 'Let us go down for breakfast.'

Branwin was soon looking after us.

'You both look better than you did early yesterday evening. Sam has already left; he has gone to Mario's to fix a blocked gutter.'

'How was the concert?'

'It was just perfect and a good turnout considering the weather. Mr Jones's band took first prize. They have already set off home, he had a meeting to attend in the afternoon. What time are you leaving?'

'Straight after breakfast.'

'I had better get on with it then.'

Having eaten and packed, we were soon saying goodbye to Branwin and setting off back to London.

Chapter 18

The weather soon improved as we left the coast behind. We made good time and arrived back in London mid afternoon. I dropped off Sophie at the Prince Edward Hotel.

'I will see you at your office at seven o'clock, James 'bye.'

I drove round to my work's loading bay and was soon parked up, locked the Volvo and proceeded to my office. Jane was hard at it, papers were everywhere.

'James, we did not expect you back in today, the weather report was terrible for the whole of Wales.'

'I must admit it was pretty poor, but I left early. How did the book run go this morning?'

'The lorry pulled into the yard at nine and was fully loaded and gone by ten forty-five. If you have any more ideas, please say. The physical effort for everyone is so much easier.'

The staff were soon going home. At six thirty Jane said, 'Goodnight James' and I was on my own.

I started the Volvo and reversed up to the conveyer. Using the new lifting gear we now had installed, the box was soon on one of the dispatch tables. I found the levers we used to open the crates for books and placed them with a large screwdriver on the table next to the box.

Sophie arrived early, 'Have you eaten, James?'

'No, you're quite early.'

'I've brought you a sandwich, can you make a cup of tea while we wait for Mrs Brooks to arrive?'

Mrs Brooks must have smelt the tea brewing, while I was pouring she came through the door.

'The taxi was early so here I am, tell me about your weekend.'

We told her about the dreadful weather, the fog from lo-lying clouds and dragging the box down the wet slippery slope to the car, while we drank our tea.

'Let us hope it was all worth it,' she said, picking up a crowbar. Sophie picked up the other one. I just wished I had a camera; two ladies, one probably 90 years of age, the other who had probably never seen a crowbar in her life holding the second one. We had waited so long for this moment; their over-the-top enthusiasm did make me smile.

'Ladies, this is my job so let me do it please, we must try to do as little damage as possible to the box.'

The acid in the timber frame of the box had eaten away the heads of the screws but I soon had the top off on the table by the box.

Sophie was the first to speak. 'Henry must have wrapped it up again after looking at it, whatever it is the material looks so old.'

'So would you if you had been in a box that long.'

'That's not a good joke, James.'

Sophie helped me lift the wrapped-up parcel out on to the table. We soon unravelled it.

There seemed to be four long wooden sledgehammers. 'What on earth would you use them for?' said Sophie.

'They are croquet mallets, you use them to play a game on a lawn, it was very popular years ago. There should be four balls of different colours, and six hoops to knock them through, and a pointed stick.'

'You are knowledgeable, Mrs Brooks.'

'When we were younger my husband played at some of the grand country houses we were invited to, working for the government we had the chance to see how the elite entertained.'

'The balls are really black, Mrs Brooks, are you sure about it?'

'I certainly am. I have played that game when I was young. James, give us your thoughts.'

'For what it is worth, I never expected to find a croquet set if that is what it is. The balls are so heavy they must be made from some kind of metal.'

'They should have been made from hardwood, the same as crown green bowls. People still play that game now, the only difference is they put weights in one side, it puts a bias on the ball. The skill was making the ball curve round and get as near to the small ball called a jack. But I am certain there were never any weights in croquet balls.'

'There is no doubt in my mind they are made from some sort of metal, Mrs Brooks, you pick one up.'

She picked one up, so did Sophie. 'Verdict?'

'You are quite right, James, but where do we go from here?'

'If it is a valuable metal, I would suggest the jewellery shop, the one with the safety box.'

'He was very knowledgeable,' said Sophie. 'Perhaps I could book an appointment for Wednesday if that would suit us all.'

'If you can make that in the morning, fine by me,' said Mrs Brooks, 'Is that okay with you, James?'

'Wednesday morning it is, I will soon pack this away safely. Can I take you both for a meal? It will make a nice end of the day.'

On Tuesday Sophie rang, 'All fixed up. Will you pick me up for ten thirty, then Mrs Brooks? She will be waiting outside her apartment for us. Appointment at eleven o'clock. Bye James.'

The rest of Tuesday was uneventful but try as I might I had a restless night. I arrived early on Wednesday at work; my mind was still full of the weekend gone. I placed a croquet ball in a strong bag and retreated to my office. The clock was going round slower by the minute, unable to concentrate any longer I told Jane, 'Hold the fort, I will be back in the afternoon.'

It was just coming up to ten thirty when I picked up Sophie from the Prince Edward Hotel.

'Morning James, did you sleep well?'

'Not really.'

'I kept on thinking about Sunday night, James. I have only read about people making love, it has made me want to do it again.'

'I have no doubt we will! Let us concentrate on our visit to the jewellery shop in Bruton Street, we need to pick up Mrs Brooks next.'

She was outside her apartment waiting for us. 'Morning, did you sleep well?'

'Sophie has just asked the same question, I did not.' When I glanced in Sophie's direction, she winked at me. We were soon pulled up outside the jewellery shop. I left them both and parked the car at the nearest carpark. When I arrived back at the shop they were seated talking to our jewellery man.

'Good morning Mr Parker. How may I be of assistance?'

'I would like you to identify and value something I have please.'

'We had better take a look at it then. I do charge for valuations if there is a great deal of time involved.'

Mrs Brooks said, 'That is quite alright.'

I placed the bag on his desk. 'It is very heavy Mr … sorry, I did not catch your name.'

'Call me Charles. Let us see what it is.'

When I opened the bag and showed him the heavy round ball on his desk, he looked quite aghast.

'This is a jewellery shop, you need to take that to a scrap metal dealer, Mr Parker.'

'If you will allow me to explain; when we came to you last, the deposit box that was in your care only contained a map. Over the last few months we eventually found the place which was marked on the map. We dug up a box. Much to our surprise it contained a croquet set, nothing more. It seemed to us that somebody had gone to a lot of trouble to hide and put a map in a safety deposit box.'

'I agree with you. To bury a box and make a map are strange circumstances. But I do not see how I can help you, Mr Parker.'

'Please, Charles, just look closely for us,' said Sophie.

'If I must, in all my years this the strangest request I have ever had.'

He soon put some sort of fluid on the metal ball, wiped it dry then scraped the surface with a knife and deposited it on a slide under a microscope.

'I stake my reputation for what it is worth,' he said 'I do believe you have a solid gold ball. I need to sit down.'

The poor man looked as if he needed a stiff drink of alcohol, Mrs Brooks said, 'I need a cup of tea!'

'What do we do next, Charles?' said Sophie.

'I will get our heavy scales, please give me a moment.' He disappeared into the back of his shop.

Perhaps it was the surprise, but we had not spoken a word when he returned with his scales. He weighed the ball, wrote some figures down and produced a calculator into which he proceeded to put his calculations. He was so pale and white looking.

'I have had quite a shock, let me lock the door before I tell you.'

'Tell us what, Charles?' said Mrs Brooks.

'Your gold ball, based on today's value of gold, comes to

£122,333.'

'There were four balls in the box, Charles.'

'Good god. I do not think I will ever get over it.'

'Do send me a bill for your time, Charles, we are so grateful.'

'Mr Parker, we have a one percent valuation fee. Today I will not be charging you. I would like to know the complete story when you get to the bottom of this. You will have to surrender the gold to the Crown. You have made my day in no uncertain terms. I wish you luck. Be careful, you have a great deal of money in that bag. Be sure to put those gold balls in a safe and tell nobody.'

We thanked him profusely. He unlocked the door of the shop, we stepped out on to Bruton Street, each to our own thoughts. I quickly retrieved the car from the car park and picked them both up. I drove to Mrs Brooks' apartment to drop her off.

'We need to give plenty of thought to this morning's revelations and what to do next, I am sure you are both aware,' she said.

'Eight o'clock tonight we will be with you, Mrs Brooks.'

I drove round to the Prince Edward Hotel and dropped Sophie at the door.

'See you at seven at The White Feathers, James,' and she was gone. I arrived back at my office and tried to show some degree of normality for the rest of the day.

At six o'clock the staff departed. I was on my own.

I placed the four gold croquet balls in the bottom drawer of the office safe, they just fitted. Having put the key to the drawer on my keyring, I locked the wooden box in my car boot, and set off for The White Feathers public house.

Arthur was there looking at his racing paper, leaning on the bar. 'Mr Parker, you are in early tonight,'

'I have had quite a day, what can I get you to drink?'

'A pint of bitter please. How are the staff getting on with the lifting gear?'

'It has had the approval of them all, we're very pleased.'

'That is nice to hear. I dropped in on Jack Berryman at the spade shop on Saturday, he asked me if I knew how you were getting on with the spade and metal detector?'

'I have totally forgotten that I need to return the metal detector. I will slip round to the shop and settle the bill tomorrow first thing. The weather held me back for several weekends, but it was a success story.'

Sophie came through the door at that moment and she soon joined us.

'I was just telling James what a lucky young man he is meeting you, Miss Sophie.'

'Flattery will get you anywhere, Arthur.'

We were soon seated at our window table. 'How did work go this afternoon?'

'Not very well. I found it so hard to concentrate. My manager was out for the afternoon so that helped.'

'Let us order and try to enjoy our meal, forget everything else till we get to Mrs Brooks' apartment.'

Two meals soon appeared like magic.

'James, I have had a letter from Nottingham to go up this Saturday to complete the handover of all the paperwork concerning the house my Aunt left me. I would really like you there, if it's possible.'

'We will not be going to Llandudno this coming weekend. I would be delighted to go with you to Nottingham.'

Having sung the praises of the chef, we said good-bye to Arthur and set off for Mrs Brooks' apartment. Sophie pressed the intercom button and we were told to come up. She had left the door open and was making tea in the kitchen.

'Make yourselves comfortable. I won't be long.' We were soon drinking our tea.

'We will help you to put all your furniture back in place, and sort all the papers everywhere before we leave tonight,' said Sophie.

'Whatever for, may I ask?'

'The mission is accomplished. We have solved the mystery surrounding George, Mrs Brooks.'

'Young lady, when that ship perished it was reported there were £60,000 on board to support the army in America. It is my belief there would be more than one croquet box on board. James, I am making sense do you not think?'

'You are in all probability right, but even if there were, how on earth could we trace them if they did exist?'

'Perhaps we should consult Dennis in Liverpool on the best way forward,' said Sophie.

'I do agree, Sophie. Our discovery will probably be classed as treasure trove. Dennis will know how to handle that. But we have all our lists of the cargo. We are not looking for agents anymore, we are only searching for croquet boxes.'

'We will know who the agent was if we can find them! Mrs Brooks you are amazing.'

'James, until the trail gets cold I feel we should go on. I am more than happy to pay all the expenses involved. This is the most excitement I have experienced since before my husband died. There is so much more to this story.'

'Yes, yes, yes!' said Sophie. 'James are you in?'

'I am in.'

Mrs Brooks went into the kitchen and returned with three glasses of port. 'Let's raise our glasses. Here's to George and the second half of this story.'

Chapter 19

We set off from Mrs Brooks' apartment, Sophie holding my arm, stopping every few yards, kissing my cheek, running round me, then kissing the other side.

'What on earth are you doing?'

'I am so excited, I thought it was all over. Llandudno, no more or Sam and Branwin. I have lived for our adventurous weekends. You must be excited, James.'

'Very much so if you must know. Could you try and constrain yourself, young lady.'

'Only till the weekend, James.'

On Thursday I was soon back down to earth. Jane informed me that we had two thousand books to pack and be loaded.

'The lorry needs to catch the boat to Ireland. It leaves at seven o'clock this evening. The driver needs to get to Fishguard.'

'I will be straight on it, Jane.'

Two of the staff were there already backing the lorry in when I reached the loading bay. At a quarter to twelve the lorry was waved out of the yard and sent on its way. I thanked the staff and made my way back to my office. Jane was beavering away.

'You have done well, James. Friday morning we have another large order but it will not be so demanding. We can start to pack and stack the books on the tables this afternoon. Four thousand three hundred in total.'

'If you can sort the paperwork, I will start after lunch.'

My lunch break had to be put on hold because I had told Arthur I would return the metal detector to Berryman's Hardware store. I was glad to see they had not closed for lunch. I paid the bill and told the young man to be sure to thank Jack Berryman and returned to my office.

I was so lucky to have someone as efficient as Jane, she had already told two of the staff to make a start putting the boxes together. I filled and counted the books into the first box, told them how many boxes to make up and left them to it.

I decided to ask Jane to work out our wage bill for the last month, plus the cost of the lifting gear and give me her estimate for next week, which was a start of a new month.

'James, are you worrying about anything?'

'No, on the contrary, I was thinking we might work a system out to pay a bonus each month based on the number of books through the door.'

'You will be pleasantly surprised. I will set it all out for you on paper. I have watched the monthly figures very closely since your father died. They have been creeping up. Tuesday afternoon would be okay for me.'

'Tuesday it is then.'

After work had finished for the day, I walked back to my apartment, thinking each step of the way that Mrs Brooks was correct in her assumption that there were more croquet boxes. Having watched the news and eaten, the time was just coming up to eight o'clock. I decided to make a start with a new search for croquet boxes, only them, no side tracking. In total I now had seventeen piles of paperwork to look through, so I had to look at all the goods that were loaded on our ship, the Albatross, in Liverpool. Much to my amazement, I completed the first pile of papers by ten o'clock. The lists were extensive; what did help was that I was now more aware I must not get distracted. Only sixteen more to go, quite pleased, I wondered how Mrs Brooks was going about it. With a cup of hot chocolate, I was soon in bed.

Friday morning, I set off to work early. Even so, Jane was still there before me.

'Morning James.'

'A very good morning to you; with four thousand three hundred books to pack, and get on their way, an early start is advisable.'

My staff were already waving the lorry into our loading bay. This was the biggest order I had been involved in. Without the lifting gear they would have struggled in the past.

'There is a call for you from the Prince Edward Hotel, James.' I had been left a message; "Two tickets booked for the train to Nottingham. It leaves the station at ten fifteen from St Pancras. Will meet you there, Sophie."

The day seemed to be going at quite a pace. By two thirty the lorry and its paperwork were on its way. I sat down with Jane, signed off the paperwork for the last working month and paid the various suppliers we used. All in all, I was very pleased with work, also our investigation for Mrs Brooks. At four o'clock I decided to leave Jane to manage and shut up the office and to finish early. The trip to Nottingham would just finish the month off nicely.

On Saturday morning I arrived at St Pancras just after ten. Sophie was soon with me. 'How come you did not need me to pick you up this morning?'

'I have been shopping, James, tonight I am going to cook you a meal!'

'You have never said you could cook.'

'My aunt taught me, from when I was very young. If I do not try now and then I will forget what to do.'

'May I ask what we are having?'

'You may not, you will have to wait and see.'

The train arrived on time. We boarded, found our seats and settled down on our journey to Nottingham. When the train stopped and we stepped onto the platform, the sun was shining.

It was a lovely day. We set off for Sophie's house.

We were soon there, with its yellow privet hedge, mellow brick wall, and metal gate that squeaked when we opened it. Mr Simpson was ahead of us and had arrived first.

'A very good day to you both. I did say we would meet at my office but after some consideration it is perhaps more fitting if we do it here.'

'Would you like a cup of tea, Mr Simpson? I have brought fresh milk with me.'

'That sounds an excellent idea. I will lay out the paperwork while you make the tea.'

'James, perhaps you can see if you can make the central heating work, please.'

'Now Miss Appleby, I have paid all your service bills, rates, etc. which I have deducted from your estate, also the cost of the headstone and funeral expenses. You also have a bank account with £4,070 from your aunt's estate in total which I can sign over to you. My bill will be forwarded to the Prince Edward Hotel in London, your place of residence at this time. I wish you all the best for the future.'

'Thank you very much, Mr Simpson.'

At that he put his hat and coat on, and we showed him out of the door, and we were left alone.

'As you now own this house officially, we had better check it over tomorrow before we leave. You are responsible for its maintenance.'

'Will you help me?.'

'You know I will, let's light the gas fire and get the beds aired.'

'We will only need one electric blanket!'

'I will make a decision on that when you serve that wonderful meal tonight, young lady. Let me see if I can get the hot water system working.'

'James Parker, I do believe you are teasing me!'

I found the immersion heater in the cupboard at the top of the stairs. I pressed the switch down and a red light came on.

By four o'clock, the house was considerably warmer.

'James, I would like to take you to our local shop, we do need to think about breakfast. We haven't got Sam and Branwin to look after us now.'

With our coats on we locked up and set off for Sophie's shop. 'We need batteries for the TV remote. Do you think they may stock them?'

'We are about to find out, this is it.' A large bell sounded as we went through the door.

'Well I'll be damned if it is not Sophie, much older if I might say.'

'Charley, nice to see you. This is my friend James.'

'What can I get you both today?'

'We would like four rashers of smoked bacon, six eggs, black pudding and a tin of mushrooms please.'

'I have never eaten black pudding before, Sophie.'

'There is a first time for everything, James.'

'Would you have batteries suitable for the remote for the TV, Charley?'

He soon found them and Sophie told him that she was now

working in London. She was going to keep the house on, and we would see him from time to time. She paid him and we said goodbye.

By six o'clock I had sorted the new batteries out for the remote and the TV was working. There were nice smells coming from the kitchen. I settled down to watch the news.

'I have put a bottle of red wine on the table, my aunt is sure to have had a corkscrew. Would you look and see if you can find one? Our meal is nearly ready.'

Having found the corkscrew, I poured two glasses of red wine.

'We are having lasagne with garlic bread and salad, I hope you will still want to kiss me after the garlic bread, James.'

Sophie produced two plates with the lasagne on them.

'Please help yourself to salad and garlic bread. I do hope it is up to your expectations, James.'

We both tucked in. It was a new experience after eating in so many pubs between England and Wales over the past months. After the meal we washed up, dried the crocks, put them away, and settled down to watch a nice old film. We both stayed awake till the end.

'What have you planned for tomorrow, may I ask? It was a wonderful meal!'

'Nothing very exciting. I thought we might sort the garden shed out. My aunt did most of the garden herself. I will need to get somebody to cut the lawn and keep things tidy. Perhaps another visit to Charley's, he must know most tradesmen around here.'

I switched the television off, Sophie turned the lights out and we set off up the stairs.

'James, I forgot to switch the electric blanket on!'

'I would say we will not be needing it tonight, my dear.'

Sophie came out of the bathroom. 'James, you are sitting up in bed without your pyjama top on!'

'That is correct. Take off that nightie and get into bed.'

Our love making was very special, with Sophie saying, 'Oh James, I do love you so much.'

We were soon asleep, wrapped round each other, it was for sure we did not need an electric blanket that night or for the foreseeable future.

On Sunday morning I awoke to the smell of bacon drifting up the stairs. Sophie was dressed and cooking our breakfast.

'I did not hear you get up.'

'Not at all surprised after last night! I cannot remember sleeping so well. I will miss you tonight when we are back in London, but I am very happy, James.'

'Let's see what the black pudding is like, then we have a date at Charley's. We have a lot to sort out before we return to London.'

Breakfast was soon over. It was as good as anywhere we had stayed at over the last few months.

'James, would you find the key to the garden shed while I wash up the breakfast things pleas?'

Much to my surprise the lawn mower was clean and well oiled as were the rest of the tools; there would be enough to look after the garden without further outlay. If Charley knew somebody reliable it would be one less worry for Sophie to think about. 'What is the verdict, James, do I need to buy much?'

'You have everything you will need; it all looks good to me. We must ask Charley if he knows a person who will look after them and the garden.'

We soon set off. Charley was there all bright and cheerful when we arrived.

'What do I have this unexpected pleasure of twice in a weekend?'

'I need a big favour, Charley, could you recommend somebody to look after the garden and the tools for me please?'

'If you go to see John Summers, two doors along, he would be the best bet for you. He is a retired engineer; he services the lawn mowers for people round here, Miss Sophie.'

'Thanks again for your help.'

He was already serving the next customer. 'Not far to go, two doors, he said.'

There was a large lion's head door knocker in the middle of the door, Sophie gave it three large swings.

'That should awaken the dead, James!'

We could soon hear noises from inside. The door opened and our retired engineer said, 'Good morning, what can I do for you?'

'Charley told me to come and see you, Mr Summers. My aunt lived just round the corner from here, she recently died. I lived with her for many years. Her name was Hilda Appleby.'

'I knew Hilda. We went to the same school together, many years ago, mind!'

'That is a surprise, Mr Summers. We are looking for somebody to look after the garden and the lawn mower servicing.'

'Your aunt cut the grass and looked after her plants. I have serviced the mower and garden tools for many years. We would be talking about two hours each week in the summer to do it all. I could manage that for you. I will need a key and a telephone number.'

Sophie thanked him profusely and we were soon on our way back to the house.

We let ourselves in on arriving.

'Where did you find the key to the shed, James?'

'In the first cupboard from the back door. The keys are all in there on hooks.'

'See if there are two for the shed please? We need to leave one with Mr Summers.'

Having switched off the water, gas, and electricity, we were soon on our way to drop off the spare key.

Mr Summers told Sophie he would ring her if there were any problems.

'I was quite fond of Hilda, we go back a long way.' We left him the key and Sophie's phone number.

We were soon on the way back to the station. We had a light lunch and boarded the train at one fifteen. With Sophie putting her head on my shoulder we were soon fast asleep.

'James! wake up, the train is pulling into St Pancras station, we are back in London.'

We descended on to the platform, passed through ticket control and out onto the streets of London.

'I have never gone to sleep on a Sunday afternoon before!'

'We do not relax much these days. I have to do some more shopping, I will see you on Wednesday.' She gave me a kiss. 'Bye James.'

I set off for my apartment; what a month, what a weekend! Climbing about on the Great Orme in the rain, finding the croquet box, the jewellery man and his valuation. Making love to Sophie.

Much to my amazement, when I opened the door the piles of paperwork spread about on top of my furniture did not dishearten me – with seventeen piles, one of which I had already looked at.

Looking for croquet boxes would be so much easier than our previous efforts. With no distractions, looking through one pile of papers per night I felt was the way to go. I ordered a takeaway, poured a glass of wine, and made a start. Much to my surprise I enjoyed my meal, I completed one pile of papers by nine o'clock without making any further progress so I decided to have an early night.

Chapter 20

On Monday I was awakened by the alarm. My main priority should be my book publishing business and my five employees, I told myself. I was already thinking about shipwrecks and gold croquet balls and the next pile of papers to look through! After quickly getting dressed, I set off for work.

'Morning James.'

'One of these days I will be here first, Jane. Did you enjoy the weekend?'

'I gardened on Saturday all day. On Sunday we had a barbecue. My husband likes to cook on the barbecue. We had friends and their children round, so it was very pleasant thank you.'

My phone rang.

'We are very pleased with the books you sent us last week and your delivery service, Mr Parker. We look forward to further business with you. Many thanks.'

'That was a good start to the day, Jane.'

'If only we could pin them on the wall, it is so good for morale, James.'

'Do you think we could keep a record of customers that are pleased?'

'We could make notes, yes, but what are you thinking about, James?'

'Once a year we could send out invitations to them, to see what we do and perhaps meet the staff. Make an evening of it.'

'It would involve drinks and nibbles, food of some sort. I do think it would make things more personal, good for our staff meetings. I will keep a record of all our 'thank yous'. It will take at least a year. It is not much extra work. We could ask Roger to give advice on choosing book covers.'

'He is certainly a fountain of knowledge, that's for sure.'

'I will get on it now, James.'

Settling down to work was becoming much easier now that I understood our filing system and the day soon disappeared. My evening also soon passed but with no further progress in my search for croquet boxes. This was my third pile, only fourteen more to go. If they weren't there what on earth would we do? I tried not to think about it.

I turned the news on. The wind and storms had done so much damage in the South and Wales that they had had extreme floods and damage all the way along the coast, didn't I know about it. I took a coffee with a book and retired to bed. The phone rang, it was Sophie.

'Hello James, I have just watched the news. The rain and wind caused havoc all along the coast of Wales so we weren't the only people getting soaked. Two weekends in a row. Nottingham was much more pleasant.'

'You have rung to tell me that?'

'I'm missing you, James! Was work okay today?'

'It was. I have just completed my third pile of papers without success.'

'Mrs Brooks must have worked all the weekend. We were on the seventh pile when I left tonight. I will see you on Wednesday, just wanted to know you were alright.'

She rang off, was I a lucky man? I put my book down and was soon asleep.

Tuesday morning, I set off for work really early. I arrived at six thirty. I had planned to look at our croquet balls in the bottom of the safe before the staff arrived. What I was going to do next I really had no idea, alas it was not to be.

'James, what are you doing coming in this early?'

Jane was sitting at her desk, paperwork spread everywhere.

'I thought if it was quiet, I might see some way forward with the staff bonus this month. What are you doing that brings you here this early?'

'I have made a start on all our well wishers for the last year. I also can think better before the staff come in and the phone starts ringing.'

'It will not be too much extra work you told me! Jane, you work above the call of duty.'

'I am very happy working here, so try not to worry about it. My choice.'

I left her to get on and made two cups of tea. 'Much appreciated, James.'

Having made my way to my office, I made a start to my day. At four thirty I informed Jane I was leaving, and would she lock up after the staff.

At six thirty I set off for The White Feathers, looking forward to meeting Sophie. As I passed through the door, I could see she was already sitting in the window seat looking dazzling.

'James, I need to kiss you a lot.'

'You will need to be patient, young lady. What is on tonight's menu?'

'The fish pie looks good to me.'

'I would agree. With white wine, it would go down nicely.' We had soon ordered, settling down to wait.

'Any more thoughts about our search, James?'

'I have turned it over several times. My conclusion is that the boxes must have been carried a short distance before they were hidden and we know how heavy they were by our box.'

'And whereabouts do you think that was?'

'Since the road Marine Drive did not exist then, it was only a path. My conclusion perhaps it was a cave, unknown to even the locals.'

'Somebody for sure knew a safe place, James!'

At that our fish pie and wine arrived. 'They certainly do not hang about here.'

'I think we should put off going to Liverpool to see Dennis until we have made another trip to Llandudno. It is possible we can add to our knowledge, however small. The lists of cargo should have been gone through over the next two weeks. When we do go to see him, he will have something to get excited about.'

'We must not give him a heart attack.'

'You can be sure even he will have palpitations when we put four gold croquet balls on his desk worth the best part of half a million pounds.'

'I will ring Sam and Branwin first thing in the morning, we will only want one room now, James.'

We sang the praises of the fish pie to the staff, gave our seats to a couple waiting and set off for Mrs Brooks. Sophie pressed the intercom button; we were told to come up. The door was open, she was in the kitchen making tea.

'I have been looking forwards all day to you coming tonight. I forgot to ask about your trip to Nottingham last weekend.'

'The house is now sorted and we have arranged for someone to look after the garden. I am very happy, Mrs Brooks.'

'James, are you still looking after your business?'

'It is far better than I expected, very happy, thank you.'

We moved into the lounge overlooking the park and sat down each with our own thoughts and a cup of tea.

'James thinks we should go back to Llandudno this weekend coming, to see if there might have been a cave where the gold was hidden.'

'It is a gamble but we might learn something more.'

'I could not agree more, James. Anything that moves us in the right direction must be investigated.'

'When we see Dennis next, I would like to ask him to advise on the best way forward.'

'We do need his specialised knowledge from this point.'

'Did you go to see George this weekend?'

'I did. He was much the same, the staff say he is not any trouble. He spends most of his time looking out over the gardens. When they ask what he can see he just smiles. It was a good decision to place him there.'

'Putting the table by the window was a good idea.'

'It certainly was, Sophie.'

'You are working through the papers at great speed Sophie informs me, Mrs Brooks.'

'I am, James, but it is proving to be quite a task. By this weekend hopefully I will finish them. When you get back on Sunday night from Llandudno, we can compare notes.'

'If we both draw a blank then what will we do?'

'Sophie, don't even think about it.'

We spent the next hour talking in circles before calling it a day. Mrs Brooks showed us out. We wished her good night and set off for the elevator. When the doors closed Sophie put her arms round me and kissed me. I felt weak at the knees when we stepped out onto pavement.

'You do realise I haven't seen you since Sunday, James Parker.'

'I have missed you too.'

'Do you think there is any chance I might stay with you tonight? I would be up early, I could make you a cup of tea before going off to work.'

'Well a cup of tea in bed does tempt me.'

'I am glad you said yes. I have brought my toothbrush.'

'I note you never mentioned a nightie.'

'You will suffer for that when we get back, James.'

'That's what I am hoping.'

Arm in arm we set off back to my apartment. True to her word Sophie left me a cup of tea the next morning with a note: I love you, James. The tea was cold, but I set off with a spring in my step for work. Mid-morning Sophie rang.

'Did your tea go cold, James?'

'Yes, it did, but thank you.'

'I have rung Llandudno and spoken to Branwin. We are booked in your room, she said they both missed us last weekend. She did not seem at all surprised that we only wanted one room.'

Jane arrived clutching a pile of paperwork.

'I will see you Wednesday evening, my treat, 'bye.'

'If you will look through these, James, we can catch the ten thirty post. The top two need your signature.'

'Straight on to it, Jane.' She left me to get on. I sorted through it all, signed the top two and posted them off with time to spare. Without any pressing matters I spent the rest of the morning visiting each department of my workers. My conclusions were that they all seemed to be happy with what they were doing. If the work kept coming in and we improved our output I would be faced with a decision about moving to new premises.

This was the first time in my life I felt that I really belonged somewhere. Meeting Sophie and Mrs Brooks had made me very happy. I now had a purpose to life. I left Jane to lock up at five o'clock and walked back to my apartment.

Having finished my tea of cod with new potatoes, washed down with a can of beer, I sat down to make a plan for the coming weekend. How to find a cave that was not known in 1812? Perhaps Sam might have some idea of how to go about it. He had lived in Llandudno all his life. Where to start? I decided at ten o'clock to call it a day, taking a warm cup of tea to bed.

Tuesday passed by quite uneventfully. There was a book run but thanks to the new lifting gear it ran very smoothly. Jane told me it was on its way soon after mid-day. At five o'clock I set off for my apartment, picking up a takeaway from the local Indian restaurant. Having tidied up after my meal, I made a start on our goods list; I couldn't help thinking of them doing exactly the same, perhaps they were getting better luck than I was. With no further progress I packed up, switched the TV to the main items of news, then went to bed.

On Wednesday morning I rang Sophie, she picked up the phone straight away.

'Good morning, James, you never ring me. To what do I owe the honour?'

'Did you do some more work on our goods lists yesterday?'

'We did, and we have not found anything new, even Mrs Brooks looked a bit down when we finished last night.'

'So it is up to us at the weekend then.'

The White Feathers was busier than usual, I was glad we had

booked. Our table in the window had been saved for us. Sophie followed me in.

'Hi James, was your day okay?'

'It was fine, thank you. How was yours?'

'We are fully booked at the hotel this week, some important conference. The manager wants everything right. He can be quite a pain.'

'If we do find the rest of the croquet balls, the reward would be a substantial amount. You could retire and live a life of leisure.'

'I could go full time with my detective agency, it is nice to dream, James.'

'We are working at the moment for Mrs Brooks! I was only joking! We had better order; they have a lot of people to find a meal for tonight.'

'Cauliflower cheese, with pork sausages for me.'

'We had better make that two, Sophie.' The waiter took our order.

'We need to hope the tide is out this weekend coming, if looking for caves is on our agenda, James.'

'I am hoping Sam might advise us. He might know where the old maps are kept, there must be some records in Llandudno.' Our meal arrived, we soon tucked in and it was delicious.

'I will try to replicate that next time we go to Nottingham, James.'

We set off for Mrs Brooks apartment, with Sophie holding my arm, it was very nice.

Mrs Brooks told us to come up. The lift was there much too soon! I pressed the button and we went down to the ground floor.

'James, what are you doing?'

'Enjoying being kissed.'

'There is a person waiting for the lift.'

'Hurry up and press the button and behave.'

When we got out of the lift Sophie said, 'I will have a red face, hope she doesn't notice.'

We were soon sitting down with a cup of tea.

'I have made little progress with all these lists, perhaps Dennis missed some. Can't say I want to go through them again. How have you got on, James?'

'Not even halfway yet, Sophie tells me you are much further on.'

'I must say the idea of a cave to hide all those boxes is more than feasible. It is another path we need to take. James, the best of luck for the weekend. It might be a good idea to look up the tide tables.'

'Sophie's thoughts are on the same lines about the tide.'

'Perhaps they did not carry those boxes! They could have rowed into a cave, it was dark. People would be looking at the ship on fire in the middle of the harbour.'

'When the morning and daylight came the tide would have gone out. The people that beach combed would be looking for anything of value and one eye looking out for the law,' Sophie said.

'They certainly would not look above their heads at the cliffs.'

'This is all conjecture, but I would guess it is as near to the truth, as possible, we will never know for sure', said Mrs Brooks.

By the time we came to leave all three of us were far more cheerful than when we arrived. We stepped out on to the pavement to a clear night sky, with a full moon to light our way back to my apartment. With Sophie holding my arm I did not ask if she was staying. I looked up and Mrs Brooks gave us a wave from her window.

Thursday and Friday were uneventful at work. I had early nights with a book, but my thoughts kept drifting towards the coming weekend.

Chapter 21

Saturday morning, I was awake early and decided to pack before breakfast. The one decision I would need to talk over with Sophie on the journey was how much to let Sam know why we were looking for hidden caves from the 1800s. Sophie was waiting outside the hotel when I pulled up at ten thirty.

'Morning James.'

I quickly put her bag in the boot and we were on our way to Llandudno.

'Would you fasten that safety belt, please.'

'You did not say that last night, James.'

She gave me a kiss on my cheek.

'Sam is going to wonder what we are up to when you ask about caves, James!'

'You have taken the words out of my mouth.'

'I do think we should promise him we will reveal all if he can have patience a little while longer.'

'We will ask him together, Sophie.'

'I thought that for a change I would make tuna and cucumber sandwiches, and a flask of tea with a cream cake for afterwards. We seem to have been in so many pubs and hotels.'

'Wonderful idea! We must find somewhere nice to pull up around twelve o'clock.'

The Jaguar purred along. We made good time and Sophie was soon telling me to pull in.

'Near that old church looks a good place for our lunch.'

'You don't think the croquet boxes, if there are more, could have been buried in St Tudno's Churchyard by any chance?'

'If they were, we will never get to digging them up, it would be quite out of the question. Until we find evidence of more boxes, try not to think about it.'

We both enjoyed our lunch and said we would do it again.

'I have been thinking, can we drive along the sea front when we arrive in Llandudno, James? It will help us if we know when the tide is fully in.' The traffic was kind and we made good time.

Spotting a gap, we were soon parked up close to the pier. We crossed the road and set off along the promenade. The tide had turned, it was on the way out.

'There is a notice: 'Fishing trips and boats for hire', let's see if they can help us,' said Sophie.

'High tide will be at one thirty tomorrow,' we were informed.

'Could you take us close to the shore, round the bay and say two hundred yards each side of the bay in a small boat, please?'

'Just the two of you would it be?'

'Yes, there would only be two of us.'

'We haven't a fishing trip booked. I will do it for you personally. Thirty-five pounds is the best, plus fuel, forty-five in total is the very best I can do. You can meet me here at twelve thirty, deposit of £20 today. We will sail wind or rain.'

I quickly paid and thanked him. We were soon on our way to the boarding house.

'I never expected we would be going out on a boat tomorrow, James, we are a good team!'

We were soon at our boarding house. Sam showed us in and took the cases to my room at the front of the house.

'When you have unpacked, come down for a cup of tea, I will tell Branwin to put the kettle on.'

He left us to get on.

'Will you broach the subject of one room when we go down?'

We soon unpacked and set off down the stairs for our cup of tea. 'There you are. You can unwind with a cup of tea. How are you both?'

'Just fine thank you. But we do feel a bit awkward about only booking one room.'

'James, we have been expecting it for some time now, the way you look at one another, have we not, Sam?'

'We certainly have, love is like a thunder-bolt when it strikes, nothing you can do about it. If you ever make it legal put us both on the list.'

'You will make them blush, Sam.'

'Thank you for that, both of you. Since you were both born in Llandudno, what do you know about caves that are accessible from the sea here?'

'That is a strange request.'

'Without doubt you are bound to feel that. We cannot tell you why, but before too long I promise you will be the first to know.'

'We will hold you to that, James. There is one important family you probably need to know about: the Mostyn Family. They have been closely intertwined with Llandudno for the best part of five hundred years. Generations of them. Now you may wonder why I am telling you about them.'

'We are all ears, Sam.'

'There are long lists of ships wrecked in the bay. That is why the lighthouse must have been placed here. A few metres to the west of the lighthouse is a cave called the Homby Cave. I think it was named after the Liverpool brig Homby which hit the cliffs below there in a storm. I am certain it was on New Year's Day 1824. A famous person visited the cave, I think it was Charles Darwin, the same year. Is that helpful?'

'We are looking for the year 1812. It would have been known as a 'smugglers cave' in all probability.'

'I do know it was said the monks would hide there from the anti-Catholic authorities. Perhaps it was only a secret to a few, James. There has been talk that the Mostyn family fitted it out as a summer house in the seventeenth century. Now this is why I told you about them.'

'There is a good chance it is what we are looking for, Sam,' said Sophie.

'What makes you think it is the cave we are looking for?'

'In all probability if it is accessible from when the tide is in, James, there will not be many caves like that.'

'We can ask the chap who is taking us out in his boat tomorrow if he knows about the cave, what do you think, Sam?'

'You can be sure he will, it is history for the tourists.'

'This is exciting,' said Branwin. 'We could have famous guests staying with us.'

'I don't want to raise your hopes, but fingers crossed.'

'We can certainly do that, James!' said Sam.

'Have you decided where you are eating tonight?'

'It won't be far. We have a long day in front of us tomorrow.'

'Sam and me are out with friends tonight, but we could provide you with cold meats, salad, and a drink.'

'Can we take you up on that?'

'No trouble, I will set it out on the kitchen table, come down when you are ready.'

At that we returned to our room.

It wasn't long before Branwin shouted up the stairs. 'We are off now 'bye.'

'They never said about starters, Sophie.'

She appeared out of the bathroom without a stitch on. 'Do you think this will do, James?'

I soon forgot about food until much later.

The next morning, we set off for the harbour. We were early, but our man was already there waiting. I duly paid him the outstanding £25 and he helped us into the boat.

'Now where would you like to start? It might save a lot of time if I know what we are looking for.'

'Am I right in saying you know this coastline well?'

'Born and bred in Llandudno, all my life spent here.'

He certainly looked the part with his rugged complexion, cable-stitched jumper, and cap.

'We are looking for a cave.'

'There are lots of caves in this area. Can you be more specific?'

'It would be probably accessible from high tide we think and might have been used by smugglers before the lighthouse was built.'

'You are talking about the early 1800s then. The lighthouse was erected in the early 1860s. You must understand most of these caves were used by beachcombers. If a ship was driven onto the rocks, when it started to break up the locals would be after its spoils. The few people that were in the town mostly lived off the fish they caught. It was very different from today.'

'Have you any suggestions then?' said Sophie.

'There was a cave below where the lighthouse was. It has been there for centuries, if you think about it, they all have. Now, did people know about it then? It is debatable but I can tell you Charles

Darwin was in Llandudno around the 1820s. He would have been a very young man then.'

'He was one of history's most famous biologists on natural history,' said Sophie. 'I remember learning about him at school. There was a famous quote: "A man who dares to waste one hour of his time has not discovered the value of life".'

'I can imagine him looking in old caves.'

'What is most important; the cave was there before he was born. Do you think you can find it please?'

'We are on our way; I will do my best.'

We were soon heading west below Marine Drive looking up at the Great Orme, the cliffs looked unclimbable from our little boat, quite frightening.

Sophie said, 'I am very nervous, James, I am not a good swimmer.'

'You have no need to worry lass, I won't let any harm come to you. I should have told you I am one of the Llandudno lifeboat crew. Now it is very calm this morning, we can get up close, no need to worry. My name is Arnold Broomfield, it is a joke among the locals. They say my ancestors made brooms for a living. Have I cheered you up a bit I hope?'

'Yes, thank you, Mr Broomfield.'

Twenty minutes later he switched the outboard motor off and dropped anchor.

'I can't see any caves, James.'

'We are still below them miss, it will be high tide at one thirty, the sea is still coming in.'

The first cave came into view after a short while.

'It will soon be under the water. I will take you to the next.'

Sure enough the second cave came into view. It was larger than the first. The floor was awash with sea water. 'We still have a quarter of an hour to high tide yet. I will see how close we can get the boat in to the next! This is the largest along this coastline and it is above the high tide waterline.'

'Would the floor of the cave stay dry when the tide is in, Mr Broomfield?'

'Most of the year but sometimes in the winter if there is a severe storm the floor would be under water.'

'James, what are you doing standing in the boat?'

'Would you be wanting to look inside then, James?'

'Is it possible?'

'Are you a good swimmer, young man?'

'One of the best at my school.'

Mr Broomfield threw a grappling iron attached to a long rope and pulled the boat in to the side of the cliff.

'I will give you a leg up. Do not let go of that rope, that is an order, James.'

I was soon on the front ledge of the cave. Much to my amazement it was quite level and would have made a good theatre setting. There was no way you would have suspected a cave looking up from low tide. Mr Broomfield was right about the floor of the cave being dry. If you stacked boxes or other goods not too high, the only way they would be visible would be out at sea with a telescope.

My theory of where the croquet boxes were hidden was more than possible. I had a good look round. The only thing there was an old rope from some previous explorer. Mr Broomfield helped me down back into the boat.

'James, keep quiet about me helping you into that cave please, I have never done that before.'

He pulled up the anchor, started the outboard motor, and we were on our way back to the harbour. It was just coming up to two o'clock when we said goodbye to Mr Broomfield. We thanked him for his efforts to help us and told him we would not be talking to anybody about our trip.

'James, we started our investigation in the Weary Traveller here in Llandudno, let's have lunch there!'

We were soon parked up and went in through the door, it was packed.

'Did you book, sir?'

'Sorry, we did not, please try to fit us in.' Sophie gave him her best smile.

'If you do not mind waiting, I will fit you in somewhere.'

'Was that you flirting with the waiter?'

'We woman do have our ways.'

'Well this is a surprise; you pair back in Llandudno again.' It was our reporter from Church Walk, Mr William Jones.

'Now if you young people would need any help, I am offering my services.'

'We may well take you up on that offer in the near future.' The waiter came back to us.

'Would you follow me, please.'

Having sat us down at a table in the next room he left us both with a menu to ponder over.

'Welsh lamb with roast potatoes for me, it is my treat, James.'

'I will join you, we are in Wales after all.'

'We got away without too many awkward questions from Snoops, he is watching us you know.'

'You are right, but he probably comes here for Sunday dinner!'

'I have not seen him with a lady friend all the times we have been down here.'

'Maybe he isn't interested in ladies.'

'He looks to me like an ordinary person dedicated to the newspaper industry, let's not forget he plays the organ on Sunday mornings.'

'I am sure you're right, Sophie.'

Our roast lamb dinner was delicious, and very little conversation flowed between us.

'If we lived here I should want to come on Sundays, James. Now, the verdict on the cave?'

'I think it holds up. Marine Drive was not built till around 1875, the total population was in the lower hundreds at the time of our shipwreck, it is more than feasible.

The cave floor was so flat it could be perfect. You would need two people, one in the boat, one on the ledge. Somebody who knew about the cave who must have been born in Llandudno.'

'That is a brilliant deduction! If Mrs Brooks should find the rest of the boxes, the agent or people that loaded them on to our ship should be high on our list. If there is a connection to Llandudno, it will prove your theory about the hiding place for them.'

'We need Mrs Brooks to have found them on the lists from the goods loaded when we get back to London, Sophie. It is the only hope we have of moving on with our search.'

'I will pay. You have a long drive back to London, let's move.'

Sophie was asleep in the car not long after we left Llandudno. I was left with my own thoughts; they were pretty mixed up. Positive action was needed for the next step. I decided to concentrate on driving and get back safely to London.

Chapter 22

On Monday morning I arrived at work early, I had not slept well. We badly needed Mrs Brooks to find those boxes.

'Good morning, James.'

Jane was already beavering away. 'What would I do without you, always here before me.'

'I need you to sign some papers later, so we can catch the midday post.'

'When you're ready, Jane.' Just as I sat down in my office the phone rang.

'James, sorry to worry you this early.' It was Sophie. 'I rang Mrs Brooks last night after you dropped me off, she has found the boxes – all twenty of them! I could not contain myself, I had to tell you. Mrs Brooks said she will know much more by Wednesday evening. I am struggling to think straight. Twenty boxes would you believe! We will give Dennis in Liverpool a heart attack when we next go to see him.'

'Thank you, that's great, but calm down and try to concentrate on your job at the hotel. I will see you on Wednesday.'

'How can you be so calm; I will let you get on then.'

She rang off. I was anything but calm but also relieved. This could only be described has a giant stride in this investigation. It was going to be a long day, but work must come first. I tried to settle down and get my immediate problems sorted out.

On Tuesday we had three book runs to pack and get on their way. My mind did not have time to think about croquet boxes. The day soon disappeared. I told Jane to have an early night and I would lock up. She accepted gratefully. On reaching my apartment I ordered an Indian takeaway and proceeded to start to tidy all the piles of paper away. With Mrs Brooks having found the croquet boxes, all twenty of them, she had told Sophie, I put the ones I had sorted into some form of order. I did not relish the thought of sorting through them a second time.

My takeaway arrived, I opened a beer and sat down at a clear table without paper files on it to enjoy my evening meal, very content at this moment. We had come so far in our quest for Mrs Brooks, since starting only a few months ago. I had been wondering about my life after my father's death. Then Sophie walked into my office, she had also lost her aunt and was on her own. Perhaps this life is planned for us. I was certainly looking forward to the next part of it.

Sophie was there before me at The White Feathers on Wednesday evening, she looked up when I came through the door. She had on a nice cream blouse with a blue pleated skirt and a matching blue handbag.

'I've been looking forward all day to meeting up, James!'

'Likewise. We could just skip dinner.'

'We have an appointment with Mrs Brooks for eight o'clock.'

'You have tied your hair in a ponytail, it's different.'

'We must still try to look business-like, after all she is funding this investigation. I will let it down later for you.'

'The fish with a glass of white wine would suit me.'

'I will join you, James.'

After our meal we complimented the staff on their endeavours and said goodbye to Arthur, who was propping up the bar reading his paper. We set off for Mrs Brooks' apartment, Sophie holding my arm.

'What is the next logical step, James?'

'We can listen to what she has discovered, then make plans. I really have no idea at this moment.'

Sophie pressed the button for the intercom, we were told to come up. The door was open, she was making a pot of tea.

'Now then, you must tell me about how your weekend went with the caves. I have been so looking forward to tonight.'

'James, perhaps you can start,' said Sophie.

'We hired a boat for high tide on Sunday, we had missed the sea turning on Saturday, lucky for us there were not any fishing trips that day. A Mr Broomfield took us out. There were three caves in total we looked at. The first one the floor was under water before high tide. The second was awash also before the tide reached its peak. The last cave was much higher, even standing up in the boat we could not really see inside.'

'Mr Broomfield threw a grappling hook and helped James climb up and in, Mrs Brooks. We are not to tell anybody, he said.'

'What did you find, James?'

'It was completely dry and looked more like a theatre setting apart from a piece of old rope from some previous explorer's visit. The interesting thing was you could hide boxes if they were not stacked too high. You would need two people to get them from a boat. They would only be visible from far out at sea. You would need a good telescope.'

'You are saying you could not see the cave when the tide was out from the beach?'

'There is no way after the tide goes out you would know the cave was there.'

'What an exciting discovery. Now I will fill you in on what I have found out. It was during the last pile of papers. I had just about given up of ever finding the croquet boxes. Then there they were, with the paperwork appertaining to them. We have the name of the agent that was responsible for loading them for the British Government.'

'Well done. Oh what would we do without your perseverance.'

'You would probably have got there, Sophie, I have no doubt about it, or James. I will make another cup of tea then we can decide where we go from here.'

We were soon drinking our second cup of tea, each wrapped up in our own thoughts.

'James, would you go first.'

'You say we have a name for the agent or person that was responsible for the paperwork and loading the boxes on to the ship.'

'We do indeed, it was Erasmus. It was a popular name at the beginning of the nineteenth century.'

'There was a famous Greek Saint by that name, I remember being told about him at school,' said Sophie.

'You can rest assured this one was not a Saint from what we have discovered so far.'

'Give me a week to see if I can find anything else. I did a lot of research for my husband; I do know the right channels to go down, James.'

'We are now at the stage where we need to bring Dennis back in. He has been researching ships and their cargo for many years, but it is your call, Mrs Brooks.'

'One week, then we will go to Liverpool. We can meet next Wednesday, compare notes, then I will book an appointment.'

'I am so intrigued with this fellow, Erasmus. I will come to help on Tuesday. It will make a nice change from endless lists, Mrs

Brooks,' said Sophie.

'It looks like your theory about how the boxes ended up in a cave that was little known could hold up, James.'

'It may be all in my imagination, perhaps there was only the one box that Henry found the day he was digging for bait.'

'What if the fire on the ship spread so quickly that they never got them all into the boat? The fire would light up the bay! They could not risk being seen. People would be waiting to help them,' said Sophie.

'For what it is worth I do believe the Albatross was sabotaged. The guy who told the tale of being strapped to a rigging pole was just insurance in case anybody had noticed them up to no good, it was a let out.'

'You are saying he was just a distraction, Mrs Brooks?'

'The fact that he was never seen again leads me to wonder why, it just doesn't add up.'

'James, it is ten o'clock, we have both got to get up for work in the morning. We will leave you to ponder, Mrs Brooks.'

We said goodnight, she showed us to the door, we went down in the lift and out into the London night. With Sophie holding my arm we made our way back to my apartment.

'You have tidied the lounge since the last time I was here, James.'

'I have put all the paperwork in one deep drawer, let us hope it stays there. Would you like a night cap?'

'Much too young, I do not think it would suit me. You might tempt me with a small glass of wine though.'

One small kiss was all it took to forget about our wine and our quest as we soon tumbled into bed. On Thursday morning there were two half empty glasses of wine on the worktop. Sophie said, 'Sunday till Wednesday without you, James. I am counting the hours down, the restraint of not seeing you, I cannot help it, I just want to make love to you. Do you think all couples are like that?'

'I would say it depends on their age. Now if we do not want to be late for work, I suggest you do not kiss me again until we are out of the door of my apartment.'

Having dropped Sophie off at the hotel with a restrained kiss, I drove on to my work.

'Morning James.'

Jane was already working away.

'We need to talk later about the 'thank you' letters from customers, I have some ideas.'

'When you are ready, Jane.'

It was three o'clock in the afternoon when she eventually got back to me.

'Is there a problem?'

'Not at all, I have already found about sixteen from the past few months. If we wait for twelve months, we could not possibly have them all at once. A smaller number would be easier to arrange and show around.'

'Perhaps we could be more selective, do you not think?'

'That is what I was coming to next, James, they are all important to us, but the ones who ordered the most books from us should be our priority, after all, it is a business!'

'I could not agree more, you have my permission to go along those lines.'

She soon left me to get on.

The rest of the week was uneventful, apart from Sophie ringing on Friday to see if she could stay with me for the weekend. I was informed she would be cooking our evening meal.

'The main course will be a prawn curry and rice, followed by 'wait and see', James.'

'It wouldn't be oysters by any chance!'

'They say they are an aphrodisiac; you certainly will not be getting them. I was more thinking the television would be nice afterwards.'

'Not having to drive home from Llandudno on Sunday afternoon will be very welcome, I will take us out on Sunday for lunch.'

The weekend seemed to end far too quickly; I had enjoyed the break from driving. Monday started with a kiss on my cheek from Sophie when I dropped her off at her hotel. My thoughts soon drifted to Mrs Brooks and what she had been up to, I guessed she would have seen George on Sunday afternoon, with the rest of her time spent investigating Erasmus. All morning I felt quite invigorated after our weekend off and the day soon raced by.

I rang Sophie during the evening.

'James, I normally ring you! Are you okay?'

'Yes thank you, the weekend was great. We must find time to do it again. I am wondering what Mrs Brooks has found out, if anything.'

'She has not rung me. I am also wondering what she has been up to. We did say a week before we consulted Dennis. We will need to sweat it out till Wednesday evening. I do not want to worry her.'

'Will you book our table at The White Feathers please for Wednesday?'

'Already booked, James. I have worries we will not get any further now with this investigation. The chances of ever finding what happened to those boxes must be millions to one!'

'You can be sure there were millions of pounds in today's money to hide somewhere. It will be for Mrs Brooks to say when we have no more leads, she is doing the paying, don't you think?'

'I do think but I wanted you to say it. You have cheered me up, James. Good night, see you on Wednesday.'

Tuesday morning, I arrived at my work just as Jane was opening up.

'You very nearly got here first this morning, James. One of our printers was misbehaving last night. Perhaps you would take a look please.'

'Who was using it last?'

'Roger will tell you when he comes in. Have a word with him, he is the best person for the machines.'

When I got to the printing conveyor lines Roger was putting overalls on. 'Morning James.'

'Jane tells me we have a problem; can I help in any way?'

'If you don't mind getting your hands dirty, I would appreciate a lift.'

'Where do we start?'

'This is a belt conveyor which is tensioned to keep it running straight. The problem is it is starting to pull apart. We need to make a new join in the belt, then re-tension the belt again.'

It was coming up to twelve o'clock when we finished, then the line was switched on. Roger showed me how to adjust the belt and we were back in business. We did not have a works engineer; without his help I would have been reliant on Arthur who could be anywhere in London working. I might be paying my staff, but I was lucky to have each and every one of them!

Jane came by at three o'clock.

'Is it all systems go for tomorrow, James?

'Roger seems happy. We had to rejoin the conveyor belt and adjust to keep the belt running centrally.'

'We have quite a day on Wednesday, so we'll soon find out. I will go over the details first thing in the morning.'

At four o'clock I decided to call it a day and save my strength.

Book runs always left me feeling drained, they were our end product. They also paid our wages I reminded myself.

Wednesday book runs ran like clockwork, the last lorry pulled out of the yard at four thirty. I was looking forward to seeing Sophie and could not wait to see if she had any more thoughts on our trip to Liverpool.

Much to my surprise, I was first to arrive at The White Feathers, so I joined Arthur at the bar.

'James, we seem to have missed one another the last two weeks, is everything running okay at work?'

'Yes, in no small way thanks to you.'

At that moment Sophie came through the door and came over. 'And what are you two planning?'

'Just a drink, what can we get you miss?' said Arthur.

'I would like a tonic water with ice and lemon please.'

We soon left him to his racing paper and took our seats at the window table, then ordered our food and two glasses of wine.

Sophie said, 'I have been thinking a lot about what to do next, James.'

'And your conclusion?'

'We need to write all our thoughts down including Dennis's knowledge from Liverpool, plus anybody else that we speak to. There will be quite a list before we make any more progress, do you not think?'

'At least that is a positive thought. Did you make any progress on Tuesday night?'

'Mrs Brooks is a real trooper. When I left her last night, she looked tired, she had put in so many hours trying to find any more about Erasmus, she said she would try again today. I am not very hopeful.'

'Perhaps Dennis will have more experience, he might get us to the next stage.'

'Without your strength, James, I would find it so hard to carry on.'

'You did want to be a private investigator!'

'Very true, let us hope the next case will be far more straight forward.'

'Can you arrange less travelling next time?'

'James Parker you are having me on, let's eat up and get on our way.'

We soon set off with Sophie holding my arm. It was a lovely evening, what else could I want? Sophie pressed the intercom button and we were told to come up. The door was open. We called out, 'Mrs Brooks!'

'Do come in. I won't be long.'

She arrived with a tea tray, 'Make yourselves at home, did you enjoy having a weekend without working?'

'I did not miss the driving, but Llandudno has become a way of life the last few months.'

'You can say that again, James! I do know it has given me something to get up for each day. Now I cannot report any new developments, but I have done some research on our mystery man's name. Desiderus Erasmus. A Dutch man from Rotterdam is the person I got back to. Desiderus was his Christian name, he was an important scholar, born in October 1466 he died in 1536 in Switzerland. He was very famous for his quotes. One of them you may have heard, "In the kingdom of the blind, the one-eyed man is king." He was also a Humanist.'

'What is a Humanist, Mrs Brooks?' said Sophie.

'I had to look it up. Humanists believe that people do not have souls, that there is no afterlife in heaven or hell nor a God who judges where people go to in the afterlife.'

'If we knew where our man went in his afterlife it would make our lives a lot easier.'

'You do make me smile, Sophie! They say they believe that we only have this life, and it ends forever when we die.'

'He was certainly making the most of it if he stole all that gold.'

'The word today is used now to mean those who seek to live good lives without religious or superstitious beliefs. You need to be careful if we talk to Dennis for, who knows, he could be one or anybody else for that matter.'

'For what it is worth, our man that was an Agent could have been descended from him but we will never find that out.'

'But he must have been well read and a scholar to have worked for the British Government, James.'

'I do agree with that. He was trusted with gold to support the war between Britain and America in the battle of independence.'

'Sophie what are your thoughts?'

'I was so wrapped up in your story, I am at a total loss. Let us hope that Dennis will throw some light.'

'This afternoon I have been on the phone to Liverpool. They say Dennis is there on Thursday next week. I have booked for two hours of his time. One thirty to three thirty. I am hoping you both can arrange the time off. I hope you do not think I was too presumptuous.'

'Not in the least. I imagine Dennis is in demand when he is there.'

Sophie said, 'I agree with you, James. Thursday it is.'

Chapter 23

Mrs Brooks told us she had been to see George again but there was no change in him. It was soon time to say goodnight to her. She let us out and said, 'Nine thirty, Thursday, I will treat us to lunch.' Sophie gave her a hug and we set off for the lift.

'I do hope I am as brave if I get to her age, James.'

'If you get to that age you won't have much choice in the matter. The best time for me in London is in the late evening, when the noise settles down. I enjoy seeing the lights come on in the windows, they are all people relaxing at the end of the day.'

'I do enjoy holding your arm going back to the apartment, James, Nottingham is not in my thoughts quite so much.'

When I dropped off Sophie on Thursday morning at the hotel it was just starting to rain. She said, 'Goodbye James, I will ring tonight.'

The day soon disappeared without any further problems. I inspected the belt conveyor late afternoon and decided to call it a day.

Eight o'clock the phone rang, it was Sophie. 'Hello, are you alright, James?'

'I have just eaten an Indian takeaway, thank you.'

'Now, a question, if you had stolen all that gold, what would you do?'

'I would retire at the first available opportunity.'

'That was my conclusion also. I am making notes for when we see Dennis next week.'

'It is more than a possibility, but how we find out is beyond me.'

'But Dennis will have far more ideas about such things. He is used to tracking people from the past'.

'The Inland Revenue, if they were working then, would know if he retired!'

'I will make a note of that.'

'In all these lists of ships and goods they must also have lots of information about people. Perhaps we should be delving further.'

'What would you like to do this weekend?'

'Since we will not be going to Llandudno I would like to stay with you, and go out for lunch on the river Thames.'

'I will do my best. See you on Saturday, late morning.' She said goodbye and rang off.

The rest of the week seemed to pass quickly. I tidied my apartment in the evenings, with Sophie coming to stay for the weekend. I was very pleased with my efforts. She arrived late morning on Saturday.

'I have been shopping on the way here, James. We are eating alfresco.'

'I have never done that here before.'

'Your balcony will be lovely for lunch as the sun is shining.'

'It is not exactly the balcony of Europe.' She gave me a long lingering kiss.

'Now would you lay the table while I prepare our lunch.'

'It would help if I knew what we are eating.'

'We are having tomato soup with garlic bread. Could you please put the wine in the fridge? It is a medium dry white from Australia.'

In a short time we were having lunch sitting on my balcony. 'This is a wonderful soup!'

'My aunt said if you put ham stock in most soups you can't fail.'

'Can I order this next time we go to Nottingham?'

'You might not be able to, I talked the cook at the hotel into letting me beg some ham stock.'

Saturday evening we watched an old film before retiring to bed. It was then Sophie told me she had forgotten her pyjamas.

'But I did bring my toothbrush,' she informed me.

'Since they never stay on for long, I will forgive you this time,' I said with a laugh.

'I will make you suffer for that, James, when I have cleaned my teeth!'

The sun was shining when we woke on Sunday morning.

'It would be nice to walk down to the South embankment and catch our boat, James.'

'I couldn't agree more.' We set off at eleven thirty to allow plenty of time to arrive and take our seats for the afternoon cruise.

'A strange thing happened yesterday morning when I did my shopping. I was riding the escalator going down when I saw George's double! He was coming up on the other side.'

'You have an over-imaginative mind; we both know he is in a home.'

'You are good for me, James, you keep my feet on the ground.' We were soon at the ticket office collecting our tickets and were shown to our table and seated. Our boat was soon on its way with views of the London Eye and so many historical buildings. A pleasant young man came round with the drinks menu and took our order.

'Would you know how long the River Thames is?' said Sophie.

'At over two hundred miles long it is the longest river in the UK, miss.'

'Do you think he warrants a tip later, James?'

'He does seem a knowledgeable young man, we can consider him later in the day.'

'If you could hire that metal detector again one weekend we could go mud larking when the tide is low.'

'I do not know what you mean, Sophie.'

'One of the staff and his girlfriend have started doing it. When the tide is low, they find all sorts of things. He has numerous clay pipes, old buckles, all sorts of artefacts. I first noticed them when I walked along the embankment one Sunday morning. This was before we became involved.'

'I will give the matter some thought.'

Our salmon meal arrived, the sun was shining and all too soon the cruise came to an end far too quickly. We set off back to my apartment.

Sophie made cucumber sandwiches followed by cake for tea, which we enjoyed while watching an old film I had recorded.

'We should add to your list Title Deeds and Land Searches. If Erasmus worked in the Liverpool docks, he must have lived not very far from them.'

'That is a good point, since people would not have had cars then. By Thursday we will have a list of sorts to give to Dennis. Can I still come to stay on Wednesday?'

'That all depends!'

'Depends on what?'

'Whether you bring your pyjamas.'

'I was thinking of more like a see-through nightie.'

'In that case I think it will be okay.'

'James Parker!'

'What?'

'Take me to bed please.'

Monday morning I dropped Sophie at the hotel, she gave me a kiss on the cheek.

'I will cook for us on Wednesday. Don't forget the list for Liverpool.'

On Monday morning I started to think about holidays and how my staff took them. I asked Jane if she could spare one hour in the afternoon.

'Four o'clock would be a good time, James.'

She arrived on the appointed hour with two cups of tea.

'My first question, holidays for the staff.'

'We all take staggered holidays. The main reason being we are a small firm.'

'So would I be right in saying my father and you always took different times for holiday breaks?'

'That is correct.'

'Second question, what is the hardest part of your job?'

'Probably what drains me most is constantly making decisions.'

'Then I have to be more aware of where we are going with the business. Do you think we could find time for staff meetings once a week?'

'That would be a good idea, if you bear in mind we have so little time on a daily basis.'

'Perhaps we could make a start next week. I would help you go through the coming publications for the following week, we must check if all are on schedule, or if anything needs postponed. If there are problems which we can solve together, or even with the staff, we can ask for suggestions from them. Would that be a good idea?'

'James if you think you are ready for it, we can go ahead. You will sleep some nights better than others.'

'I will give it a go; I have always slept well, Jane.'

'The rest of the world is just waking up when we go to bed. I sometimes send emails and text messages these days in the middle of the night.'

'I had no idea you were taking work home, that's on top of a long day here.'

'I do like working in this book publishing business, James,' she left me to get on.

When I'd eaten my evening meal my mind drifted back to my father's business which I had taken over and how little I knew about it. I had a long way to go to step into his shoes. I realised emails are a blessing for me, they are the platforms which enable us to stay in contact with our readers all round the globe. How on earth he did it without them I guess I would never really know. Jane was right, I had not slept well when I awoke on Tuesday morning.

'We do send books overseas, Jane?' It was nine thirty and she had brought two cups of tea into my office.

'We certainly do.'

'That means several different languages.'

'We have been doing it for a number of years now.'

'I am not sure about any of it, languages were not something I was good at.'

'You do not need to worry, I will break you into it gently. The staff are all behind you, James.'

I decided there and then that at the end of the year we would have a party for them all and their partners. I just had to survive that long.

Chapter 24

Thursday morning soon came around. I was up early and decided to walk to my works where I picked up the Volvo estate car in which I had put the croquet box, complete with wooden mallets and four gold balls in the back, covered over the night before when the last of the staff had gone home. I left a message for Jane to lock up at the end of the day.

Sophie was already waiting when I arrived at the Prince Edward Hotel.

'Good morning James.'

'Good morning to you.'

'Perhaps it would be a good idea to put Mrs Brooks in the front with more legroom, I will mind the gold in the back, James.'

'I hope if you are riding shot gun in the back you have a weapon of some sort.'

'It is a bit early for jokes like that.'

Mrs Brooks was also outside her apartment waiting to be picked up and we were on our way.

'We did make it last time in time for lunch, James, but I have looked the mileage up and the total miles from London to Liverpool without detours is two hundred and twenty miles.'

'I will keep the speedo at seventy once we are away from London. Not to worry, we will be in time for a quick lunch when we get there.'

It was just coming up to twelve forty-five when I pulled on to the car park of the Liverpool Maritime Museum. Sophie quickly got a ticket from the machine, while I helped Mrs Brooks out of the car.

'The nearest place for food will do, we have not long, one thirty is our deadline,' said Mrs Brooks.

'The Best Fish and Chips' was the notice over a door, so we filed inside.

'Could I have plaice and peas, please,' said Mrs Brooks. I ordered three cups of tea with fish and chips twice for Sophie and myself.

'I did enjoy your tale about the liver birds the last time we were here,' said Sophie.

'We are not sight-seeing today. In the two hours at our disposal we have to get the most out of it that's possible, Sophie. I will say the view from here is spectacular though.'

With little said between us, each to our own thoughts, Mrs Brooks paid and we set off for our appointment. The electric doors of the museum opened, and Lillian was at her desk.

'Hello again, Dennis told me to take you straight through to his office.'

We set off following her down the corridor to Dennis's office.

I could feel the hairs on the back of my neck lifting, we were surrounded with so much history on the walls, old maps and pictures from the past. Lillian tapped on a door and we were told to enter. I had forgotten Dennis's fine striking face and silver hair. I was glad he was willing to help us.

'How nice to see you. Please take a seat. I was wondering if we would see you again, now, how can I help?'

'James, will you tell the story so far,' said Mrs Brooks.

'We have been going to Llandudno most weekends. George was on the way there when he had that terrible accident. Now George had tied a key to a bracket clock some time before and told Mrs Brooks' husband to guard it with his life. We traced the key to a jewellery shop in London. It opened a deposit box there, inside which was one half of a map, nothing else.'

'Please go on, you have been busy!'

'We traced Henry's brother to a nursing home, and from there to his landlady, where he and Henry had both lodged. It appears the three of them had grown up together in Llandudno. She said there were tales of shipwrecks in most pubs, the locals got their beer paid for that way. She had been very fond of both of them, but she was unable to help.'

'Several weeks later a parcel arrived, it was from their landlady. She was cleaning out a shed where Henry and William kept tools, paint, screws, things for the repair of boats. She had found an old newspaper (the writing was hard to read) about the Albatross when it went down, also clipped to it was an old map. They were in a biscuit tin.'

Mrs Brooks said, 'Would you mind, Dennis, I need a drink please.'

'I will get Lillian to bring us all a cup of tea. This is an intriguing story. Please carry on, James.'

'Much to our surprise it was the missing half of the map we had already found in the deposit box. When we joined the two halves together, we discovered that Henry had buried something on the Great Orme. It was behind St Tudno's Church, slightly higher up the slope.'

'Well I never,' Dennis said.

Lillian appeared with a cup of tea and biscuits for us all.

'We decided to hire a metal detector. When the weather forecast was grim, and the rain was pouring down, one Sunday afternoon we went for it. We dug up a box, the same box Henry had found early one morning in the sand all those years ago. We put it in my Volvo and drove back to London the following day.'

'We were so cold and wet we stayed an extra night there. The roads were awash with water,' said Sophie.

'We all three met at my work on Monday evening when my staff had all gone home for the day. The top came off without too much damage. There, wrapped in an old cloth of some sort was a croquet set. There were four wooden mallets and a stick plus four balls. The unusual thing was the balls were made of some sort of metal.'

'I am quite sure they should have been hardwood,' said Mrs Brooks.

'You are certainly right about that,' said Dennis.

'I thought they could be possibly cannon balls, but why put them in a Croquet box,' said Sophie.

'We then decided to take one to the jewellery shop, where we had found the deposit box key in London. The man behind the counter said we should have gone to a scrapyard with it.'

'He really was quite put out, but James asked him please to have a better look at it,' said Sophie.

'When he had examined it, he locked the doors to the shop. He then got his heaviest scales and he said it is solid gold. The poor man, he looked quite pale. He did some calculations based on today's prices, and it came to £122,333 in value.'

'There were four balls in the box, Dennis,' said Mrs Brooks.

Then Sophie picked up the bag with the gold ball and placed it on the table in front of Dennis. He sat there looking at it, he was speechless.

He gathered himself together. 'In all my years, I've never heard anything like it. Where are the rest of the balls and the box?'

'They are in the back of my Volvo; I have covered them up.' Dennis looked flabbergasted.

'You had better show them to me.'

Dennis had a limp but with his stick I had a job to keep up with him. We had left Mrs Brooks and Sophie in his office guarding the gold ball. I opened the rear hatch on the Volvo and took the lid off the box.

He soon said, 'There are three more balls and four mallets. I have seen enough, cover them up, James.'

We were soon back in his office. Mrs Brooks said, 'There were twenty boxes on the Albatross when she went down, Dennis.'

'Also, we have found the agent's name who was responsible for loading them on the ship, it was Erasmus,' said Sophie.

'I can tell you this chap Erasmus would be quite high up to handle cargo of this description. I will make a start tomorrow to find out more about him. Now how many people know about this croquet box with its gold balls?'

'Only the three of us and you, Dennis,' Mrs Brooks said.

'We need to keep it that way. If the lid comes off this story, Llandudno will be inundated with treasure hunters digging up the Great Orme and newspaper reporters from all over the country. It is a big responsibility. You will not be able to leave them here. We cannot risk them coming to light on the days I am not here. Where did you keep them before?'

'James looked after them and the box at his office,' said Sophie.

'My suggestion is you move it, there must be too many people around your work, James. Four balls comes to half a million pounds! To a museum you could double that easily. What about the jewellery man?'

'We never gave him any of our addresses.'

'If you did, that would be five people already. When you leave here on the way back to London, decide on the safest place you can think of. I do not want to know where, is that clear?'

'If you say so, Dennis.'

'My next request is that we meet in London on Wednesday

evening, I will come by train. I can manage it if I finish here early.'

'I will book you in at the Prince Edward Hotel, it is where I work.'

'Hopefully we will have more to go on about this Erasmus chap when I see you next.'

'Do you think you can find more about him, Dennis?' said Mrs Brooks.

'There are a lot of people I have got to know over the years, we all do favours for one another, we have a good chance.'

Mrs Brooks said, 'Take me home now, please James.'

Halfway back to London Sophie said, 'Dennis made the point of deciding where to put the croquet box and gold balls; I could not have them in the hotel, we certainly cannot bury them in London, what are we going to do?'

'Why not put the box in my apartment?' said Mrs Brooks.

'We can take the box up in the lift, that is if you do not have a better idea, James.'

'It will keep me from the temptation of looking at them. Good idea. It would be better if they are with you. I have been dreading Jane asking why I have locked one drawer in the safe, we do both have keys for petty cash.'

The journey back to London took longer, it was just coming up to seven when we arrived at Mrs Brooks' apartment.

'I will go ahead and hold the lift door open, James.' With two of us we had soon loaded the box in the lift.

'If you take it into the lounge, we can put it under the table, I have a large tablecloth which nearly touches the carpet,' she said.

'I have had enough excitement for one day. We will see what Wednesday brings.'

We wished her well and went down in the lift out into the London night.

'Where would you like to eat, James?'

'The White Feathers, since we both seem happy there.'

'The table in the window is booked, Mr Parker, but I will find a nice table for you both if you give me a few minutes,' said the landlord. 'What would you like to drink while you are waiting?'

'Two glasses of white wine please.'

Some twenty minutes later we were shown to a nice table in an alcove, very private for us, but with a good view of the rest of the room.

'This is nice, James. We do not have to rush our meal, it being later than normal. This is my treat so let's look at the menu.' After much debating we both chose pork with new potatoes.

While we were waiting, Sophie said, 'Do you think we have come to the end of our investigation, James?'

'What makes you think that?'

'If we are right then there were possibly nineteen more boxes in total, plus the one Henry found in the remains of the hull of the Albatross. Erasmus would soon start spending when he thought it was safe to do so.'

'That would be a lot of money to get through, even in this day and age. It is for sure he would have got through some of it, I am firmly convinced the bigger part of it is still out there somewhere. Now, will we ever find it? Only time will tell.'

Our pork with apple sauce arrived.

'I needed you to stop me thinking we have come to a full stop, James.'

The meal was delicious, we ordered two more glasses of wine and stayed until nearly closing time.

'You are over the limit for driving, James.'

'I will have a word with the landlord, I think he will let us leave the car in the carpark.'

Sophie settled the bill while I asked about the car.

'That is quite alright, Mr Parker, you do not need to ask.' We set off back to my apartment.

'James, I hate to say it, but we have just left the Volvo in a pub carpark with the croquet box and four gold balls in the back!'

'You can correct me if I am wrong but the last I remembered we put them under Mrs Brooks' dining table.'

'Oh! I did have two glasses of wine. James, I am sorry, it must have gone to my head.'

'You need a good night's sleep. You will be fine tomorrow; it has been a long day for us all.'

Chapter 25

On Friday morning Sophie woke me with a cup of tea. 'You do have to go to work today. I am going into work early. My manager will be watching me after taking yesterday off. I will let myself out.' She gave me a kiss that made me want her to stay.

Having taken a quick shower, I soon set off. It was mid afternoon when Jane brought two cups of tea and a biscuit to my office.

'It seems a good time, Friday afternoon, the end of the week.

Tell me more about books in other languages please, Jane.'

'Where to start … When we translate a book into another language you radically broaden the market for the author. We have over sixty-five million people in the British Isles. Could you hazard a guess how many people there are in Europe in total?'

'My geography was better than my foreign languages at school, I would guess six hundred million.'

'You are warm, James, but it is nearer to seven hundred million.'

'They do not all buy books.'

'That is correct, and the disturbing thing is there are now fewer people reading books than there were ten years ago!'

'Please go on, Jane, I am not sure about any of this.'

'There are various reasons for fewer books. People can look and read on the internet; they say even newspapers will be read online in the future.'

'You are saying we face an uncertain future in this business?'

'Your father had a saying – "Let's wait and see". The antique world slowed down after nine-eleven in America, when people stopped flying. The hotels were soon empty all round the world; less people, less staff, less money to spend on things like books and luxury holidays. This was when he changed to this business ...'

'He must have thought this was a better bet, Jane.'

'Most certainly he did, but he kept it small without too many overheads.'

'You are saying we need to be careful in going after this world market?'

'That's it in a nushell, James, this world is changing all the time, he taught me that. We want book sales but if we expanded, we would need larger premises. I will say he was not a young man, perhaps if he had been your age he may have chased those big orders, we will never know. I think you will make your own decisions. But my advice is, tread carefully. You have more than enough to think about now. I will start to lock up. Sleep well, we can talk further next week.'

She left me to my thoughts. I soon switched the lights off in my office and set out back to my apartment. You can switch lights off, but when you run your own business you can never become complacent unless you want to fail. I picked up a takeaway and watched the news and then had an early night. The driving to Liverpool on Thursday was still catching up on me.

On Saturday morning Sophie rang to ask if I would like to go out to lunch. 'You will need a warm coat.'

'Am I allowed to ask where we are eating?'

'On a boat if I can book it. I have some shopping to do but I aim to be with you for twelve if that is okay.'

'Looking forward to it, see you later.'

Sophie was on time and we set off, it was coming up to twelve thirty when we finally boarded the boat she had chosen for lunch. With its white tablecloth and two glasses of wine we ordered and admired the view.

'Any more thoughts on Erasmus and all that gold, James?'

'I'm afraid I have been neglecting our quest for Mrs Brooks. Sorry. I have found out we send books from time to time all over Europe. It's quite daunting. Without Jane and my work force behind me I just would not know where to start.'

'James it is only a few months since you took it all over, it may take a couple of years or more before you start to make big decisions. If necessary, I could help with paperwork for the running of it. Let us enjoy the meal when it comes. We both need a weekend off without too much thinking.'

Our waiter arrived with the starter, Sophie had ordered a salad, mine was the soup of the day which was tomato. We soon tucked in.

'I must tell you the latest gossip at the hotel. There is talk of a firm building a giant Ferris wheel on the South bank of the river, it will be a tourist attraction.'

'A giant wheel! Will people ride on it?'

'They certainly will. You will be able to see all over London when you are at the top.'

'You do seem well informed about all this, Sophie.'

'One of the staff overheard the manager talking to a building contractor at the hotel. The receptionist said he was very important, he worked in many countries worldwide. That might be because he always left a good tip for the staff. Don't forget I am a private investigator!'

'Perhaps we might even take a ride on it one day.'

'One thing is for sure, if it ever gets built we will be a lot older, James.'

The main course arrived; lamb with new potatoes. Sitting there letting the world go by enjoying dinner with Sophie made for a perfect Saturday afternoon. At three thirty Sophie paid for our lunch, I left a tip for the proprietor to split between the staff. We then set off along the Thames embankment, watching the street performers and artists peddling their wares.

'I would like a nice picture of London for my Nottingham home, James, but not today.'

'You have made me wonder, is there a gallery in Llandudno?'

'Why would you want to know that?'

'If we could see some early pictures of the landscapes there it might help us to guess where the gold was moved to from the cave we found.'

'No more theories, let us enjoy the rest of the day. We will see if Dennis comes up with anything new on Wednesday.'

Saturday evening we went to bed early and got up late on Sunday morning.

'What would you like to do today, James?'

'After a cooked breakfast, which I will cook for you, I will take you somewhere, one hour's drive from London where you have never been before.'

'One step at a time, I will get dressed and wait for the chef to surprise me.'

Sophie was soon seated at the table. I had cooked smoked haddock with scrambled egg, the look on her face made the effort all worthwhile. 'There is a pot of fresh English tea, toast and marmalade to follow.'

'Eating breakfast in itself is not some part of the day I have ever given a lot of thought to. But this is very special, James! I had no idea you could cook like this.'

The outcome of this was that we both had to get undressed and back into bed for the next hour, with Sophie telling me she would love me forever.

At twelve o'clock we eventually drove out of London. 'We are going to the Chilterns where we will walk along one of the ridges, the views are spectacular. And the hills will be alive with red kites. Do you remember Devil's Bridge, the first time I took you away to Wales?'

'Definitely, and Maisie your parents' housekeeper.' Sunday came to its end far too quickly.

I dropped Sophie off at the Prince Edward Hotel on Monday morning and proceeded to work.

Jane was already sorting through a huge pile of paperwork. 'Good morning James.'

'Good morning to you,' I said in passing, and made my way to my office.

Wednesday afternoon soon came around, there had been two problem-free days. Sophie rang, she said, 'Dennis is on the train safely so I will entertain him when he arrives. He has good news, but his phone line kept fading. I will bring him with me tonight, must rush, have promised to meet him at the station, 'bye.'

It was with some degree of trepidation that I entered The White Feathers. But Dennis was all smiles and was looking at the menu with Sophie. When he saw me arrive at the table he immediately stood up with an outstretched hand to welcome me.

'I trust the train journey was okay?'

'It was fine, James, and when I stepped down on to the platform there was Sophie waiting to greet me.'

The waiter came over with three glasses and a bottle of white New Zealand wine.

'I did ask Sophie about the wine before I ordered, but now you are here it is not too late to change.'

'Is the fish on tonight?'

'Dover sole caught fresh this morning, sir.'

'Sounds about perfect.'

'That is all three of us then, James.'

'Sophie told me you mentioned good news on the phone, so tell me how you got on.'

'I have found the agent Erasmus who was responsible for the croquet boxes that were loaded on the Albatross, but, what's more, he retired two years after the ship went down in Llandudno bay.'

'You are amazing, Dennis,' said Sophie.

'Thank you for that. Now be prepared to be even more amazed. He moved to Wales in 1815. Where in the whole of Wales do you think he retired to?'

'You are not going to say Llandudno?'

'I am indeed.'

Sophie said, 'That is too much of a coincidence! He was up to no good.'

'You make a better investigator than me.'

'You have been doing very nicely before I became involved, James.'

'Here is the waiter with our orders and we haven't even poured the wine yet. Would you do the honours, James?' said Sophie.

We all three settled down to enjoy our meals. It wasn't long before there were three empty plates and Dennis poured us each another glass of wine. The waiter soon cleared the table.

'Let us raise our glasses to this venture into the past,' said Dennis.

'Good gracious, it is ten to eight. Mrs Brooks will wonder why we are late, we had better make a move.'

With Dennis in tow we set off for her apartment.

When we arrived, I pressed the intercom button and we were told to come up.

Mrs Brooks gave Dennis a warm welcome and made a pot of tea. We were soon seated.

'Now, have you made any more progress, Dennis?'

'I am pleased to say in the affirmative.'

'Please tell me more.'

'Let us start with Erasmus, I have found him in some old records of the docks in Liverpool.'

'Well done, Dennis.'

'Next, he retired in 1815, some two years or more after the Albatross went down in Llandudno bay on that fateful night. The next part came as quite a shock; he retired to Wales. You will find it hard to believe, to no other place than Llandudno!'

Mrs Brooks looked quite taken aback.

'Are these all established facts, Dennis?'

'I'm sure of them.'

'James, Sophie, you must have heard all this earlier this evening, what on earth is the next step?'

'Looks like it is back to Llandudno,' said Sophie.

Dennis said, 'I would like to join you there, if I may.'

'We would all three like that very much. James, any idea where to start?' said Mrs Brooks.

'That is a big question and the answer can only be that we need to find out where he retired to, or the place where he spent his last days. He may have even moved on from there.'

'There would have been only a small number of people living there in the first quarter of the 1800s. The roads would only just be beginning to be laid,' said Dennis.

'We need more local knowledge in my opinion, for what it is

worth. Have you any suggestions, James?' said Mrs Brooks.

'I would say our reporter would be a good bet, and perhaps Sam at the place where we stay when we are up there.'

'Why Sam, James?'

'I remember him telling us one evening about helping his father who was a general builder replacing slates and chimney pots when he was young. They used to push a hand cart round loaded with slates and ladders. His father would have known most of the old houses and roads.'

'This is a lot to take in, I think it's time to call it a day. We can all regroup next week with any fresh thoughts,' said Mrs Brooks.

Sophie cleared the cups and saucers for her, and she took us to the door.

'I am very grateful for your help, Dennis, please let me have the bill from the hotel and your rail expenses.'

'There will be no need, I will be able to make a claim towards our investigation. This is of national interest and about the history of Wales. You have my full backing at all times. Good night, Mrs Brooks.'

We went down in the lift, out into the London night, and began walking back to Sophie's hotel. We left him in the entrance of the Prince Edward Hotel, having arranged with Sophie to book him in for the following Wednesday.

'It is now four people united in our quest, James.'

'Dennis will be of great use to us now, he has already helped immensely.'

'I hope we can get our reporter to help, he must have records if he will share them with us.'

'When we tell him that the story would be his exclusively to write about in the paper, he will want to be part of it, you can rest assured.'

'I do like your confidence. Since we will not be going to

Llandudno this coming weekend, what would you like to do when it comes?'

'Am I right in saying you still have one day's holiday owing, and if so, is it possible to take it this Friday coming?'

'It is short notice, but I can ask my manager. What have you in mind?'

'I would like to walk along the Portobello road looking at the antique stalls and shops.'

'You sound like you are treading in your father's footsteps. I have never been there, but I have heard about it. I will do my best; it will have to be the first opportunity I get in the morning. I will ring after work tomorrow evening.'

Thursday was uneventful at work. I was beginning to think Sophie could not get the day off. It was nine o'clock when the doorbell rang. 'Sophie, this is a surprise!'

'I hope it is a nice one, James. There was so many papers to sort out at work my manager said if I stayed to finish then he would okay it for me. I have just finished.'

'Put your feet up. I will make a cup of tea and see what I can find to feed you with at this time of night.'

Sophie had soon eaten so I poured two glasses of wine and we watched the ten o'clock news together. 'I suppose you are stopping the night?'

'James Parker you are going to suffer for that remark.'

Friday morning I slipped out of bed, made two cups of tea, and took them back with me. Sophie was still fast asleep. After a good deal of shaking she woke up.

'What time is it?'

'Six thirty, antique dealers start to work very early, they will be starting to pack up just after lunch time.'

'You never told me we had to get up this early.' She was soon dressed, and we set off.

'I have heard the staff at work talk about the market there, James. Tell me about it.'

'Where to begin? The Portobello road is probably the world's best-known market. Though famous for antiques, there is much more. It is a haven for fashion, food stalls, books, music. If you are looking for something unique, you can spend many happy hours there.

I first came when I was very young with my father. He once bought me a clockwork mouse, you would wind it up and it ran around everywhere. We catch the train here to the tube station at Notting Hill.' When we came out into the daylight, there they were, hundreds of stalls.

'On by the way, keep your hands in your pockets. When you get distracted by street performers there are often pickpockets at any markets, just be careful.'

We set off browsing the stalls moving from Notting Hill towards the Ladbroke Grove end. By ten o'clock we were both hungry, we had missed breakfast due to our early start. The notice over a door said, 'Breakfast all day.'

'Can we go in here, James, I am starving!'

We ordered poached eggs with baby spinach on an English muffin, with two cups of tea.

'There are people here from all over the world, I have been listening to them talking. It was a super idea, I am enjoying it, James.'

'There are also weirdos and eccentrics. They seem to be drawn here. But I have always wanted to come back for more.'

It was while we were talking, Sophie said, 'The pictures and the ornaments on the shelves are all for sale.'

We were soon drawn to a glass case with a model of a ship in it.

'The label on the case says it is a Brig Sloop from the first quarter of the 1800s. Do you think it would make a nice memory of our investigation, James?'

'I like it very much. What's more, it can be our first joint purchase.'

We asked the proprietor to lift the glass top off so we could look more closely. Having placed it very carefully on one of his tables, he said. 'My best price to you young people is £125. It is quite hard to find a good example like this anymore.'

'What can you tell us about it?' said Sophie.

'I only bought it last week from a dealer in Liverpool. The person who he acquired it from said it had been in one family for many years, and it came from America. I do know they were in the forefront of glass technology. It was the first big industry in America. The glass is totally original. If you look closely you will notice little bubbles and waves. The case, to my mind, is totally from that early period. Brig Sloops also belong to that same time. Where are you based?'

'About seven miles from here.'

'I will throw in the delivery to your place if that will help.'

'We would like to purchase it,' I said.

He stuck a piece of paper on the glass.

'Write your address on it please, now what day will you be there?'

'I have given you my work's address, any weekday to suit you.'

We said goodbye and thanked him for his help. 'He seemed a really nice genuine guy.'

'Running a café and antiques business, my father would say he is definitely a person to make a friend of.'

We set off back the way we came, heading for Notting Hill tube station. By twelve o'clock some of the dealers were already starting to pack up.

'They are dismantling the stands already, James.'

'Some of these dealers have come here from other parts of the country. They would be on the road to drive here in the small hours of the morning. If they are not selling at weekends, then they are far from home buying stock. It is not the easiest way to make a living.'

'I imagine it is terribly exciting.'

'To become a general dealer the broad spectrum of knowledge needed takes a lifetime to acquire just to brush the surface of it. That is why my father specialised in antique clocks.'

'If you had not taken your father's publishing business on, you may have become part of the antique world, James. We could have had a shop and lived over it. I would have looked after it while you went off buying stock.'

We had reached the tube station, went down on the escalator to the platform. The train was due in five minutes, it arrived on time, taking us back towards home.

Having let us in, Sophie was walking round the lounge looking at each wall in turn. 'Big decisions, James, where are you going to put the glass case when it arrives?'

'I will make a cup of tea then we can think about it.'

'You sound just like Mrs Brooks.'

'You can sit in the middle of the lounge while I make the tea.' When I came back with two cups of tea, Sophie was sitting on a chair in just her underwear. 'What are you doing!'

'Trying to distract you, James.'

Needless to say, there were two more cold cups of tea.

The weekend soon passed. We did decide where to put our ship in its glass case. I dropped off Sophie at the Prince Edward Hotel on Monday morning and returned to work.

Chapter 26

On Wednesday afternoon Sophie rang to say Dennis was safely on his way and she would pick him up from the station.

I told her that our glass case with ship had arrived late on Tuesday afternoon.

'Looking forward to seeing it, 'bye.'

Both Monday and Tuesday had passed by without any problems. I had decided to adapt my father's adage; "wait and see".

I was the first to arrive at The White Feathers. Arthur was looking at his paper, so I decided to join him at the bar.

'You have picked all the winners, Arthur?'

'If only I could, Mr Parker. Is everything okay at work?'

'The lifting gear has made a real difference. I am very happy with it, what can I get you to drink?'

'A pint of lager would do nicely, thanks. The landlord says it is good for the waterworks.'

'You are not drinking water these days, Arthur!'

'No miss, we were talking about a job,' he said, giving me a wink.

Sophie, with Dennis in tow, had just arrived whilst we were talking.

'Now what can I get you both to drink?

'A glass of red wine for me please, James.'

'One half of lager for me,' Dennis said, giving me a wink also. He had certainly heard more than Sophie of my conversation with Arthur.

The waiter showed us to our table in the window, leaving us to look at the menu. We all chose jacket potatoes with salad and a nice glass of merlot would compliment that, we all agreed. 'Have you found out any more about Erasmus, Dennis?'

'My colleagues have given me several hours of their time, but we have all drawn a blank, and, believe me, they know how to conduct a search.'

'So, it is back to Llandudno?'

'That is the only way forward, Sophie.'

'What about this reporter James mentioned last week while we were at Mrs Brooks apartment?'

'James thinks he will try to help if we promise him the sole rights to printing the story.'

'I've not got any better ideas, how do we get hold of this chap?'

'He plays the organ on Sunday mornings at a church we know, in Llandudno.'

'What do you reckon, James?'

'It looks like we are all going to church on Sunday!'

Our meal arrived at this point. While we were eating Sophie said,

'I will try to book us all in with Sam and Branwin first thing tomorrow morning.'

'What about Mrs Brooks?' Dennis said.

'We can ask her later tonight; she might want to go to see George. You will like Sam and Branwin, Dennis.'

'I am sure I will. If you can book me in at your hotel for Friday night, I could travel with you if you do not mind?'

I decided to tell Dennis more in depth about Llandudno over our meal, then we set off for Mrs Brooks' apartment. When we arrived,

Sophie pressed the intercom button, we were told to come up. The door was open.

'She will be in the kitchen making a pot of tea, Dennis,' said Sophie.

'I will be with you in a minute, make yourselves at home.'

She was soon with us carrying a silver tray with a teapot and four china cups and saucers.

'Do you take sugar, Dennis?'

'No thank you.'

'Now, what have you got to tell me?'

'Not any more than last week I am afraid, my colleagues and myself have all drawn a blank. The only way forward is back to Llandudno. I have agreed to go there too this coming weekend.'

'Do you want to be there, Mrs Brooks?' said Sophie.

'I will only slow you down, so I will go to see George if you do not mind. Have you made a plan?'

'We thought if we went to church on Sunday morning the reporter might look on us more favourably.'

'Since he has been following you all round Llandudno, he might welcome it. You will have to tread carefully with him, James.'

'Remember the carpark he followed us into, Mrs Brooks, I feel James has his measure.'

'Sophie I am just saying be careful, nothing more.'

'The best way forward would be that we introduce him to Dennis, he will then realise the importance of why we want him helping us. When I tell him we will give him exclusive rights if we find the gold, to print the story in his paper, the full story! I think he will not need much persuading.'

'James, I am going to enjoy working with you,' said Dennis, 'that sounds a good plan.'

Four people well and truly hooked is how I would describe us, Dennis's eyes seemed even more blue than ever, or perhaps I was just imagining it. The weekend could not come quickly enough. The atmosphere round that table was electric. I stretched my foot out and touched the croquet box under the table. It was there although I could not see it. Whatever next!

Mrs Brooks showed us to the door. 'I will ring on Sunday evening; I will not be able to wait till Wednesday evening. Take care of one another,' and she shut the door.

We set off for the lift.

'I did forget to tell Mrs Brooks I found out Erasmus was forty years of age when he retired to Llandudno. There is no doubt in my mind we should form an alliance with this reporter chap, and Sam's knowledge of Llandudno will be invaluable.'

When we arrived at the Prince Edward Hotel, Dennis said, 'I will see you late on Friday night if you are still up, Sophie. I can find my own way here from the station.'

'It is no trouble for me to meet you,' said Sophie.

'It is a chance for me to see a London show, so I will take advantage of it.'

Sophie took my arm and we set off for my apartment.

'James, were you playing footsies under the table at Mrs Brooks?'

'Whatever gave you that idea?'

'I thought you were being romantic!'

'No such luck, I was feeling for the croquet box.'

'I will make you suffer for that comment.'

'Let's step it out, I can't wait.'

Thursday and Friday I helped Jane with the dispatch of twelve hundred hardback books all going to Germany. She took it all in her stride.

'Remember the filing cabinets, James, it is easier now that you have mastered them, you will get there.'

I decided to take the work's Volvo estate car for the coming weekend. If Sam and Branwin joined the search it would be a much better vehicle for transport.

At five o'clock I told Jane to get off home and enjoy her weekend. 'I will lock up.'

She accepted graciously and said 'Good night, James' when she left. I admired the brig ship when I got home; I was very pleased with our purchase. Sophie had told me she would eat with Dennis at the hotel, so having ordered a takeaway I took a shower and had just about laid the table when it arrived. The decision to go back to Llandudno did mean a long drive in the morning. I had an early night after watching the news.

Dennis and Sophie were waiting by the entrance to the hotel on Saturday morning, I loaded their bags and we set off. We greeted each other and I asked Dennis what he went to see at the theatre. 'It was The Mousetrap,' he told me. 'It is a murder mystery play by Agatha Christie. It has been running since 1952, the longest running West End show in the history of London.'

'What is it all about?' said Sophie.

'If I tell you that, you might not go to see it, that is the secret of why it has run for such a long time.'

'James will you take me to see it one day?'

'I most certainly will, I am just as intrigued as you.'

'When will we arrive in Llandudno, James?'

'It will be mid-afternoon when we get there. I am hoping to stop in Shrewsbury for a late lunch. If you need to stretch your legs, I will pull over anytime.'

When we pulled into the kerb at the boarding house, Sam seemed to appear from nowhere. He carried Dennis's case and showed him to his room, it was the one Sophie used to stay in.

'After you have unpacked come down for a cup of tea, I will leave you to get on.'

Sam and Dennis soon hit it off, they had both spent a good part of their younger lives at sea.

I decided to ask Sam and Branwin if they were busy on Sunday. 'There is nothing we can't put on hold. What's it about?'

'We would like you both to come to church on Sunday morning with us.'

'It is not my thing but I could make an exception, James, tell me why?'

'You did wonder once what we were up to, coming down so many weekends to stay here. I did say when the time was right, I would let you know. This is the time to come out with it. There is another person who we want to tell when we are all together if you can have patience till tomorrow.'

'I will need to know the time of the service so I can plan breakfast,' said Branwin.

'It is on Church Walks, ten o'clock it starts.'

'Breakfast at nine and we can walk from here, weather permitting.'

We decided to take Dennis to Tribell's fish restaurant for our evening meal, our hosts had already made other arrangements and declined our offer to join us. It was just the three of us. It was the first time we had a chance to discuss our lives before we had met up.

The reason Dennis became involved in the Liverpool museum was that, after his wife died from a long illness, he wanted something useful to do. Since his whole life had revolved around the sea it was the perfect job for him, he told us.

We told him how we had come together and at the end of the

evening I felt he would become one of our special friends. We walked back with the lights on all along the promenade. It was becoming like a second home here. Very different from the lights in London.

Sunday morning, I awoke on my own, Sophie was sitting in the bay window reading.

'It is only seven o'clock, you are already up.'

'I couldn't sleep, thinking about today. When we started this investigation, it was only you and me, it is now becoming so much bigger. If this story breaks it will be all over the country. I am finding it hard. I really need you, James.'

'If it is any consolation, I am not feeling much better about it, but we are both nervous and we are going to see this through to its final conclusion, whatever that may be.'

'We have now found so many facts on this investigation but I am not sure about any of it, perhaps I should say conjecture.'

'Give me an example, Sophie.'

'Most of the crew of the Albatross went off drinking and whoring the night before setting off to America. The total population of Llandudno was in the lower hundreds. When we set off down here trying to find the pub Henry died in there were so many. We only visited a few. Another fact I have come across, Llandudno did not have a pier in the early 1800s. It was not till 1877 when the first pier was built. People travelled round the coast to get from one town to the next.'

'Is this all relevant do you think?'

'The main reason people travelled round the coast that way was because there were not many roads, if I have remembered it right. That leads me to think there would not be even any pavements, never mind pubs.'

'No wonder you could not sleep, I will get dressed and we will go down to breakfast.'

Dennis was there before us; he was seated drinking coffee at the breakfast table.

'Now we are all here, help yourselves to cereal, I will start to cook the bacon, one egg or two?' said Branwin.

We all three said one. At which point Sam joined us.

'Sam, would you mind if I ask you a question?' said Sophie.

'As long as it is not too difficult.'

'When was the first pub built in Llandudno?'

'It is on record that the King's Head, in Old Road, dates back to the late 1700s. You will find it if you go up Church Walks, it is on the right behind the Victoria station. You can travel up to the top of the Great Orme in the summer season from there.' At that point Branwin arrived with our cooked breakfasts.

'There is not much Sam will not know about the pubs round here, Sophie. He will have done work for most of them when he was younger with his dad. Eat up, we do not want to be late for the start of the service.'

When we collected our coats from the bedroom I said, 'Now you know there were pubs even before the ship went down do you feel better?'

'I do, much better, James,' and gave me a kiss on my cheek.

The five of us set off for the church.

When we arrived, we managed to find five seats together and were soon seated. The sun was shining through the stained-glass windows, casting a lovely light inside the church. After greeting the congregation, the vicar said,

'Would you all now stand for the first hymn, number 163.' The congregation all stood up and the organ burst into life.

Eternal Father, strong to save,
Whose arm doth bind the restless wave,
Who bidd'st the mighty ocean deep
Its own appointed limits keep; Oh, hear us when we cry to thee
For those in peril on the sea.

There were three more verses in total.

Sophie whispered, 'That hymn was very appropriate, don't you think, James?'

The service lasted about one hour. When it ended, I signalled to our party to hang back. 'Let Snoops make his way outside then we will join him.'

'He will not take kindly to you calling him 'Snoops', James,' said Sophie.

We followed him out of the church.

'Mr Jones, could you spare a minute please?'

'I am always at your disposal and for all the residents of Llandudno. Did you enjoy the service?'

'Very much so, but we do have a proposition to put to you. I think you will be more than interested.'

He stood holding his chin, thinking it over.

'I remember you from a while back. All five of you?'

'I am afraid it is, sir.'

'If you will follow me, I will make a cup of tea at my apartment and we will discuss the matter.'

He showed us into his apartment and went to make the tea, leaving us sitting round a long table.

Chapter 27

Dennis said, 'This a wonderful old building with its spacious rooms and high ceilings.'

'If my memory serves me right this one is Helm House. There are many more in Llandudno like this. They were the homes of ageing magnates, industrialists, and wealthy influential businesspeople. Their upkeep and gardens cost so much. Most are divided into apartments now,' said Sam.

Mr Jones came back into the room with our cups of tea on a tray.

'Help yourselves to milk and sugar. Now, how may I be of assistance to you?'

'We have decided that James will be our spokesman. So, James, would you begin,' said Dennis.

'What I am about to disclose to you, Mr Jones, Sam, and Branwin could well be of national importance to the country. You do know that Sophie and I have been coming here to Llandudno most weekends for several months. We have now enlisted Dennis who is a curator of the Liverpool Maritime Museum. Sam and Branwin own a boarding house where we have been staying while we have been here. You have this apartment in Church Walks where we are gathered here today. We have also a sixth person who is not here today, Mrs Brooks, a lady in her early nineties. She is the lady who first started this investigation. A few short months ago a fisherman by the name of

Henry Hendon was telling a tale in the Weary Traveller public house, when he had a stroke and died. George was with him.'

'I am well aware of that, James, please go on.'

'Henry must have known it was serious as he thrust a piece of paper into George's hand, who is Mrs Brooks' brother-in-law, saying, "Gold, gold," repeatedly.'

'I was told about that, but I was not there to confirm it.'

'George drove back to London, put the piece of paper in an envelope which he gave to Mrs Brooks' husband to put in a safe place. He told him to guard it with his life. George did run a fine line with the law, but since it was not money this time, Mrs Brooks' husband took the envelope to a jewellery shop in Mayfair. It was put in a deposit box. He returned home and tied its key to a bracket clock key. He told his wife we'll be sure not to lose it there. Several weeks later George was driving back to Llandudno when he had a terrible accident. He did survive but is now brain dead, unable to talk or communicate. Mrs Brooks' husband passed away some time afterwards.'

Branwin said, 'Oh the poor lady. To lose her husband and his brother.'

'This is now where we come into this. Sophie had advertised in a local paper for work as a private investigator. Meanwhile, Mrs Brooks decided to start to downsize, thinking she might move. She put the bracket clock in an auction amongst other things. My father bought it. With the upset of her husband dying and his brother very ill she forgot all about the key tied to the bracket clock. Some several weeks later she remembered about the key. She had kept the invoice from the auction which she gave to Sophie to trace my late father, with instructions to try to buy the bracket clock back.'

'This seems to be getting complicated, James,' said Sam.

'If you will bear with me, I will do my best to keep it as simple as I can. Sophie, with my help, traced the key to the jewellery shop where we retrieved the envelope containing Henry's piece of paper from the deposit box. We took it back to Mrs Brooks and then found out it was one half of a map. Mrs Brooks then said, "I owe it to George to find out more. Would you two young people like to go to Llandudno and see if you can find anymore about the missing piece of paper which would make up the other half of the map. I will pay all your expenses".'

Mr Jones said, 'I should stop you there, James. You must understand it is my duty as a reporter to report to the nation anything, be it sport, deaths, births, crimes, even wars.'

'If I was to say you could have exclusive rights to report this story before any other newspaper in the British Isles, would you put on hold what I am about to reveal?'

'If we could put a time limit of say six months, I might be able to compromise. I will need you to tell me more, then I will make a decision.'

'Sam, Branwin, what about you?'

'We could go with that, James.'

'Then I will continue.

'Henry had a brother who we traced to a care home. He had also died, in fact before Henry. The matron at the care home said the few things he had we could have for a small donation to the Christmas party. She said she should have disposed of them long ago since nobody had claimed them. There was just a carrier bag with pyjamas, a small travel clock, and two books.'

'It is not much at the end of a lifetime, I'm afraid.'

'Much to our surprise the two books were on shipwrecks. The same ship, the Albatross, had in both books a circle drawn round them. The circles were in pencil, somebody had rubbed the pencil marks out but Mrs Brooks was using an eye glass when she searched through the books and discovered them. On investigating more, a Brig Sloop named the Albatross had gone down in Llandudno Bay in 1812. It seemed the crew had gone whoring and drinking in the pubs that night, leaving only seven people to look after the ship.'

'Can you back all this up, James?' said Mr Jones.

'I can, sir.'

'Please carry on.'

'A fire had started, with not enough crew on board to contain it. In a short amount of time it quickly spread and the Albatross was doomed. Now the ship was setting out for America the very next morning. Dennis searched through records at Liverpool on the history of the Albatross. With his help we found she was carrying goods to support the war between America and England. This was the Battle of Independence. Amongst the goods on record it showed she had £60,000 in gold on board, this was to support the war out there. At a loss, to go from there we traced the landlady that William and Henry had both lived with. She said they all three had grown up together and she missed them both. She did say they could tell a good tale but not to put too much store by it. She was unable to help us.

Mrs Brooks said perhaps we had missed something, so we went back to the books again. It was then we discovered a loose page in the one book without a number on it, lo and behold it was the other half of the map! It matched the half in the deposit box from the jewellery shop.'

'Henry and William must have kept half each for safe keeping,' said Branwin.

'The following week I received a parcel from their landlady. After our visit, she decided to have clear out of their things. She had been cleaning out a shed in the garden where Henry and William kept paint and things useful for boats. Her words were that she had found a tin in a tin so to speak. There was an old newspaper cutting about the wreck of the Albatross, it must be old some of the words were difficult to understand.'

Sophie said, 'Would you mind if we have another cup of tea please, Mr Jones?'

'This is a fascinating story. We could all do with one. Would you do the honours please? The afternoon seems to be racing away. Please go on, James.'

'Now you will remember the incident at the hospital carpark.'

'I remember it well. You left me feeling somewhat frustrated.'

'At that time we did not know you were a newspaper reporter. You had followed us from Saint Tudno's church on the slopes of the Great Orme down into Llandudno.'

'That's what reporters do, James.'

'Let us now cast our minds back to the night Henry died in the Weary Traveller. The tale he was telling George that night was that he had gone at first light down to the beach to dig for rag worm bait for a fishing trip later in the day. There, protruding out of the sand, were the remains of part of a stern of an old ship. He went over to take a closer look and discovered a long wooden box in the sand. He put it in his trailer and drove home.'

'That has happened many times when we have had a storm the night before. Within a few days they are soon covered over again by the shifting sand. There have been countless wrecks over the last three hundred years,' said Sam.

'The big thing is we found out Henry had buried the box again behind the church on the Great Orme.'

'How on earth did you find that out?'

Sophie came back with more tea for everybody at this point.

While she was passing the cups round, I thought of Mrs Brooks' advice. "If he tells you it is just another fisherman's tale, reel him in! My husband said never play all your cards at once".

'We must now get back to the two halves of the map. When we put them together there were three crosses marked on them. One cross was where we found the box buried.'

'You are going to tell me you found gold in the box.'

'I am, sir. The box contained a croquet set with four balls and four wooden mallets. The balls were cast from gold.'

'That is as good a tale as I have ever heard. Henry was a master at telling tales, you can't expect me to believe it.'

'James?'

'Yes Sam?'

'If you do not mind me saying this, your imagination must be running away with you!'

I decided to play my trump card. 'Sophie, could I have your handbag please.' I took out the gold croquet ball and placed it on the table.

'Do you believe me now!'

The room went suddenly very quiet.

It was Sam who regained his composure first.

'I don't know what you have got into, but I would like to be part of it. How do you know the croquet ball is gold, James?'

'The jewellery shop in Mayfair did a valuation.'

'How much did he say it was worth?'

'At today's prices it came to £122,333 to be precise. There were four balls in the box making, it close to half a million.' Mr Jones went to a cabinet and came back with a bottle of brandy and poured some in his tea.

'If anybody else would like some, please help yourself. This is a

Sunday afternoon I will not forget in a hurry. Where do I, Sam, and Branwin come into this?' said Mr Jones.

'I will leave Sophie to explain more.'

'Firstly, Sam and Branwin; you both have extensive knowledge of Llandudno, you were both born here. Sam, you helped your Dad working on most of the old buildings when you were younger.

Mr Jones; you have extensive knowledge of the people that have lived in Llandudno plus hopefully some records of them. Now there is a record, which Dennis can confirm, of twenty croquet boxes loaded on to the brig the Albatross in Liverpool. We believe the gold was to support the Battle of Independence in America. James and I are convinced the gold was taken off the Albatross the night she went down in flames. The gold was put in a rowing boat, with gunpowder exploding everywhere as the ship was carrying many cannons to protect it from pirates. It must have been like a modern-day firework night. With all this distraction it was rowed to the land and hidden in a cave we found above the high-water line. You could not see it when the tide was out. You would only become aware of it if you were out at sea using a telescope.'

Sam said, 'Do you mind if I come in here?'

'That's what we want from you, please go ahead.'

'When I was young, I would go with my mates looking in the caves below the Great Orme. Our parents told us to keep out of them, you will be trapped when the sea comes in, they are very dangerous. One day we were throwing stones from the beach at the cliffs above us when we disturbed a flock of pigeons who seemed to fly out of the cliff high above us. The next day we came back with a ladder. If my father had found out I would have been in big trouble. Lo and behold when we got to the top of the ladder there was a secret cave that the tide never reached. Now to cut the story short we decided to call it pigeon cave. When you stand on the pier you can see many caves now but since the pier was built many years later your story holds up.'

Branwin said, 'You never told me about that, Sam.'

Sophie said, 'I will carry on now. Dennis helped us to trace the agent who was in charge of loading the ship. His name was John Erasmus. He must have been high up in government circles to be trusted with that sort of cargo.'

'You must have extensive records, Dennis, to be able to pin him to that date in time.'

'Four of us, including Mrs Brooks, spent many weeks before we got there.'

'Now be prepared to be surprised, Mr Jones,' said Sophie. 'In 1815 Erasmus retired, some two and half years after the Albatross went down. He was forty years of age. Now where on earth in the whole of Wales do you think he retired to?'

Mr Jones said, 'You are not going to tell me Llandudno!'

'I am indeed. And our conclusion is he was up to no good.'

Branwin said, 'That would be one of hell of a coincidence.'

'Those were my words,' said Sophie.

'So, am I right in saying he nicked all that gold?' said Mr Jones.

'We think he did, and James thinks he could not have spent it all. Twenty croquet boxes equate to ten million pounds. You would have a job in this day and age to get rid of it without the tax authorities finding out.'

'So James, what is the next step?' said Mr Jones.

'Both Sophie and myself think that you, being a reporter, will know a lot about the history of Llandudno. When the roads were built, that sort of thing. If Erasmus moved here, he could well have died here, unless he moved on.'

'Well I can tell you the population was in the lower hundreds in the early 1800s here in Llandudno.'

Sam said, 'Can I come in again please. My father told me that his great-grandfather had told him that Llandudno Bay was mainly marsh land. It was auctioned off around 1850. That is when the first hotels started to be built and the roads laid out.'

'If he moved here in 1815, he must have lived somewhere,' said Branwin.

'I would like to come in here,' said Mr Jones. 'Church Walks, where we are now gathered, was named after Saint George's Church which was built in 1840. After the great storm of 1839 removed the roof of Saint Tudno's, it was realised there was a need for a more conveniently situated church. The town's population was increasing and mainly centred on the lower slopes of the Great Orme. We are slightly higher here in Church Walks than the marshland.'

'Sam, you did say at breakfast this morning that the oldest pub in Llandudno is the King's Head on Old Road,' said Sophie.

'I did, that is correct. The Victoria Tram station is on Church Walks, the pub is directly behind it just a few yards along from where we are now. It dates back to the 1700s. You can take the tramcar up the slope of the Great Orme to the top. It is well worth the ride if you have not done it before.'

Mr Jones said, 'Can you tell me more about the newspaper cutting, the one the landlady sent to you, James?'

'It seems a local chap went down at first light the next morning after the fire, to the beach. He found a man tied to a rigging pole. He was alive and said he was a sail rigger. The story he told was the crew and the cook had gone on the drink on shore, leaving just seven men to look after the ship. They were sailing to America the next morning. The ones on board decided they deserved a drink, got merry, and then lit a fire to cook some fresh meat. He had a stomach bug, so he moved to the other end of the ship. Now, the Albatross was carrying cannons and lots of ammunition. She was well armed to protect its cargo from pirates. A spark ignited one of the barrels of gunpowder, which set off a chain reaction all down the length of the ship. He grabbed a rigging pole and jumped overboard. His next memory was waking up when the local found him.'

'That is quite a story, James.'

'Now the paper tried to find the only survivor who had told the story to the local chap. But the sail rigger had just disappeared and the local was accused of being liberal with the truth. Both Sophie and myself think he was there to make a distraction the next morning, just in case somebody had seen anything during the night.'

Mr Jones said, 'If you will all come with me please.' He took us into a large high room with metal cabinets from floor to ceiling. There was a long table in the centre with chairs placed round it. The only other thing in there was a high pair of stepladders. 'This is where I keep my records through the years made by my predecessors and myself. My library is a growing evolving organism which I have spent most of my life dedicated to. This is at your disposal. It may take many hours to find John Erasmus, but if he married, had children, died in Llandudno, he will be here. Where would you like to start?'

'The year 1812 is when the Albatross went down,' said Sophie.

'If we are all in agreement, let's make a start, 1812 is a very early date, but it might be here.'

To our amazement he soon produced a large old folder. We then went back into his lounge, where he laid out on the table various old newspapers with dates.

'I do know they are not complete from this early period. We shall see what was saved. Ah, I do believe this is what we are looking for.

Here is a Llandudno Echo dated 1812, with a picture of the Albatross on the front page.'

It confirmed the piece of paper, word for word, in the biscuit tin found by Mrs Thomas in Chapel Street, who was William and Henry's landlady. I think even Dennis was taken aback; five people absolutely dumb-struck.

Mr Jones was the first to speak. 'If you do not mind me repeating Sam's words, I am not sure what you have got into, but I will do my best to help. I am the last in a long line of reporters in my family. If I could retire after this is all over, with my story making headlines of the century, I would be a very happy man!'

Branwin said, 'It is getting late now, you have a long drive ahead of you, James.'

Mr Jones said, 'If you can come next Saturday and Sunday, my home is at your disposal. Between us we will find him, even if it is a long time in the future.'

We said goodbye to him, and I drove Sam and Branwin back to the boarding house.

'Shall I book the three of you in for next weekend then, James?' said Sam. We all said, 'Yes please'.

I set off back to London with Sophie and Dennis soon fast asleep in the car.

Chapter 28

On Monday morning, when the alarm went off, I had to drag myself out of bed. It had been coming up to midnight when I had dropped Sophie and Dennis back at the Prince Edward Hotel. Sunday had been a long day for all three of us, mentally and physically. I made the decision that four o'clock would be the latest we would start back from Llandudno in the coming weeks. Sophie rang at mid-morning.

'You made it to work then, James?'

'I did, but I could do with a quiet day.'

'Dennis told me before he left that he had rung Mr Jones and told him he could start work down there next Saturday morning. He has rung Sam and Branwin and booked for Friday night with them. He is going down on the train Friday afternoon. I will leave you to get on. See you on Wednesday evening at The White Feathers, 'bye James.'

Monday and Tuesday were both uneventful. By Wednesday afternoon I was much clearer in my head and looking forward to Sophie staying the night. I was the first to arrive at The White Feathers public house. Much to my surprise, Arthur was not propping the bar up. When I enquired, the barman said he was away on some big project. He had not been in since the weekend. I took two drinks over to our table in the window. Shortly after, Sophie arrived. She had on a silk cream blouse, with a blue tight-fitting skirt, matching shoes, and handbag. She made my heart skip a beat, and quite a few of the customers in the pub by the looks she was getting. 'Hi James.'

'Nice to see you,' I said. 'I have taken the liberty of ordering a glass of white wine for you, was that okay?'

'That is fine. I need it, we have had a busy day at the hotel, some important guests are here till Friday. We have been told to be on our toes, no mistakes, the waiters and cooks have a stressful time. Clockwork precision is how the manager says it must run and woe betide you if it doesn't.'

'My father always said customers must come first at all times.'

'You are right, James. I am starving, what's on the menu?'

'The cottage pie looks tempting to me.'

'Let's make that two then please.'

We both enjoyed the pie with carrots and peas. Sophie had taken off her shoes and a foot kept getting under my turn-up on my trousers. I was soon distracted from our conversation. 'Would you stop playing footsie under the table, we have to go to see Mrs Brooks next.'

'You are right, but I have not seen you for three whole days. I count the days when we are not seeing each other, I do need you to kiss me a lot, James!'

'You will have to be patient for a little longer. We have to report to Mrs Brooks.' I settled the bill and we set off. We were soon there, and I pressed the intercom button and was told to go up. The door was open, and we let ourselves in. Mrs Brooks was pouring tea for us.

'There you are, make yourselves at home. Now what have you found out over last weekend?'

'Sam and Branwin agreed to help and Mr Jones said he would be at our disposal for the coming months, but he did say he had a duty to the wider public. When I told him he could have exclusive rights to the story, he soon became more interested.'

'Well done, James, what happened next?

'You could have heard a pin drop when James put the gold ball on Mr Jones's table, Mrs Brooks,' said Sophie. 'And what's more Mr Jones has records from when the Llandudno Echo paper first started. We now have his permission to search through them. If Erasmus lived in Llandudno, married, or had children, he reckons we will find him. His records go back to the night when the Albatross went down. It is all there. We just have to trawl through it, to use a nautical term. Week by week, year by year, and every decade.'

'When people are born or die, or there are special occasions, they do get announced in the local papers. Mr Jones, I can see, is going to be a great asset to us in our quest,' said Mrs Brooks. 'You have done well.'

'With Dennis helping also, he will be used to searching through paperwork. We can now make a fresh start next weekend,' I said.

'How did you find George, when you saw him last weekend, Mrs Brooks?' said Sophie.

'Much the same, but I do talk to him about what we are trying to do. If he only understood he would be so pleased.'

It was soon time to say goodnight and we went down in the lift out into the streets of London. With Sophie holding my arm we walked back to my apartment. I put the key in the door, and we stepped inside. The first kiss developed into pure lust for both of us. We never made it to the bedroom; we pulled each other's clothes off in frustration, making love in the hall.

'That was a surprise, James, I thought it was only me that was frustrated.'

'We have spent too long with other people and not had enough time with each other on our own, is what I think, Sophie!'

'The coming weeks are not going to be much different, but where there is a will there is a way,' she said with a laugh and took her clothes into the bathroom.

When she came out, she said, 'I had still got things I wanted to talk about but now I can't think about any of them.'

I made us both a night cap then climbed into bed. 'What do you want to talk about?'

'Ask me tomorrow, make love to me again, please, James.'

The next morning, I was awake first. I made us both a cup of tea and took it back to bed. Sophie was just coming out of the bathroom. She was already fully dressed.

'Morning, I had the best night's sleep I have had for a long time!'

She sat on the side of the bed drinking her tea with me. 'Are you going to get back into bed with me?'

'I am certainly not, James Parker, we have both got to go to work today. If I turn up late my manager would probably give me the sack, after the warning he gave everybody yesterday.'

I took Sophie's advice and got dressed while she did toast and found the cereals. It was five minutes to eight when she got out of my car at her hotel. When I arrived at my work the gates were already open and the staff were reversing a lorry in to load up today's books for dispatch. My day passed quietly, and I took an early night.

Friday morning Sophie rang, 'Any great thoughts about the coming weekend?'

'I suggest we ask Dennis with Mr Jones to draw up a plan of attack. They will know the best way forward.'

'You are brilliant, we have asked for help, let's take a back seat. See you on Saturday morning. My manager has just come in, he looks on the warpath.'

And she rang off. I decided to not worry Jane with explaining to me about how we exported our books later in the day. I needed a clear mind for the weekend.

'It is all in hand, we all know what to do, James, we can leave it till you are ready,' said Jane. 'Leave me to lock up. We will see you on Monday.'

At five o'clock I wished everybody goodnight and set off back to my apartment. Taking a back seat was going to be a new experience for us both in this investigation.

The bell rang and I went to the door at quarter to seven on Saturday morning. When I opened it there was Sophie with her case.

'Morning, I couldn't sleep so I got up early.'

'Come in and we will have a cup of coffee before setting off. This is a surprise!'

With both bags in the car we set off at seven o'clock. 'You managed to not get the sack then, Sophie?'

'I did, I kept my head down, but one of the waiters was in trouble. He served a red wine with the fish, when they had all ordered white, not sure if he will be there on Monday.'

I decided to drive there without a break and by twelve thirty we were pulling up at the boarding house. Sam said, 'You must have made an early start! We thought it would be nearer two when you arrived. I will take your cases up. Join Dennis and Branwin in the kitchen.'

We said hello to them both, Branwin was making a soup for our lunch.

'What is the plan, James?' said Dennis.

'We are hoping that you, with Mr Jones's help, will be advising us since you both have more experience on searches involving paperwork.'

'Right, let's make a start then. One of the most difficult things about searching through paperwork is not to let your mind drift away from the main criteria of what you are searching for. I will try to explain more clearly. There are two men, one on each side of a car, the car is about to be resprayed. One man masks the passenger side windows. He puts newspaper to cover the glass held on by masking tape. The paint sprayer then puts the new paint on. The second man masks the driver's side windows, the same procedure. He never finishes in the same time as the chap on the other side of the car. The paint sprayer allows the same amount of time for each side of the car, but he is always late starting on the second man's side. Now why would that be?'

'Are the windows the same on both sides of the car?' said Sophie.

'They are indeed.'

'Then they should take the same amount of time. Dennis, I do not understand.'

'I will now explain why. The slower man kept on getting distracted by the football pages, his mind would wander thinking about football, his main hobby. Now do you understand? We have a century and a half of newspapers to search through.'

'It will be incredibly hard to not get distracted,' Sam said, who was listening in the background.

'After lunch, when we arrive at Mr Jones's apartment, I will ask him to print a list of things that we are searching for. We will have one each to look at. If your mind is tired or drifting by something that has caught your eye you must focus on that most important list.'

'I feel worn out before we start,' said Branwin.

'I will admit a search of this magnitude is daunting, thousands of newspapers. It will be a new experience for me,' said Dennis. Branwin put out the soup dishes round the table. 'The sooner we start the quicker we will be off.'

We went to get our coats from the bedroom after lunch. Sophie said, 'I am glad we are not doing this search on our own, James.'

'It would be grounds for a divorce for any sane man.'

'You will be made to suffer for that remark later this day, James Parker.'

We went down and joined the others in the hall. Sam locked the front door and we set off to Mr Jones' house.

'Come in, make yourselves at home, can I get you a drink, tea, coffee?'

'We have just had lunch so perhaps a little later,' said Branwin.

'Right let us make a start. I have put chairs round the table in my records room. Since there are six of us, I have allocated each of us a year to search through, starting with the year 1812. Would that suit you all?'

Sophie said, 'James and myself have decided to let you and Dennis guide us with this search. Dennis has a request if he may, before we start, Mr Jones.'

'You have my full attention, how can I help, Dennis?'

'Because of the magnitude of the task facing us, I would like each of us to have an A4 piece of paper with the places we need for our search clearly shown in large print. It will stop us being distracted.'

'That is a valuable point, Dennis, there will be interesting facts pulling us away from the task in hand. Let us make the list of what is important to us.'

'Sophie, perhaps you will go first?'

'Deaths and Obituary columns.'

'James?

'Births and Marriage occasions.'

'Sam?

'Anniversary wishes if he was married.'

'Branwin?'

'I think court notices.'

'Why do you say that?' said Dennis.

'Well once a crook always a crook so the saying goes. This guy was at it big time.'

'He could have committed something, even if it was small it would probably be put in the paper. I will print us all a list to focus on. Perhaps you ladies would make us all a drink, then we can make a start.'

By five thirty we were glad to call it a day. Mr Jones said, 'It is my opinion that Erasmus would lay low for the first few years, for what it is worth.'

'Dennis said we have nearly searched the first twelve years with six of us at it. On a lighter note, where are we eating tonight?'

'The best fish and chips is Tribell's restaurant in Lloyd Street. I could get Branwin to book us a table for eight o'clock,' said Sam.

'If we are all in agreement, we meet at eight,' said Mr Jones.

On the way back to Sam and Branwin's, Sophie said, 'If we have searched through the first twelve years in a Saturday afternoon, by the end of tomorrow, we should have another twenty-four years looked over.'

'That might not ring true. As papers became more available to the people, there will probably be more pages. The old English should be easier to understand though. Let us not miss anything. I would not like to face going back a second time,' said Sam.

I lay on the bed when we got back and was soon fast asleep. I was woken by Sophie shaking me.

'James wake up, it's seven o'clock, you still have to get changed.'

We set off for Tribell's fish restaurant at seven thirty. It was a nice evening for walking.

Sam and Dennis told us some of their earlier escapades in the navy when they were younger. Mr Jones joined in; it was a most enjoyable evening. I walked back to our digs with Sophie holding my arm. I felt very happy. When we got back Dennis said, 'We leave at nine thirty in the morning, goodnight to you all.'

'Aye aye, captain,' said Sam. 'Breakfast for eight thirty. We will all be joining you. It has been a long day.'

On Sunday morning the sun was shining as we made our way back to Church Walks.

'It would be a lovely morning to walk round the bay,' said Sophie.

Mr Jones made us welcome when we arrived. We soon had our heads down. It was twelve thirty when we all agreed we needed a much-earned break. Branwin had made up pork and stuffing sandwiches last night when we were all in bed. Mr Jones showed her how to work his stove to warm them up and produced a bottle of wine to go with them.

'This is a nice surprise,' said Dennis.

'Food for the brain, my father used to say,' said Sam.

When it was three thirty, I was beginning to think about the long drive back to London when Mr Jones said, 'Well I'll be blowed! We have got a lead.'

Dennis said, 'What have we got?'

'We have a Gavin Erasmus born in 1825 who was deported to Tasmania on the Lord Auckland in 1846. It says he handled stolen goods that were the property of a local merchant.'

'He must have gone on a convict ship. I remember my history lessons from school. They were not the nicest of ships. Quite a few of the convicts never made it, they died on the way there of some terrible diseases.'

'Is there anymore?' said Sam.

'That is the lot I'm afraid, we need to persevere. We are making headway. We can carry on next weekend.'

Dennis said, 'I have records of all the convict ships in Liverpool at my disposal. During the coming week I will see if I can find out more about Gavin Erasmus.'

'We need an address, Dennis,' I said.

'I can't promise that, James, but I will leave no stone unturned.' We thanked Mr Jones for all his help and set off back to the boarding house. Sam helped to load our cases.

'I will book you in for next weekend.'

'I will travel down on Friday evening, so I will need an extra night, Sam,' said Dennis.

We wished them both goodbye and set off for London. It was quarter to ten when I pulled onto the carpark of The White Feathers.

'I hope they are still serving,' Sophie said.

We were soon inside. I asked the waiter if we could still order. 'We have started to clear up. I will ask the manager, Mr Parker.' He was soon back.

'If you can settle for cottage pie, he will okay it. What would you like to drink?'

'Red wine for the three of us, please.'

There were people starting to leave so we soon found a table. 'Do you think you will know more by next weekend, Dennis, or are we still clutching at straws?'

'This period of the convict ships and the deportment of people is covered both in England and Australia in great detail. Many people want to trace their ancestors from both sides of the world. We will learn more of that, I am in no doubt. You will have to wait till next weekend before I report back. This coming week I have to search through records on Hidden Liverpool.'

Three glasses of wine arrived with our cottage pie order. Sophie said, 'Tell us about Hidden Liverpool please, Dennis.'

'Not many people realise that until just over the last thirty years Liverpool had its own stock exchange. It was founded in Liverpool in 1836. Liverpool was the principal market for cotton and was rapidly becoming the richest port in the world.'

'So our investigation is a drop in the ocean,' I said.

'I would not say that, it is just one of many we investigate. Do you want more?'

'Please do go on.'

'This investigation we have been asked to look up is all about shares. The East India Company is widely recognised as the world's first public trading company. Put simply; sailing to the other side of the world was too risky for any single company or person. The investors realised that putting all their eggs in one basket was not a smart way of doing things. So, investors purchased shares in multiple companies. If one ship was taken by pirates, two more would make it back and they could still make a profit.'

'I always wondered how the stock market was formed, good luck with your search.' I paid the bill and tipped the waiter, being among the last to leave, and we set off back to Sophie's hotel. We pulled up in the car and said goodnight to Dennis.

'James can I come back with you tonight?'

'You are saying we just need more you and me time?'

'Something like that.'

I parked the Jaguar and we let ourselves into my apartment. 'The Brig Sloop in its glass case is the perfect thing for our memories, James. I did enjoy our day at the Portobello Road Market.'

'The room looks much better since all that paperwork we had from Dennis has been tidied away.'

'Poor Mr Jones now has paperwork on every table and flat piece of furniture.'

'Mr Jones has his sights set on the scoop of a lifetime; you are not to be unduly perturbed about him. I do find though he seems a very nice chap. To quote Mrs Brooks, I will put the kettle on. What would you like to drink?'

'One hot cup of tea please, James.'

'That will be a first, you will need to keep your clothes on a little longer.'

'I will do my best but do not make me wait too long.'

Chapter 29

On Monday morning, having dropped Sophie off, I proceeded to work. Sophie stopping the night made me realise we did need time together besides work, she was good for me. What had started as an adventure, going to Llandudno nearly every weekend all those many months ago, now was our every waking thought. It was an obsession that we must keep going to its final conclusion. I wonder if the great archaeologists in Egypt looking for tombs going back thousands of years felt like I did. Perhaps one day I would take Sophie to Devil's Bridge, and we could also walk along the coast watching the waves and seagulls.

'James, are you okay?'

Jane had come into my office and disturbed my daydreaming. 'Quite alright thank you. Good morning, did you enjoy your weekend?'

'Saturday night my husband took me out to the theatre, then the children came over for Sunday dinner. It was very nice, thank you.'

'Is there anything I need to be concerned about?'

'The monthly turnover is up by six percent on last year's figures and the previous last two months. You did say we might invite some of our best customers for nibbles and to meet the staff one evening. I have been working on a list for you on who we might invite.'

'For it to go well they will need plenty of notice, then the staff will have to be considered. Can we handle it, Jane?

'We can but try, I will give it my best shot.'

She left me to get on with checking last week's turnover and the wages paid. It was not until Wednesday morning Sophie rang to confirm our table was booked at The White Feathers.

'You have not heard from Dennis by any chance?'

'He did say it would be the weekend before coming back to us. We just have to be patient.'

'It is starting to run thin on the ground I'm afraid.'

'It is all that driving. We need to think of a way to eliminate some of it. See you at seven, 'bye.'

I was the first to arrive at The White Feathers. Arthur was back, propping up the bar, reading his paper.

'Evening, Mr Parker, what can I get you to drink?'

'I would like a pint of bitter please. The staff tell me you have not been in for some time now?'

'I have been away installing a conveyor for a food processing plant in the Midlands. It is up and running now. We had problems but hope they are now in the past.'

'I am very grateful for the work you carried out for me; I wish you luck.'

Sophie had arrived.

'What are you two planning then?'

'James would like a monorail up to Llandudno to save the driving, he has asked me for an estimate.'

'You have to be kidding, Arthur.'

'I am, miss, what would you like to drink?'

Sophie said a glass of red wine would be perfect then we took our drinks over to our table in the window and the waiter gave us a menu to study.

'You have told Arthur about the driving to Llandudno, James?'

'Only in passing.'

'I have been having some thoughts also, let us order and I will tell you about them while we are eating.'

We both ordered the lasagne with salad and garlic bread.

'Amaze me with your thoughts, my dear.'

'Now you will need to think about this quite seriously, James!'

'I am all ears.'

'Since we have met, we have not had a proper holiday. What if we both take a week's holiday and go up to Llandudno. We can then visit council offices or solicitors. At the weekends they are all closed. If we are to find more about where Gavin Erasmus lived, we need to be there in the week. And take nice walks, sit on the pier, and let the world go by.'

'You never cease to amaze me; I am all for taking you up on that idea.'

'Just think of the nights, James! If you are serious, I will inquire at work about time off.'

'Let us get this coming weekend over first, there will be six in total of us at Mr Jones' apartment, plus Dennis's input from records in Liverpool.'

I told the waiter to compliment the chef, gave him a tip to share with him and settled the bill. We set off for Mrs Brooks' apartment. Sophie pressed the intercom button; we were told to go up.

'Come in make yourselves at home, the kettle is on, we will have a nice cup of tea.'

She was soon back with a tray with three cups of tea. 'Now, what have we new in our search?'

'It is good news; we have now established Erasmus had a son called Gavin.'

'This is all very exciting. What do we know about him?'

'He committed a crime here in England and was deported to Tasmania on a convict ship.'

'Like father like son, you have done well. Have you worked out the next step?'

Sophie said, 'Dennis says the convict ships are well documented, he reckons he will know more when he has searched through the records at Liverpool.'

'Do we know how many years he served, or if he came back to England?'

'Not at this stage, but Mr Jones said if he did come back home it will be in the papers in his past records.'

'We have not established where he was living, but there is a good chance that it could be in the Church Walks area.'

'Why do you think that, Sophie?'

'Llandudno Bay, as we know it today, was all marshland, it was in the 1850s before it was cleared and the hotels were starting to be built. Church Walks is on slightly higher ground and also we have the oldest pub there, in Old Road at the start of the Tramway to go up the Great Orme.'

'My word, you have been busy.'

'Is there any change in George?'

'He is much the same, I have found a taxi firm to take me there at very reasonable rates because it is a regular booking. I shall tell him everything you have told me.'

It was soon ten o'clock and she showed us out and we went down in the lift.

'When I went to the toilet there was a man's toothbrush and comb on the window ledge, James.'

'Perhaps she has a man friend, it is no business of yours.'

'I was just curious.'

It was just starting to rain when I put the key in the door of my apartment.

'James?'

'Yes dear, how can I be of assistance?'

'You will soon find out! But I am worrying about the gold croquet ball you put on the table at Mr Jones' apartment, what did you do with it?'

'That was several weeks ago, it is back in the box under the table at Mrs Brooks' place. There is no need to worry, I have everything in hand. I will make us a drink to take to bed.'

When I took the tea to the bedroom, Sophie was reading a book.

'This is a surprise.'

'I read each night at the hotel when I am on my own, James. It is a good way to switch off at the end of the day.'

'I know a good way to switch off.'

'What is that?'

'Put that book down and I will show you.'

'But the tea will get cold.'

The following morning, I was up first and made a French breakfast with coffee, croissants, and jam, which I took back to bed on two trays.

'I shall not want to go to work when you do me breakfast like this.'

It was ten to eight when I dropped Sophie at the hotel, all in all we had had a nice start to the day.

Thursday and Friday were uneventful, perhaps things were getting easier. I was still glad the week had come to an end. I turned the lights off, locked up, and set off to my apartment. On Saturday morning I drove to the hotel and arrived at seven. Sophie was already waiting at the door.

'Morning James, take me to Llandudno.'

'You seem chirpy.'

'I have just finished my book and it had a happy ending.'

My Jaguar purred along, perhaps it was catching, I was enjoying the drive.

I pulled up at the boarding house just before one o'clock. Sam appeared like magic to take our cases in. After unpacking we went down to join them in the kitchen.

'Dennis is not back yet; he was gone quite early. He said to start without him if he was late. I will start to warm the soup, it is leek and potato,' said Branwin.

She was soon serving us in the dining room when Dennis arrived.

'There you are, you are just in time, do please come and join us we are having soup for lunch.'

Dennis told us he had been to the other end of the bay, doing research. The little Orme is part of our history, just on a lesser scale.

We arrived at Mr Jones' apartment at two-thirty and he made us all welcome.

Dennis said, 'I will start first. I have confirmed he was deported on a convict ship. It was a six-hundred-ton barque built in Calcutta in 1835. It sailed on the 19th of April in 1846, arriving on the 25th of August at Van Diemen's Land the same year. He later returned to England in 1858.'

'Around twelve years in total, Dennis.'

'He must have qualified for a ticket to leave, James. Having served his time, he would have been given a ticket to freedom. Over a period of eighty years some one hundred and sixty thousand convicts were deported to Australia. About one thousand eight hundred of them were from Wales. He was just one of them.'

'You have been busy, Dennis. What have we about an address?'

'We are no further forward. It is my opinion that the first proper paths to be laid were where we are now, in Church Walks. His father would be living in the best part of Llandudno to my way of thinking.'

Mr Jones said, 'I will try the council office records in the coming week. But our best chance for an address may lie in my newspaper records.'

'There are lots of sprawling mansions in landscaped gardens; homes to ageing magnates, foreign diplomats, industrialists, and members of the aristocracy. We have had them all at one time or another. Church Walks would fit for my money,' said Sam.

'We must push on. The afternoon will soon disappear,' said Mr Jones.

By five o'clock we were all ready to pack up, it had not been a fruitful afternoon.

Branwin said, 'I have put a meal in the oven for tonight. Perhaps you would like to join us, Mr Jones.'

'I would like to take you up on that offer, if you don't mind me not being with you till eight o'clock. On Saturdays I have to report on the local sports results.'

When we got back to the boarding house Sophie said, 'I will see if I can help Branwin in the kitchen. Why not try to take a nap, James, you drove all the way here without a break this morning.' Branwin served up a Welsh stew with dumplings. Sam opened a bottle of red wine. The evening passed quickly; Mr Jones seemed a nice man. He told us he had never married and lived on his own all his life. It was decided that ten o'clock was early enough to start work on Sunday morning.

It was Sam who found our next clue, we had had lunch and it was coming up to three o'clock.

'I have a John Erasmus in the Obituary Column. It says he departed this life on the 9th of June 1855. He resided in Church Walks, we have found him, but we do not have a number.'

'Perhaps they did not have numbers if the roads and footpaths were still being laid,' said Branwin.

'He died before his son Gavin came back to Wales then?'

'He must have done, James. You can be sure the council will know the details of what houses were built in that early period,' said Sam.

Mr Jones came in at this point.

'I know most of the councillors and should be able to pull a few strings.'

'Without arousing suspicion to our real reason for asking?'

'I am in and out of their offices several times a year for all sorts of reasons. Discretion is the word at all times, James.'

There was a general uplifting of spirits in the room. We were all satisfied with our efforts for the weekend.

'Let's call it a day, I will see how I get on during the coming week,' Mr Jones said.

It was Wednesday morning when Sophie rang to say Mr Jones had been on the phone with her for quite some time.

'He had made discrete enquires with the council about locating the house. One of the people working there said his father was an historian, he had been to see him. There is not a shadow of doubt the house where John Erasmus resided was called Wisteria House. The chap was well into his nineties. When he was young there was a sign at the front of the house in the garden. He reckons Erasmus must have been a keen gardener. The story of how the house had got its name is mired in controversy.

'I had to write the next part down, James. The first Wisteria plants were introduced to Britain in 1816 by a Mr John Reeves from Canton in China. At that time there were only two varieties of Wisteria plants known to the wider world. It is not known when Erasmus bought the plants from him. But by research, it appears the historian reckons he must have chosen both. You will be amazed by the next bit, James.

'Wisteria floribunda, which has clockwise climbing stems, and Wisteria sinensis, which has anti-clockwise climbing stems, Erasmus planted one each side of the main entrance door to the house. The house was on the opposite side to the church further along. He believes the house has not been occupied since the second world war, but he can remember the Wisteria plants climbing across the front of the house. It had never been sold due to the dilapidated state of it. The last owner was a Mrs Hancox who is in a care home. She is now a centenarian. Until she dies it is a pain in the backside for the council. He stresses we will need to contact her for the key and her permission to enter it. The council would absolve itself from any injuries or accidents. He could arrange for us to have the key when we have obtained her consent.'

On Wednesday evening we went to Mrs Brooks' and told her of the latest developments.

She said, 'This is all very exciting. It looks like another visit to a care home for you both.'

'Mr Jones has booked an appointment for Saturday afternoon to see Mrs Hancox. The historian can fix us up with the key once we have got her permission to view the house.'

'You will need to take two good torches with you. If the house has cellars, I would make a start there. You will need some steps to look in the loft.'

'It is doubtful he would put all that heavy gold in a loft, Mrs Brooks,' said Sophie.

'In the past the lofts in the old houses were not like they are today. There were huge lead tanks to catch all the rainwater, they did not have fresh water from the mains like today's modern home. It would be the perfect place hide those croquet boxes; it is the last place anybody would look. You say Sam knows about old buildings. Get him to check for false walls or bricked-up chimneys.'

'Will you be coming to Llandudno with us if we obtain permission to look the house over?'

'No, I would only slow you down, I will go to see George.'

By ten o'clock we had taken the house apart brick by brick and put it back together again. The fact that Erasmus had died there would probably not give any more leads. I told her we would ring with any fresh news on Sunday night. We said goodnight and went down in the lift out into the London night. Sophie linked her arm with mine and we set off back to my apartment.

'I hope the next case I take on is not so long drawn out, James.'

'You did want to be a private investigator.'

'I still do.'

'Then my advice would be to take on jobs with less travelling. We are spending half of every weekend in the car. It leaves very little time to spend at Nottingham or my house at Devil's Bridge in Wales.' When we reached my apartment, we soon tumbled into bed with Sophie telling me, 'I do love you, James.'

On Thursday morning the sun was shining when I opened the curtains. We had both overslept. I shook Sophie.

'Wake up, we are late for work.'

'I will meet you at the car, I only hope my manager is occupied somewhere else when we arrive at the hotel.'

It was ten past eight when I dropped her off and she ran straight inside.

'Bye James.'

Mid-morning, Sophie rang to say, 'We got away with it, James.'

'I am pleased to hear that.'

'My manager had been away for the weekend also; his train broke down coming back into London. He was in a foul mood, snapping at everybody.'

'If we had known I would have made breakfast for you, then made love.'

'James, be serious. I need this job. If he is in a better mood tomorrow, what about if I ask him if he would consider me taking the first three days off next week. I have days owing me still to take.'

'What has brought this on?'

'I have been thinking. If we get permission from Mrs Hancox on Saturday afternoon, then try to get the key from the council even with Mr Jones' help it will be late in the day. In all probability it will be Sunday morning before we start our search in Wisteria house.'

'It sounds good to me. Sunday morning we will only be five if Mr Jones is playing the organ at the church, but I'm sure he will join us later. We will have two full days after the weekend on our own. If nothing turns up, it will enable us to retrace our steps if we need to. I will sort two torches out and pick up a metal detector from Mr Berryman's spade shop in Shylock Street. Best of luck with the manager, ring on Thursday evening to let me know how you got on. I will need to sort things out with Jane about opening and locking up. 'Bye for now.'

Chapter 30

It was quite late on Thursday when Sophie came back to me.

'It is all systems go, James, my manager has okayed for me to take Monday through to Wednesday evening holiday. Sorry, I have worked late, I did not want to worry you. On Friday everything needs to be in hand before I leave.'

'I will sort things out with Jane first thing in the morning.'

'Do not forget to see Mr Berryman, not too late on Friday.'

'I will have it all in hand. If you would like to come here when you finish work, and bring some old clothes for scrambling about in Wisteria House, I will order a take-away meal for eight o'clock.'

'I'm really excited about the coming weekend, let's hope Mrs Hancox likes us, and we get that key.'

We said goodnight and I put the phone down. I also needed to switch off if I was going to get any sleep.

When I told Jane on Friday morning she said,

'We all need a break sometimes, James, you get off and forget work, we can survive for a few days. Give my regards to Sophie.'

'You have noticed then?'

'We have, James, and everybody here is very happy for you.'

I decided to take Sophie's advice and visited Jack Berryman's hardware and spade shop in the morning. I picked up the metal detector, a good strong spade, a crowbar, and a pickaxe. I then enquired if Jack was in today.

'Mr Berryman only comes in Saturday mornings now,' I was informed.

Friday afternoon passed quickly. I stayed and locked up for Jane. Having said goodbye to all the staff I decided the Volvo estate was the best car for the job. I packed my morning purchases in the back under the tonne au cover, then drove round to my apartment. I put a pair of old jeans and a jumper from my college days in a bag, then locked the car and waited for Sophie to arrive. At quarter to eight the doorbell rang. She greeted me with a kiss.

'I feel like we are going on holiday, James.'

'It looks like you are, with two cases.'

'We must do our best to impress Mrs Hancox, it all depends if she takes to us. I expect you to be like a long-lost son to her.'

'I will ring for the take-away while you get sorted.'

Our meal soon arrived and I opened a bottle of white wine, it felt to me we were going on holiday also. When we had eaten, I packed my various attire for the coming weekend. Then we settled down to watch the news, before retiring to bed. We had left the curtains open and when I woke the sun was shining in through the bedroom window. It was six thirty. I made two cups of tea and took them back to bed.

'James you are spoiling me, what did I do to deserve this?'

'I will need to give the matter some serious thought, my dear! You have thirty minutes before we leave for Llandudno.'

I packed the car and we were on our way, not quite on time, but I was very happy with our start to the day. The Volvo seemed to eat the miles up. We decided not to pull up for a break on the journey and arrived at one o'clock. Sam helped us in with our cases.

Dennis was there ahead of us, seated at the table talking to

Branwin in the kitchen.

'There you are, come in and sit down. I have made soup and sandwiches; you must be tired. Mr Jones will be here when he has made an appointment with Mrs Hancox for you.' At a quarter to two Mr Jones finally made it.

'Sorry I could not get to you earlier; Saturday is always a busy time for newspaper reporters. I did get permission for you to talk to Mrs Hancox quite early in the day. The care home said she takes a nap after midday lunch. If you arrive at three, they will make sure she is awake for you.'

'We are very grateful to you, Mr Jones. It looks like Sunday morning before we can start with the search.'

'We still need the key, remember, James.'

'James will charm the bed socks off her, Mr Jones,' Sophie said.

'Let's hope he does, we have a lot riding on it.'

He had written the name of the care home down for us on a piece of paper, the Glades Rest Home. Sam said, 'Can I see it? You can walk from here, if you set off at quarter to three. I will draw you a quick map.'

We unpacked and set off with Sophie clutching Sam's map. When we got there it had beautiful large bay windows with a porch that had a Minton tiled floor and stained-glass windows each side, with an art nouveau style door, all very tasteful. There was a mat with 'Welcome to the Glades' in front of the door. We pressed the large polished brass bell and stood waiting anxiously for somebody to hear it. We soon heard footsteps and the door opened. A lady in a very smart grey suit, probably in her early fifties, said,

'How can I help?'

'We have come to see Mrs Hancox for a three o'clock appointment.'

'You must be the people I spoke to Mr Jones about this morning. If you follow me, I will take you to her.' We went up to the second floor. 'It is room five on the left, there is a nurse with her now. She is a centenarian, one hundred years old. She can be quite difficult at times. I will leave you to it.'

I tapped on the door and a voice said, 'Enter.'

The nurse propped her up with pillows, 'You have some visitors this afternoon, Mrs Hancox.'

Her skin was wrinkled, and she looked tired of life.

'I don't want any visitors. If you're from the council I told you I ain't got no money.'

'We do not want your money, Mrs Hancox.'

'She can hear you, but sometimes chooses not to.'

'Mrs Hancox, am I right in saying you own a house in Church Walks?'

'What if I do, do you want to buy it, young man?'

'We do not. But we would like to look it over, you might have something of value there.'

'You won't find anything, only broken windows and the roof leaks.'

'We would still like to look if that is possible, Mrs Hancox.'

'Now listen to me; my great-grandfather bought that house in 1865, he was a tea merchant. When it was eventually passed down to my father, before the first world war, it was in a bad state of repair then. My father was killed in France during the war. My mother loved the place so much, she said she wanted to die there, but we did not have an income. She died of tuberculosis in 1930. We had sold most of the furniture by then. I had to move out. The cost of the repairs and the upkeep put buyers off. It has been empty ever since. You would not be the first to look, there have been many more, young man.'

'I would still like to take a look.'

Laugh lines bracketed her old twinkling eyes and she said, 'It is going to cost ya.'

'I do believe you are trying to blackmail me, Mrs Hancox!'

'A bottle of whiskey it will cost you, I do like a spoonful in my tea.'

'And what if we find anything of value, Mrs Hancox?'

'I would like to be buried with my Bill on the Great Orme.'

'Where was he buried Mrs Hancox?'

'In St Tudno's graveyard. That is where I want to go when I leave here. You can pay for that.'

'I will promise to do my best, Mrs Hancox.'

'Get a move on then, I haven't got long at my age.'

The nurse popped her head round the door at this point, 'Are you all alright?'

'We are, very much, thank you.'

'This young man will be coming back with a bottle of whiskey for me. You can show them out now, nurse.'

It was the first time I had ever seen Sophie speechless. When we left the care home, she soon regained her composure.

'We have got permission to look in Wisteria house, James. That was our main objective this weekend. The key is the next part. If Mr Jones can sort that today, it is all systems go tomorrow morning.'

'Erasmus's son must have sold the house to Mrs Hancox's great-grandfather in 1865. He probably could not afford the upkeep,' said Branwin when we got back.

'I very much doubt we will ever find where he went after the sale,' said Dennis.

'The fact that he sold the house, there is a good chance he did not know about the gold,' Sam said.

'We may need to still speculate after tomorrow, if we should draw a blank.'

'Sophie, we do not solve them all,' said Dennis. 'We will solve this one.'

Mr Jones said, 'I am off, let's get this key sorted.'

On Saturday night we decided to go to Tribell's Fish Restaurant, there were just four of us. Sam and Branwin had been invited out by friends. Both Mr Jones and Dennis told tales of earlier days in their youth.

Sophie told them how we met. The evening soon ended.

Mr Jones gave me the key to guard, 'I will join you when the service is over.'

We set off back to the boarding house. When we got back Branwin had left a note saying "Make yourselves a hot drink. Sleep well, see you in the morning." My next memory was of waking Sunday morning with a cold mug of chocolate on my side of the bed on the bedside cupboard.

'It was nothing to do with me, James.'

'If it was, I do not remember anything about it, Sophie.'

'You were fast asleep before I got into bed. These next three days will pick you up, it is all the driving every weekend you have been doing.'

Branwin banged the dinner gong in the hall, 'Rise and shine. Cooked breakfast ready to serve. We have a house to search.'

There was an urgency over breakfast, we were all infected with it, we ate up and were soon on our way to Church Walks.

We drove down on to the promenade and along to Church Walks. We passed the church on the left side of the road, then fifty yards on Sam said, 'This is it on the right.'

There was a six-feet-high brick wall with a gap you could drive your car through. The gates had given up the job of keeping people out many years ago. The drive sloped upwards and we parked in front of the house.

Sam said, 'The garden must be at least half an acre.'

Dennis said, 'We should inspect the doors and windows from outside before we go inside.'

The windows had been three-quarter boarded up to keep out intruders and stop them looking in.

'At least the top panes of glass have not been covered over. We will get some natural light inside,' said Sam.

There were two steps leading up to the huge front door at the front of the house. Sophie pointed to wooden stumps coming out of the ground each side of the front door.

'We have got the right house, but there is not much left of Erasmus's prize wisteria he bought from Canton in China.'

I put the large old key in the lock and much to my surprise we were soon standing in what looked like a medieval banqueting hall. There was a balcony on three sides, with a large imposing grand staircase at the opposite end to the front door that we had come through.

'James, where to start? You are in charge,' said Sophie.

'Thanks for the confidence. Mrs Brooks said check the cellar first then the loft. Perhaps you could go with Sam and check the attic. While Dennis and myself do the cellar.' I gave Sophie a torch for their search and told them not to forget to look in the water tanks.

Sam said, 'I will get the steps from the car.'

'Branwin, would you make a note of all the rooms, please be careful.'

'Will do, James, no need to worry, I will make a start.'

On the left of the staircase I found a door which gave access to the cellar. Dennis had also brought a torch. The door opened without any trouble and we went down the steps. Much to my surprise it was quite a nice temperature. With Dennis behind me I felt braver than I expected. On the one side, covered in cobwebs, was a line of barrels.

'They certainly liked their alcohol, looking at this lot, Dennis.'

'We must not forget people drank a lot of ale and wine. Rain water was the only supply when this house was built, James.'

There were rows of tea chests piled one on top of another up to the roof of the cellar, all empty. Mrs Hancox had said her grandfather was a tea merchant. We found empty old wine bottles in recesses and packing timber. It was all covered in a century of dust and cobwebs. The floor was remarkably dry. It looked like it had not been disturbed from when the house was built.

'I feel confident the croquet boxes were never hidden down here, James.'

'I agree. You could not lift the floor of the cellar and put it back without it showing. I will bring the metal detector down and make sure on Monday morning, just to be certain. We have seen enough.' We went back up the stairs to join the others. Branwin was the first to join us.

'You could get lost in this house. The paint is coming off the walls in most rooms, and the plaster. I would not like to be here at night, even if you paid me. The smell and the floorboards creaking, I did not linger, it made me quite nervous.'

'What was upstairs like?' I said.

'You can see the sky in some of the rooms. I told Sam and Sophie to be careful when they climbed into the attic. They then found a door into a further loft. I am worried about them, James. The floors are not safe, never mind the roof. I will take you to where I left them.'

Dennis followed me up the steps into the attic room. Sophie was the first to come through the door from the loft with Sam close behind her. It was Sam who spoke first.

'You can forget the lead water tanks in the loft. If the gold was hidden there it vanished with whoever pinched the lead. They must have cut them up for scrap many years ago. When it rains the gutter pipes are still coming through the walls where they would carry the rainwater to the tanks. The loft must be like a great watering can when it rains. It is no wonder they can't sell it. You would need to pull it down and start again.'

They both had black faces, I had never seen Sophie with her hair so bedraggled.

'I would not go up there again if you paid me, I need a bath.'

'Branwin, did you find anything that might be remotely significant?'

'There are eight rooms upstairs. I have been in them all. There are empty wardrobes each side of the chimney breasts in some of them. Downstairs they have a scullery, a book room without any books, just empty shelves. There are various other rooms also, completely empty, James.'

'Hello, hello.' Mr Jones had arrived. 'How are you getting on?'

'Not very well. Was the service okay?'

'My organ playing was not at its best, my mind was here wondering what you had found.'

'Well, Dennis and myself have checked the cellar while Sam and Sophie climbed into the loft. We have drawn a blank up to now.'

Branwin said, 'We have eight empty bedrooms to look at next.'

'Branwin, if you will lead the way, let's make a start.'

We went up the grand staircase at the end of the hall, then we filed into the first bedroom.

Sophie said, 'What sort of things should we be looking for?'

'Sam, you were a builder before the navy, any ideas?' I said.

'If you look for hidden cupboards, tap the walls to see if they are hollow, take note of the floorboards, there should be no tongue and grooved ones. The boards should be held down with nails or slotted screws. We need to know if they have ever been lifted.'

It was some fifteen minutes later when we finished the first room. We were all in agreement there was nothing we had missed. Sam said, 'Let's move on to the next.'

The next bedroom was much the same but hanging from the ceiling there was an old wooden chandelier covered in cobwebs. 'You would have put candles in the holders when this house was built,' said Sam.

By five o'clock we had gone through all the bedrooms with a fine-tooth comb. We decided to call it a day.

Mr Jones said, 'Where are you eating tonight?'

'I think Tribell's restaurant is good value for money,' said Sophie. 'If we are all agreed let's go for it. What time would suit everybody?'

'I would like to join you. I could make it for seven thirty,' said Mr Jones.

We said goodbye to him, and I locked the sturdy front door. We drove back to the boarding house. When we got there Branwin put the kettle on and magically produced a coffee walnut cake, which needed eating.

'After you have all washed your hands,' she said.

We all sat around the kitchen table and Sam was the first to speak.

'I hate to say it to you both but short of demolishing the house brick by brick, getting a mechanical digger and bulldozer in the garden, you will in all probability still find nothing. If you asked a gambling man to fund it, I do not think you would find many takers.'

'We still have the downstairs to do tomorrow morning. Let us give it our best shot,' said Sophie.

Sam said, 'I need to take a bath after climbing about in that loft.' It was seven o'clock when we had all showered and we set off for Tribell's. On arriving we ordered drinks while waiting for Mr Jones. We were still choosing our meal when he joined us. Over dinner he asked me, 'This enormous task you have taken on, James, what about the cost of coming here to Llandudno nearly every weekend?'

'I think Sophie is the person to answer that question, Mr Jones.'

'I believe I have told you how I met James. Mrs Brooks said she would fund this investigation. She was on her own, what with George being brain damaged, then losing her husband. It has given her a reason to fight on in this world. She is in her early nineties. She told us to go off and enjoy ourselves, you do not need to work all of the time. We were both on our own in London, so we took her up on it.'

Branwin said, 'When you first came here it was separate bedrooms all those months ago. Both Sam and I are happy you have got together. Who knows, it could be wedding bells in the future!'

'Now don't you go embarrassing them,' said Sam.

'Mr Jones has spoken my thoughts,' said Dennis. 'The sheer enormity of what you have taken on, frankly just amazes me. You must both realise that after tomorrow there is nowhere else to go with this investigation. Wars and certain times in history are well documented, but not when it comes to material things. They are more perishable; most searches never turn up the goods. The problem with gold, it could have been melted down to make jewellery or exchanged for other precious things in this world. We only win a small percentage of searches, Sophie.'

The rest of the evening seemed to disappear too quickly. We arranged to meet Mr Jones at Wisteria house for nine thirty the next morning, complimented the staff on a wonderful meal, and set off back to the boarding house.

It had been a long day for us all, we wished Sam and Branwin good night and climbed the stairs to go to bed.

'I think Dennis is under the impression we have gone as far as it is possible, James, to find the gold.'

'Let's think positive about it, we found each other. That is far more important.'

'James you are so good for me, make love to me please.'

We were seated at the breakfast table on Monday morning when Branwin told us, 'The weather forecast is good till the end of the week.'

'You will not get me in that loft again, rain or no rain. That house needs pulling down,' said Sam.

'We can forget the loft, Sam, I will be taking the metal detector with us, starting with the cellar floor, just in case we did miss anything. There were wooden shutters folding in on some of the windows with rusted up hinges. There could be a recess behind one of them.'

'I think we are at the end of the line. But we will try everything we can think of today.'

Sophie said, 'I will help Branwin wash up. Let's make a start.'

Mr Jones was there before us, looking very thoughtful when we arrived. 'The odds are Erasmus would bury the gold; it would be the safest place. I am sorry, I forgot to say good morning.'

'Morning to you, William, but where? The garden must have been tended until the first world war in some sort of fashion. Remember it was full of quite exotic plants, in its day he may have had many people here visiting.'

'Looking at it now, it's so overgrown you would need a bulldozer to level it before you could start. You are not going to get the council to give permission for that. They would need Mrs Hancox to okay that. Even if she did there would be the problem of who would pay for it,' said Sam.

'Let's make a start inside the house.' I unlocked the huge old front door with the hinges creaking under protest and we were back inside. Having set the metal detector up, I started down the cellar with Sophie following me.

'I would like to look down there,' she said.

We spent over one hour searching, even lifting tea chests up to be sure we had not missed anything, then we joined the others in the scullery.

'The floor is made up of old tiles in here, for what it is worth I would check it out, James,' said Branwin.

By one o'clock we were running out of ideas, so we made a stop for lunch. Branwin had made cheese and pickle sandwiches, with two flasks of tea to wash it down.

'James, your arm must be aching, let me have a go for the next hour. You can supervise.'

I set the metal detector up and we followed her like the pied-piper. Mr Jones eventually took over, but it was all to no avail. At five o'clock Sam said, 'Somebody must say it, we have nowhere to go from here, we must call it a day!'

'Let's pack up. We can think about it tomorrow before we give the key back,' said Sophie.

When we had returned to the boarding house, Branwin asked us if we would like to join them for our evening meal.

'We have not had you stay over after the weekend before, on a Monday night. It will be jacket potatoes with cauliflower and a cheese sauce. Sam likes bananas with custard for his desert.'

'We would like to take you up on that offer please.'

'It will take me an hour. I will sound the dinner gong when it's ready.'

I lay on the bed while Sophie took a shower, pondering about Mr

Jones and Sam's thoughts about the garden. Short of asking Mrs Brooks to buy Wisteria House so we could demolish it and bulldoze the front garden, we really had come to a stop. Dennis had said, 'We do not solve them all.'

'James you look really quiet'

'I have run out of ideas; we have to give it up.'

'Tomorrow it will be just you and me, we can take our time over it, you never know.'

'Optimistic is the only word for you. I will take a shower.'

On Tuesday morning the sun was shining and staying true to the weather forecast. Sam and Branwin said the best of luck. We said goodbye to Dennis and set off for Church Walks in the Volvo.

'A miracle is what we need, James, just a small one. I am thinking the same as you. I did not sleep well last night.' I parked up and let us in to Wisteria House.

'If you are waiting for an inspiration, Sophie, I have not got one.'

'Let's split up. You go round the upstairs bedrooms and I will do the ground floor.'

With the view of the Great Orme from the back bedrooms, the view at the front looking out over the town to the sea in the distance, old Erasmus had chosen well to build his house here and with his interest in exotic plants and the money to pay for them. The garden must have been something to behold in the past. My heart was not in our search and by twelve o'clock I found Sophie downstairs and said, 'Let's go for lunch in the King's Head.'

Built in the late 1700s, it had been there from the beginning of Llandudno. There were old pictures of local life on the walls. It was a much-needed break from our search.

It was three thirty when I said, 'Let's call it a day.'

'Hold the steps, James, I want to look in those tall cupboards on each side of the chimney-breast in the room we were in.'

'They are not big enough to put in anything like we are looking for.'

'Nevertheless, I want to look.'

Standing on the top rung of the steps she was still unable to see properly so she scraped the bottom and brought out some old black and white photos that were lying there in the cupboard. She passed them down to me.

'It looks like the garden here. Even in black and white he must have had the best garden in Wales.'

We put the steps in the car and the rest of the tools. I could see Sophie was close to tears when I locked the front door for the last time.

'Let's see if we can drop off the key with Mr Jones on the way back.' Sophie agreed.

'Yes James, we can say goodbye to him. We will be going back to London tomorrow.'

'Mr Jones was at home and we returned the key for safekeeping. We both thanked him for his time and the use of his records.

'I want you to know you are welcome to my home anytime. It has been my pleasure to spend time with you both. I will return the key first thing in the morning.'

We drove back to the boarding house. I unloaded the steps for Sam to put away. Branwin made a pot of tea.

'Tell me, how did you get on?'

I told her we had returned the key to Mr Jones and we were no further forward. Sophie showed her the photos we had found in the cupboard.

'Why not take them with you when you say goodbye to Mrs Hancox, I expect she will enjoy recalling her youth from when those pictures were taken. What are you doing about a meal tonight?'

Sophie said, 'I am not very hungry, thank you.'

'There, that's not like you, Sophie. Tomorrow is another day, it has been a disappointment to you both, but you will survive. I will do a nice breakfast for you before you leave in the morning.'

We went upstairs to our room and started to pack for the following morning.

I switched on the television at eight o'clock and we tried to watch a film, needless to say our hearts were not with it. When I woke up in the morning Sophie was sitting at the dressing table, combing her hair.

'Sophie are you alright?'

'I am, it will take a bit of time, but I will get there.' Branwin, true to her word, did give us a marvellous breakfast.

'You will come to see us from time to time now this all over, both of you?' said Sam.

'We have enjoyed every minute of our weekends with you. Llandudno has become like a second home to us.'

They both came out to see us off when we said goodbye. We drove round to the Glades nursing home. 'You need to dry your eyes before we get out of the car, Sophie!'

'I will be alright, James.'

She pressed the brass bell button and we could hear it ringing inside the hall.

It was a nurse that came to the door. 'I am afraid the manager is out this morning, can I help?'

'We were here a few days ago to see Mrs Hancox. If possible, we would like to see her before we travel back to London today.'

'Are you the people that gave her that bottle of whiskey?'

'Guilty I'm afraid.'

'She certainly cheered up, but she is not so well at the moment. I will show you up. Try to not tire her. Mrs Hancox you have some visitors, I will prop you up so you will be able to talk to them.'

'I don't want any visitors.'

'Morning Mrs Hancox, you said that last time.'

'It is you again, what do you want this time?'

'We have brought you a present to look at.'

'Can I drink it?'

'You cannot, too much whiskey is not good for you, but we hope you like it.'

'Well, where is it then?'

'I will leave you to it, call me if you need anything,' the nurse said.

Sophie took the photos out of her bag. 'Mrs Hancox, we found these pictures in the bottom of one of the high cupboards in Wisteria House. We are both hoping it will bring back memories of when you were younger.'

When she looked at the first picture her old wrinkled face broke into a smile. 'We had a beautiful garden when I was young. My mother liked to sit in the Gazebo in the afternoon when the sun was up.'

'What is a Gazebo, Mrs Hancox?' said Sophie.

'It is like a small bandstand you see in some of the parks. They were in fashion then. I sold it when she died to pay for her funeral. We had sold most of the furniture to pay for the bills by then.'

'The pictures were all we found, but I hope we have cheered you up a bit,' said Sophie.

'You have made me think about my youth. My mother told me that during the Industrial Revolution local authorities said we needed more open spaces where people could relax. My father's friends would come with their wives to play croquet or bowls on our lawn. My mother did jugs of lemonade and cucumber sandwiches. She served them in the Gazebo. I think it sold to the Botanical Gardens in one of the cities.'

'My aunt took me to the park one Sunday afternoon in Nottingham when I was young, there was a brass-band playing in the bandstand. You have brought back memories for me, Mrs Hancox.'

She had gone to sleep while Sophie was talking to her.

I called the nurse. 'She drifts off like that sometimes, you are not to worry. I will make her comfortable.'

We thanked her and went down the stairs and out to the car.

'I would like to sit on the pier for one last time before we leave. We can buy a drink and a sandwich for lunch.'

It was halfway through our lunch when Sophie said, 'Erasmus must have put the croquet boxes in a safe place. He had, we think, the best part of twenty of them.'

'I thought we were enjoying lunch, Sophie!'

'If he put them in the garden, he would have built somewhere to hide them. Henry only had one box to worry about for safe keeping. That is the reason he buried it behind Saint Tudno's church.'

'So, your logic is he put them in a secret place in the garden. Would you like to tell me where?'

'When I went with my aunt to see the brass band playing in the bandstand in Nottingham it was raised so the people could see the band playing their instruments and hear the sound all over the park.'

'Can we get to the point?'

'Find the Gazebo base and we still might find the gold!'

'You have done it again! I feel all on edge, Sophie.'

'How do you think I feel? Let's find the car.'

I drove along Church Walks, turned through the gates and pulled up in front of Wisteria House. I set up the metal detector, gave Sophie the spade, and said, 'Lead on.'

The garden was like an obstacle course. It had not been touched probably since the first world war. There were trees and shrubs all gone wild.

'If the Gazebo had a floor there will be a flat piece of ground somewhere. There would not be enough soil for a tree, James.'

It was four o'clock when the detector picked up a strong signal. Sophie used the spade to thump the ground and she hit something like a plank, then another one.

'This could be it, James!' We set to and over the next hour we dug out a six-sided wooden floor. The metal detector started to go crazy. I went back to the car to fetch the crowbar.

'We have found the base of the Gazebo. If there is trap door, we need to find it,' I said.

The oak planks had swollen and were determined not to give up the job they had been laid for. With me on the spade and Sophie pulling on the crowbar we eventually managed to move one. We could see a dark space below.

'You rest. I will get a torch from the car, James.'

With the torch light we could see steps going down beneath the floor. We set to with renewed vigour. After much huffing and puffing we got the next board loose.

'Would you go down first, James, I will follow. There might be booby traps, please be careful.'

'This is not an Egyptian tomb. It is a Gazebo in a garden, Sophie.' We went down the steps to the bottom and waited while our eyes got accustomed to the darkness. The area we were standing in was about twelve-feet-long by six-feet-wide with a ledge seat on both sides of the room against the walls. The room was totally empty. Sophie sat down on one of the ledges.

'I really thought we had done it, James.'

I could see she was upset, I put my arm round her. 'What we are in is an air-raid shelter from the war, people would go down in them to be safe. Unless there was a direct hit you were safe from the bombs that were dropped during the war. Come on now, let's put it behind us and pack the car. It will be well after midnight when we get back to London.'

We went back up the steps, into the daylight. I could see Sophie was still quite emotional.

'It's been a long day for us both, Sophie.'

'Please listen to me. This is not an air-raid shelter. The house has been empty since the '30s. Mrs Hancox told us. She should know, she did own it, James. I do not remember being told there were planes in the first world war.'

'During world war one the German military made extensive use of Zeppelin balloons to raid our country. They had one big problem; they were filled with hydrogen, the slightest gas leak and they set on fire. They were still around in the second world war, but they were filled with helium, it was safer. I do not believe they did bombing raids.'

'Mrs Hancox said her father was killed in the first world war. I do not think he had the Gazebo built. Before we give up, take the metal detector down for me. Then it will set my mind at rest. We can set off back to London with no regrets, please James.'

I started in the middle of the floor. Each time I made a pass between the ledge seats on the outside walls. On both sides of the room the metal detector made a positive noise.

'Perhaps they put reinforcing bars under the ledges. I will get the pickaxe from the car.' I knocked two of the bricks off the ledge. Sophie put the torch in the gap.

'I can see wood, James. Loosen some more and we will be able to see better.'

With the pickaxe I soon loosened more, and we put the bricks on one side. Sophie switched the torch on to look. She grabbed my arm and dropped the torch.

'It's a croquet box, James!' and she burst into tears.

I picked the torch up from where it had fallen and took a look.

The tears started to run down my cheeks. I pulled Sophie back up the steps out into the sunshine and held her.

'Now dry your eyes, let us see how many we have got.' It took two hours to get them all up to the surface. We had dug nine boxes from under the ledges. We knocked the planks back into place on the floor of the Gazebo then loaded the boxes into the back of the Volvo and set off. Every few miles I kept looking over my shoulder to see if the boxes were still there. What had started has an adventure all those months ago had been a traumatic journey for both of us. At ten o'clock I decided to pull up at a pub that was lit up, there were still plenty of cars on the front by the road.

'Why are we pulling up, is there anything the matter, James?'

'Nothing to worry about. Can you see if they are still serving? I will find a phone and ring Mrs Brooks. We cannot turn up at one o'clock in the morning without ringing first. Hopefully there will not be to many people about at that hour. We can take the boxes up in the lift.'

'You are not taking them back to your work?'

'I do not want to be responsible for them.'

I left Sophie to find something to eat and went in search of a phone. Mrs Brooks picked up the phone, 'Hello.'

'It is me, James. Sorry it's so late. We will be arriving sometime after one o'clock. You will need to stay up please.'

'This all sounds very exciting, James, am I allowed to ask about it?'

'Let's say you will be very pleased when we get there.'

'In that case I will put the kettle on when you buzz to come up. See you later,' she rang off.

Sophie had found a table, and there were two glasses of wine on it.

'I have ordered two pasties with chips and peas; they were about to stop serving. What did you tell Mrs Brooks?'

'I thought it better to wait till we get there to explain about the gold. I apologised about ringing so late and said we had a nice surprise for her if she could manage to stay up.'

'Very good, at least if she has a heart attack we will be there.' The waiter arrived with our order.

'Looking at our clothes, James, who would guess we had over four million in the back of the Volvo!'

'Eating pie and chips and very happy. If we had not to drive back to London, I would have said order a bottle of champagne.'

'Perhaps we can do that over the weekend. Mrs Brooks will say, "Put it on the bill", I have no doubt. You will still love me when this is all over, James?'

'That is not a question you need to ask, but less driving on the next case please. Eat up, we still have a long way to go.'

It was just coming up to one o'clock when we pressed the intercom button at Mrs Brooks' apartment.

'You have made it at last, I have been worrying about you both!'

'We are here now so there is no need to worry any more. We need to put some things in the lift, so give us about fifteen minutes please and we will be up with you.'

It was very quiet, and we quickly carried the nine croquet boxes from the Volvo to the lift. There were no awkward questions and we had not spoken to anybody. We pressed the button and the lift went up. In no time it seemed we were at Mrs Brooks' door. We carried the first box in, and Mrs Brooks looked flabbergasted!

'You have found another one, I feel quite shook up.'

'It is best you sit down; we have nine in total. We need to get them off the landing then we will not have to answer any awkward questions from your neighbours.'

They fitted under the table with the other box we'd retrieved from the Great Orme. The tablecloth covered them all nicely. Mrs Brooks looked in a state of shock. Sophie poured the tea and we told her how we had given up. Then Sophie found the photos in the bottom of a cupboard and we took them to show Mrs Hancox before we came back to London. She then told us about the Gazebo in the garden when she looked at the photos. How we had gone back for one final shot at it, before coming home.

'You have hit the jackpot, but where we go from here is anybody's guess.'

'Sophie has to work tomorrow, and I have things to attend to at my work. Our heads will be clearer by the weekend. Shall we regroup then?'

'I have arranged to see George at the weekend. What if we meet on Wednesday at eight like we normally do? On my estimate we are talking about very nearly five million pounds under that dining table. This will be a daunting task, even for Dennis.'

'There would be thousands of people descending on Llandudno if this leaked out Sophie, or from you, Mrs Brooks.'

'We both know what is at stake, James.'

'It is now after two o'clock, we both need to be in work tomorrow. Let us pack up now. We will see you on Wednesday evening, Mrs Brooks.'

We let ourselves out and went down in the lift.

'She was quite shaken up, I will ring to check that she is alright later tomorrow.'

'We are all shaken up and tired, let's get you back to the hotel before people start getting up.'

It was quarter to three when I dropped her off. I drove to my apartment and parked up. I would not be forgetting the last twenty-four hours for many years to come.

Chapter 31

On Thursday the alarm woke me, I had placed it out of reach from my bed. There was no alternative but to get out and switch it off. It had been well after three o'clock when I had climbed into bed the night before. After two cups of black coffee and a shower, I was ready to see what the world had in store for me at work. 'Morning James. Did you enjoy your long weekend?'

Jane was there at work before me, as usual. 'It was most enjoyable, nice weather and good company, thank you for asking. Have there been any problems while I was away?'

'No problems as such. We have some big orders to get out this coming month, but better that way than too little, we will cope.'

I made my way to my office, looked at the papers waiting to be signed on my desk, then tried to get on with my day. Mid afternoon Sophie rang.

'Hello James, are you hard at it?'

'In a fashion, I am trying to put the weekend behind me.'

'I have been thinking; if you could take the metal detector and the other tools back to Jack Berryman's hardware shop on Saturday morning, we could meet up and I could take you out for lunch.'

'I will take you up on that offer, any other requests?'

'It would be nice to spend Saturday evening just you and me, I could make us a meal, we could put our feet up and watch the television.'

'Perhaps I had better have oysters on the menu!'

'James Parker, you won't be needing oysters when I get my hands on you.'

At that she said, 'Mr Berryman's at one o'clock, 'bye James.'

Much as I wanted to leave work early, I stayed till the last of the staff departed, then locked up and made my way back to my apartment.

After a good night's sleep, on Friday morning I was feeling much better. The fact that I did not have to drive the next morning to Llandudno was very nice. The time raced by and I was looking forward to Sophie taking me out to lunch the next day. On Saturday morning I decided to put it to good use, by bagging all the paperwork we had from Dennis concerning the Albatross.

It would not erase the memory of the countless hours we had all spent going through it. I wondered if Mrs Brooks and Sophie were doing the same. Having put the vacuum round, at twelve o'clock I set off for Jack Berryman's hardware shop. When I arrived, there was a notice saying 'Wet Paint' but the door was open. Mr Berryman was behind the counter.

'How may I help, sir?'

'Just returning the tools I borrowed.'

'I recognise you now, sir. You know Arthur I believe?'

'I do indeed. I see you are having the shop re-painted.'

'We are providing a service to trade and private people alike. Appearances are very important to us.'

He gave me the bill which I paid and thanked him for his help.

Sophie was waiting outside for me when I stepped through the door, carefully avoiding the wet paint.

'James, fancy meeting you here!' and she gave me a kiss on both cheeks, linked her arm in mine and we set off for lunch.

'I passed a cafe with tables outside on the way here. It looked very nice. We can take advantage of the weather with the sun shining and sit outside.'

'That would suit me fine.'

It was a good choice in a not too busy road. When we got there, we were soon seated, and the waiter gave us a menu to study. We both chose the cauliflower soup with garlic bread. Sophie ordered a white wine and I had a small beer.

'I have been shopping on the way here, you will not be having oysters but I hope you will enjoy it.'

'Did you bring your pyjamas in that bag?'

'You seem to be in a lively mood, I have brought them with me since you would like to know. But it is a secret what you will be eating, James.'

At that the soup with garlic bread and our drinks arrived. 'What have you been doing this morning?'

'I decided to tidy all the paperwork from Dennis into one place and put the vacuum round.'

'I took my set of papers to Mrs Brooks a while ago after my manager complained, so that saved me the bother. You are right, I cannot see us wanting them again. I am at a total loss of where we go from here.'

'Dennis must be our guide. Mrs Brooks will have some idea of the next step. They must take it between them now. We have done what we set out to do.'

'This is nearly the end for us. It makes me feel sad and happy all at the same time.'

'You can always put another ad in the paper.'

'It would be too stressful on my own, James.'

'I did say with less driving, you know I will help you. Now eat up that soup. Shall I order two coffees?

'That would be nice, thanks.'

It was three o'clock when we set off back to my apartment, enjoying the afternoon sunshine. When we got there, I let us both in and Sophie produced a bunch of flowers she had bought earlier in the day.

'I am hoping you will have a flower vase, James, I should have asked before purchasing them.'

'I have a beautiful antique Lalique glass vase my father bid for at an auction many years ago. It will be nice to see it being used. It has been in the back of a cupboard for far too long.'

She spent the next ten minutes arranging sprays of gypsophila, small sprays of white flowers, mixed with some pink carnations.

'I had no idea you were a flower arranger, Sophie, they look wonderful.'

'My aunt used to help with the flowers at our local church in Nottingham, some of it brushed off onto me. I will say that antique vase has lifted it to another level. If you can find a nice film to watch tonight, I will start to think about our meal.'

I found two films so that Sophie had a choice. I then laid the table with a nice cotton tablecloth, my best cutlery, and wine glasses. She gave me a bottle of French white wine to put in the fridge, still leaving me to ponder what was going to go with it.

'Time for you to open the wine, please, you are about to be waited on.'

'So now can you tell me what exquisite dish I am about to be served with?'

'I can indeed. It is meatballs in a tomato sauce full of Mediterranean flavours with a Moroccan twist.'

'What is the twist bit?'

'I have added dried apricots, oregano, and chilli to the tomatoes. Help yourself to salad, let's make a start.'

While we were eating the conversation soon drifted to Mrs Brooks with all that gold we had carried into her apartment.

'I do feel quite guilty about putting all the croquet boxes under her dining table, Sophie.'

'She did ask us to find Henry's gold, it is not our responsibility anymore. On Wednesday evening she will tell us what she is going to do with it.'

We soon ended the meal and cleared the table, putting everything in the dish washer. Sophie chose the film she preferred and we settled down to watch it.

On Sunday morning I awoke with a start, Sophie was prodding me to wake up.

'It is ten thirty, James! I have cooked us both bacon, sausage, egg, and tomatoes for our breakfast.'

I sat up and she put a tray on my lap with breakfast and a cup of tea.

'To what do I owe the honour?'

'I have to keep you interested, James. Eat up, we are going for a walk along the embankment later. The sun is shining, and it is a lovely day.'

At twelve o'clock we set off. The day soon raced by. We stopped for lunch at a small cafe on the embankment then spent the afternoon watching the birds and people mud-larking along the Thames. We did manage to keep our clothes on till nine o'clock back at my apartment, then Sophie said,

'I would like an early night!' and gave me a wink.

When I dropped Sophie off at the hotel on Monday morning, Wednesday seemed a long way off. The sheer enormity of our search and findings had left me with mixed feelings about the future. Sophie was right, Dennis and Mrs Brooks would take it from here. A car horn tooted, and I realised I was holding the traffic up, so I drove on to my work. Monday and Tuesday were uneventful. Wednesday seemed like the longest day of my life. At five o'clock I left Jane in charge and drove round to my apartment, showered, and dressed then there was a knock on my door. It was Sophie. 'What are you doing here?'

'I must tell you; a recorded package came with three keys. One was to get into the building, one for the front door, a third key we will understand when we get there.'

'I hope she is alright; it must have been quite a shock us turning up with all those croquet boxes long past her bedtime.'

'It is just me being silly, James, and worrying, it will all get sorted when we get there. I will take a shower and we can find out what's on the menu at The White Feathers.'

It was quite crowded when we arrived and despite being earlier than usual there was a reserved notice on our table by the window.

'They do try to look after us here, James.'

'We are regular customers. Let's look at the menu, the fish, chips, and peas would suit me fine.'

'Let's make that two.'

The waiter was soon over and took our order. I chose the best white wine for a treat.

'You are being extravagant tonight.'

'We can afford to, there are ten croquet boxes in total sitting under Mrs Brooks' dining table with a minimum value of five million.'

'Mr Jones will be the happiest reporter in the country. I would give the world to see Dennis's face when Mrs Brooks told him.' The waiter was back with our order, 'Let's tuck in!'

Before long we were on our way to Mrs Brooks' apartment. 'This the first time we have not used the intercom to get into the building, Sophie,' I said.

The first key let us in to the apartment block and we took the lift up to the second floor. Sophie put the second key in the door, and we stepped inside. The kitchen door was open and there was a large envelope leaning against the kettle. Sophie picked it up.

'It says, "Put the kettle on, make a cup of tea, sit down and open the envelope".'

My dear Sophie and James, I do have a lot of explaining to you both. When we first started to look for Henry's gold it was all above board. George had that terrible accident; I was trying to make amends for George. Your company and the energy you brought with it was so good for me. When George was discharged from hospital and he was put in the home, you were the reason I found the strength to carry on. I did not expect George would ever recover back to normal. The hospital said it was possible it could happen but highly unlikely with his head injuries.

You were down in Llandudno one weekend when I visited him on my own. I had made him a cup of tea and asked him how his head was. He suddenly put his arms round me and said, "I'm back." The shock knocked me for six I might tell you. "We will soon get you out of here," I said, "and take you home with me". George said he had been thinking about it for several days. He told me we are too old to go chasing all over the British Isles looking for Henry's gold. You were making amazing progress so let's see how far you both could get.

Now when George was young, he had done a bit of acting, so we both agreed to give it a try. The next time you went with me he couldn't resist lifting his arm so that Sophie saw it. I could see you looking at me, James, they were not tears you could see, I was trying not to laugh. The next time I visited I really told him off.

'I think Mrs Brooks needs telling off when we see her next, James, how could she do it to us!'

'Carry on reading the letter, you can decide what to do or not to do when we have read it all.'

Now I hope you won't be too angry with me. George was my husband's younger brother and he did sail close to the wind sometimes, but my husband and I both loved him. I had a wonderful life travelling with my husband all over the world. He was very well paid, but I sometimes spent weeks at a time without seeing him. It was a very lonely life working in different countries. George came to see me on one of his many visits, to keep me company when my husband was away.

Perhaps it was the drink one night, we were young, and he told me he had always loved me and that was why he had never got married. To cut a long story short we soon became lovers. George was full of fun and I looked forward to him staying when my husband went away on business. He always managed to make me laugh, he was full of surprises. The day Sophie thought she saw him in London, going up the elevator when she was going down, he thought the game was up, but he bluffed it out. He had come to London to spend the weekend with me. He was sure you would be in Llandudno. A loveable rogue is my best description, but I do love him so much, even at my age.

Now I must come to the third key; it will fit a deposit box at Turton Street at the jewellery shop. In the drawer you will find a cheque made out to Sophie for £50,000, which I hope you will split with James. You will need to draw on it tomorrow as I will be closing my account on Monday coming. You will find the one croquet box which you dug up on the Great Orme where we put it under the table. I believe Dennis will help you to declare it treasure trove. You should have quite a substantial amount from its value when the Government has decided what to do with it.

I have enjoyed our time together and I am so fond of you both. I just love George so much. It is time to say goodbye, you will always have a place in my heart.

'James!'

'Yes Sophie?'

'I hate to say it, but Mrs Brooks is a crook!'

ABOUT THE AUTHOR

I am a retired horologist and clock restorer, 78 years of age, living in the Georgian town of Bewdley Worcestershire.

This is my first book.

Printed in Great Britain
by Amazon

69933789R00169